Dale Mayer

WHALEN 05
SHADOW RECON

WHALEN: SHADOW RECON, BOOK 5
Beverly Dale Mayer
Valley Publishing Ltd.

ISBN-13: 978-1-773367-34-7
Print Edition

Books in This Series:

Magnus, Book 1

Rogan, Book 2

Egan, Book 3

Barret, Book 4

Whalen, Book 5

Nikolai, Book 6

About This Book

Deep in the permafrost of the Arctic, a joint task force, comprised of over one dozen countries, comes together to level up their winter skills. A mix of personalities, nationalities, and egos bring out the best—and the worst—as these globally elite men and women work and play together. They rub elbows with hardy locals and a group of scientists gathered close by …

One fatality is almost expected with this training. A second is tough but not a surprise. However, when a third goes missing? It's hard to not be suspicious. When the missing man is connected to one of the elite Maverick team members and is a special friend of Lieutenant Commander Mason Callister? All hell breaks loose …

The last thing Whalen expected when he was called in to investigate the strange events at the arctic training camp was to find his old girlfriend, Chrissy. And as the first meeting showed, she was still angry at him. Not exactly the type of under cover existence he'd been hoping for.

Chrissy joined the military because of Whalen. Not to chase after him but to understand why he did what he did – or more to the point why he'd chosen this life over her. Now older and wiser, but still as in love with him as ever, she finds herself in the kitchen of the camp from hell. She only wants to finish her tour and head back home to open a bakery with her best friend.

Too bad some one at the camp has other ideas. And it's going to take everything the two of them can do to keep both of them safe… Even as others show up dead.

Sign up to be notified of all Dale's releases here!
https://geni.us/DaleNews

W HEN WHALEN BROWN woke up the next morning, it was almost noon, but he'd been up half the night, dealing with generator issues. He was now in the kitchen, and he smiled to see both Barret and Avalon come in together. "There they are. The sleepyheads finally decided to show up."

She flushed as she walked over. "Hey. How're you doing?"

"I'm doing fine. Maybe not as good as you two are though."

She laughed. "Nothing quite like finding out what the hell happened to make all the rest of it go away."

"And to make you guys take another step in your personal world."

She flushed and nodded. "Still, it was a good choice."

"It was, indeed. Barret's a good man," Whalen stated.

She smiled and grabbed two cups of coffee and came back. "I got to sleep in for the first time since … God only knows how long."

"And you won't get it again," Chef announced from the counter. "I told Steven to shift out of the kitchen."

She stared at him in dismay. "But then it's just the two of us again."

He nodded. "Rather have you in my corner any day," he

declared, with a big fat smile. "But somebody new is coming in, and I might shanghai them too."

"Who's that?" Avalon asked.

"Her name is Chrissy, and she's a baker. Although I'm not sure that she wants to be doing any of that work here. Let me just say she was a baker before she signed up."

"So, you'll shanghai her into the kitchen, will you?" Avalon repeated in a teasing manner.

"Absolutely. At least if I can." Chef looked over at Whalen and frowned.

Whalen frowned right back.

Chef laughed. "Do you know her?" Chef asked. "You know her from somewhere?"

Whalen shook his head. "Don't think so. Don't think I know anyone named Chrissy."

"That's because it's Crystal," Chef clarified.

At that, Whalen stiffened, and he nodded. "Yeah."

"I figured you knew her, but I can't remember why."

"That's because we were an item a while back," Whalen shared. "If it's even the same person, which I don't know for sure that it is."

But then a bright and cheerful woman walked into the room. She stopped when she saw Whalen, and the smile fell away. "*You*," she said, almost a bit venomously.

He groaned. "Hi, Crystal."

"It's Chrissy," she stated. "You're the only one who ever called me that."

"Because it's your legal name."

"Doesn't matter. I always preferred Chrissy."

He nodded. "Point taken." He looked over at Chef. "Yeah, I know her." Whalen stood and looked over at her. "How you been?"

"I've been fine. How about you? I mean, after all, the last thing I heard from you was, *I'll see you after work.*"

He winced. "Yeah, that was a while ago."

"Five years," she declared, as she crossed her arms over her chest. "I joined up because of you."

He stared at her. "Really?"

She nodded. "I wanted to understand the draw that made you choose this life over me." And, with that, she gave him a fat smile and added, "And now I get to find out for myself." **Not quite what I thought I'd find up here, Mason. WTF?**

DAY 1

WHALEN WATCHED AS Chrissy turned and walked out of the kitchen. He let out his breath in a hard *whoosh*, only to hear Barret and Avalon chuckling. Whalen shook his head. "Not sure there's anything to laugh about in this case."

"It's not so much *laughing* about it," Avalon corrected. "It's more a case of realizing that, no matter what you try to do in life, sometimes it comes back around to haunt you." With half a grin, she added, "Think of it this way. It's a good time to clear the air and to move forward."

"I have moved forward," he declared, maybe too forcibly, considering the raised eyebrow and the look both her and Chef Elijah were giving him. Whalen groaned and took a step back. "But, maybe for her sake, I can try."

At that, Avalon burst out laughing. "You can tell yourself whatever you need to"—she had a big smile on her face—"but, the bottom line is, she's here, and apparently she'll be working with us." Avalon turned to Chef Elijah. "Did she really agree to help us out?"

He nodded. "I've known her before, although not a whole lot. I heard she was here and had that baking history, and I just thought that we could, ... that everybody could use the change of pace."

"And yet I've been doing a ton of baking for you."

"You have, but I also know that you want to get back

out and to do some training, while you can."

"Sure, I want to, but I don't necessarily have to do it all the time."

"Exactly." Chef nodded. "So I thought maybe Chrissy could come in for a little bit of work, and you could get a little more time off."

"Perfect," Avalon replied, all smiles.

WHALEN LISTENED TO the play-by-play with only half an ear, as he tried to sort out the fact that Crystal was here. *Chrissy*, right. He'd always called her Crystal, and she'd always preferred Chrissy, but he'd had his reasons, and she apparently had hers. Thus it was a bone of contention between them. Looking back, he was probably an ass to not have honored her preference regarding her name, but he'd been trying to point out to her that her name was beautiful. She had loved it until that incident in her family, which she'd never dealt with, so she changed her name rather than doing so.

But apparently one could only deal with this shit when they were ready, and it was, in a way, almost karmic that he was here and so was she.

Whalen grabbed a cup of coffee and headed over to the equipment area, where he was doing inventory for the day. Not that it should take all day, but, given the amount of stuff that people were *not* putting back in place, maybe it would take longer after all.

As he walked in, he looked over to see someone familiar—Smolen—who had a big grin on his face.

Whalen shook his head, as he stared at Smolen. "Anytime you smile like that, it makes me worry." He circled his finger toward Smolen's facial expression, including his grin and his ticking jaw.

Smolen laughed. "I was just thinking about this equipment room, as you came in."

"Yeah, what about it?" Whalen asked cautiously.

"It's the area that gets the least attention."

"This is a base," Whalen stated. "Maybe it's not a normal or a traditional base, but it still should be well maintained."

"*Should* be absolutely." Smolen chuckled. "But has it ever been? Now that is a completely different story."

Whalen got to work, but the only thing on his mind was Crystal. He didn't have many misgivings in how his life had turned out and about the roads he had taken and the opportunities not pursued. Still, he had regretted not contacting her afterward. So maybe Avalon was right, and Whalen would at least get a chance to clear the air with Crystal now.

Certain things in life he regretted, and not talking to her and explaining his decision was one of them. Yet it had been too easy to bury himself in work and in all the other things that happened in life, rather than go back to something he considered already done and closed—whether he'd been happy about it or not. Probably not a good choice on his part, but five years ago he'd been young and much more idealistic and much more confident in what he thought would happen in his life.

Instead life had a way of doing things to people that they weren't quite prepared for. But to think that she'd enlisted because of him? That gave him a weird feeling. It wasn't the life he particularly wanted for her and didn't think it was what she wanted either. Therefore, to think that he would have had such a negative effect on her that she would enlist was more disturbing than anything. And, with that, he realized Avalon was right.

Even if not for himself, Whalen needed to find closure for her because that sucked as a way to go through life and certainly sucked as a way to enter any military service. Motivation was everything, and using unresolved issues as a means to make important life decisions wouldn't be very fulfilling.

Since they had split up about five years ago, he wondered at what point in time she'd signed up. If it had been soon afterward, then theoretically she could almost be at a place where she could walk away again—if she had found enough closure to do so.

For the first time he realized just how much of an impact he'd had on her life—and not in a good way, something he wasn't proud of. Groaning, he ignored the smirk from his friend, who didn't have a clue what was on his mind.

Whalen had only been half listening as Smolen gave the rundown on the equipment area. Whalen stepped forward, took a closer look, and froze. The room was a mess. Full of equipment tossed on the floor. He turned, his jaw dropping, as he stared at his buddy. "Who the hell allowed this to happen?"

"One of the guys who passed away was in charge of this," Smolen explained. "We are short-handed, so we've just had a rotating crew assigned in here, nobody permanent. Thus the mess ever since."

"But that's not ..." Whalen was absolutely dumbfounded that anybody would allow the equipment room to be in this condition. All the military services were about precision, organization, dedication, looking after equipment, looking after themselves. Here, in this survival training base, such a nightmare was hard to fathom. He shook his head. "Oh my God, this will take all day."

"Yep, it will," Smolen agreed, with a cheerful smile. "I'm going out on shooting practice though."

"Shooting?"

"Yeah, we're setting up blinds and simulating tracking down our enemy in whiteout conditions."

"Great, that sounds wonderful." And it did; it sounded a whole lot better than what Whalen had set out before him. He groaned as he stared at the room. "At least nobody's coming back in here for hours."

"They'll be back here at the end of the day," Smolen pointed out, "if they can get in here."

"Oh, they'll get in here," Whalen vowed. "I don't know about the rest of it though."

"I think it's pretty funny that you got nailed for this job." Smolen chuckled. "Somebody must not like you."

He rolled his eyes at that and shrugged. "Whatever. It is what it is."

"Yeah, you say that now. We'll see how you feel about it in a few hours, when you're still here, trying to make sense of this catastrophe."

Whalen glared at his friend Smolen, who gave him a cheerful salute and took off, chortling happily. Whalen was glad that his buddy had something to laugh at, but honestly, this room was a disaster.

However, there was a reason why Whalen was here, so that was an important stage of why he was doing what he was doing. But, damn, nobody told him it would be this much of a shit show. He turned his attention to the mess in front of him, grabbed the clipboard with the itemized list of equipment, and got to work.

CHRISSY STARED DOWN at her trembling hands. She'd come for this. She hated to admit it, but it's why she was here. Somebody, a friend, had told her that Whalen had applied to come up to this station but had been refused, so she'd thought maybe she could apply and pull one over on him. Except then, at the last minute, she had heard that he would be here after all.

Now here she was, one of the odd ones out because the military wasn't accepting anybody new for this current training session. However, out of the blue, she'd been asked by the chef if she was willing to come up for a few weeks. She'd agreed immediately. Of course now, knowing that Whalen would be here, had just confirmed how she was meant to be here, to confront him finally. Yet, now that she'd seen him, she couldn't believe how strong her reaction to him had been.

Ever since she'd first met the man, she knew he was it, the one for her. Somehow he didn't get the same memo. When he had promised to come back that night five years ago, then hadn't shown up, she'd made multiple phone calls, until she'd realized he had gone out on a mission and hadn't told her. After mutual friends had reluctantly told her that he was out of the country again, she had calmed down enough to realize that, no matter what she had thought about their future, Whalen hadn't been on the same page.

It had hurt, and she'd done her best to move on, but only as time went on had she realized she just wasn't moving on. She'd dated again. She'd dated multiple people, but nothing ever had the same feeling, the same staying power. It had all felt temporary, as if she were waiting for Whalen to return, and that pissed her off more than anything and made her realize that she needed to do something.

It hadn't taken her long to sign up, to put herself into his orbit again, only to realize how foolish that had been. She'd made it through basic training, and she'd made it through everything they'd thrown at her, mostly by gritting her teeth and carrying on, just putting one foot in front of the other.

She hadn't necessarily regretted her decision, but she'd realized just how foolish it was to have taken on the military service for such an emotional reason. And she hadn't ever thought she would consider herself a fool, but in this instance? Regardless, she ended up enjoying her time in the military. However, she had no intention of signing back up again.

It had been a very worthwhile time, but she'd also just confirmed one of her dreams to have her own business, her own bakery, because that's really where her heart was. In order to have that, she would leave military service. She'd saved a ton of money during her five years, to the point that she might even pull off her bakery now, which would have made this stint even more important to her. Still, with Whalen here, she'd been given another golden opportunity to walk away from him, this time for good, and to have that future that she wanted for herself.

Even after all these years, whenever she thought about him, she just got angry. Angry at what he had done to her, angry that she had allowed herself to care that much, and angry that she had made so many life decisions around him, only to realize that he wasn't on the same page, which just made her angry all over again. She'd been so sure that what they had was special, and yet it had only been special to her.

What a sobering realization to figure out that *the one*—who you thought loved you in a way that nobody else could possibly even understand—just didn't care and probably wasn't even capable of it.

Clenching her fists, she walked back into the kitchen and smiled at Chef Elijah. "I hear you're looking for a baker," she murmured.

He gave her a nod. "Morale's been a little on the low side," he noted, "so I figured upping our game on baked goods would help."

She nodded. "They always do, don't they?" She turned and introduced herself to the other woman. "Hi, I'm Chrissy."

"Hello, I'm Avalon." She gave her a mischievous smile. "Sounds as if you'll liven things up a bit."

She winced at that. "Sorry. Obviously you know now that Whalen and I have a bit of history, but ..." Then she let her voice trail off.

Avalon immediately picked up on it and nodded. "But, you know, maybe having some history will give you a great opportunity to find closure."

Chrissy stared at Avalon and then slowly shrugged. "That's what I was hoping for. I hadn't realized how much closure might be needed, not until I saw him."

Elijah snorted in the background. "Oh boy, now we have another couple in the making," he muttered, with a grin, looking over at Avalon.

At that, Chrissy immediately shook her head a little too hard. "No, no, no, no. Don't get me wrong. There won't be any relationship between the two of us," she declared, still shaking her head. "I wouldn't mind finding closure on this, but I certainly don't expect to find him interested in me. It was my fault in the first place. I should never have made some of the life decisions that I did." She sighed. "But, now that I'm here, well, I need to face the music, … whatever that means."

"If you say so," Elijah quipped. "You might just find that it's not quite as hard as you're expecting it to be."

She grimaced. "I find that, if I no longer have expectations, it's much harder to have them broken."

He stared at her and laughed. "You're too young for such a complicated, negative view of the world."

"Maybe," she agreed, "but it doesn't take long before the world beats you down. I decided not to stay that way, so I should at least get points for that."

"You do, indeed," Chef declared, "and you're here. So, while you are"—he grinned at her—"the two of you will split up the duties, each working part-time, if that's all right with you."

Chrissy faced him and smiled. "Now that is even better news. I was afraid I would be here and not doing any of the training."

"No, everybody here needs to be part of the training," Chef noted. "Have you been informed on some of the negative aspects of being here right now?"

"Yes," she replied. "I heard about several accidents and something about a nurse and her boyfriend having a drug issue."

"Let's just say there have been several incidents," Avalon added. "Some of them were deliberate, and some of them weren't. Elijah and I have been doing our best to keep the kitchen running. Other than us, Chef prefers to keep the kitchen to himself."

"I would agree with that too," Chrissy stated, with a smile. "Do you want me now or later?"

"Now would be great," Avalon replied immediately, "as I have to head into a meeting and do some more debriefing," she explained, with an eye roll for Elijah. Then, with that, Avalon quickly prepared to leave. As she walked out, she smiled at Chrissy. "Welcome aboard."

Feeling happy, at least about the welcome part, Chrissy laughed. "Thanks. Hopefully I'll appreciate that welcome in a little bit."

"I hope so," Avalon agreed. "Otherwise it'll be a very long session for you."

"I'm only here for a few weeks," she shared, with a shrug. "I can handle anything for a few weeks." She turned to look at Elijah and asked, "Where do you want me? What do you want me to deal with right now?"

"Something for dinner would be the priority at the moment," he said. "We haven't started anything yet. Supplies have been a little on the scant side. We were doing okay, but then … it always depends on when the next supply run comes in."

"A lot came in with me," she stated, "although not so much on the baking side."

Chef nodded. "We'll make do with what we can."

She shrugged. "I spent a lot of years making do," she replied, "so I'm not bothered by that at all." And she got to work, first sorting out what she had for options. She looked back at him. "Do you have a menu planned?"

He nodded, then pointed to the board that she'd missed on the side. She walked over and studied it. "How about I get to work making up a bunch of pies? You've got quite a bit of lard, flour, and fruit—canned and frozen. I can make pies for a couple days, and we can dole them out slowly," she suggested, as she contemplated the other options. "Pound cakes are great too, as they just get better as they age."

Chef listened and nodded to everything she said, though she didn't know whether he was just relieved to have something off his plate or if he really appreciated her ideas.

When he just said, "Go for it," she realized she would have a good share of autonomy here.

And, with that, she got to work.

DAY 1 LATE MORNING

CHRISSY FINALLY LIFTED her head after putting fourteen pies in the ovens. She had another fourteen to go in, and a couple more that she would turn into cream pies. Chef watched her work several times, probably just checking out that she really knew what she was doing, but he never said anything untoward.

When she finally put on the teakettle, signaling time for a break, Chef finally spoke. "That was a good bit of work today."

She nodded. "I wanted to make sure that we got somewhat ahead, so we weren't up against the calendar and working with time constraints all the time."

He chuckled. "Most people don't realize just how much that calendar, that schedule, can get to you."

She nodded. "In my case," she murmured, "I prefer to have things done well in advance. So I'll work hard for a couple days and see if we can't get a whole lot built up, and then you can offer it at your leisure. After this"—she pointed to the tea—"I'll get started on some batches of cookies."

"Cookies, tarts, anything would be great," Chef declared, giving her a huge grin.

"I do still have some pastries that I want to try out." She looked back at the mixing bowl. "However, I was wondering about just hanging on to that for another day."

"You're free to do that too," Chef replied. "If you've got something in mind though, let me know, so I don't use up your stuff."

She laughed. "Even if you do, it's easy enough to make up more."

"Easy enough, sure, but I don't always have enough supplies here. So we can't overdo anything. We might have to inventory it all."

"Right, that makes sense too." She frowned. "I'm not used to being in a position where the supplies are on the low side."

"Here they're on the low side because everything's got to be airflighted in. We've got a few ways to do that, but none of them are easy," he noted, with a smirk.

"And how much? ... Is it supposed to last for three to four months? To the end of this session of training here at the base?"

He nodded. "Doesn't mean that it will though. Sometimes the timing doesn't work out. I've already thought half-a-dozen times that we would have been shut down already, but we keep going. It is a valuable base."

"Even if it's only for people to learn and to understand what it's like to be together and to get along during times of hardship, you know? Remember that experiment where they put people—what was it? Eight people or maybe ten?" she began, as she stared off in the distance. "They put them into this special unit, where they didn't get to see anybody outside for a year. Everybody volunteered for the assignment, but it was ... pretty traumatic for them."

"I imagine it would be," Chef agreed, "and I do remember hearing something about that. It was more of a science project to see if people could survive being out in a remote place, such as Mars, all on their own."

"Because that's a one-way trip, right? And everybody would have to see the value of that one-way trip in order to handle it, and yet you don't want anybody who'll see it as a one-way trip without the science behind it," she added, with a shrug. "I don't know that I'd be up for it personally, but that's just me."

"No, I'm not sure I would either," Chef admitted. "I do like to have peace and quiet, since I don't like people all that much."

Chrissy burst out laughing and nodded. "That's one of the things that really surprised me when I joined up," she shared. "The lack of privacy, the inability to just disappear into my room when I wanted to and to shut out the world. Always bunking with somebody, always doing something with somebody, always being assigned a job with somebody." She shook her head. "It took a bit to get used to."

"And it's not for you?" Chef asked.

"Not long-term, no. On the other hand, it's taught me an awful lot, a lot about who I am on the inside, a lot about what it is I want out of the world," she said, with a smile. "So, it's definitely been a valuable experience."

"Good. Then you won't hold it against Whalen, *huh*?"

"Wasn't planning on it," she said, frowning at him.

Chef nodded. "He's proven to be a good guy here."

"I have no doubt about that," she replied. "He was a good guy in my world too, until he wasn't." And, with that, she gave Chef an eye roll.

He burst out laughing. "I'm glad you have a sense of humor. I wasn't sure. ... I was a little concerned when I realized you two might have some history."

"We all have history," she stated. "And this job throws

us together in different combinations on a regular basis. So I'm sure lots of people here have history in some way or another."

He studied her and then slowly nodded. "You got that right, and some of the history goes way, way back."

Such an odd tone filled his voice that she looked at him and asked, "Meaning?"

Chef shrugged. "Just meaning that … these military connections can go way back in time. I've been working with the CO here for a very long time," Chef noted. "Not here of course, but all sorts of places. I'll probably retire when he does. It would be hard to shift to somebody new after all these years."

"Oh, that I can imagine," she confirmed with a nod. "Not sure I could even do it."

"Exactly." Chef smiled. "Glad you understand. It's a weird relationship that we have, but, hey, it works for us, so it is what it is."

And, with that, he got back to work—as if she'd been cut out of the conversation, not in the know enough to ask any reasonable questions. Not knowing if anybody here would stop her from asking anybody else too. She could potentially ask Avalon but was afraid that would be seen as prying, and that Chrissy didn't want to do.

She had only just arrived here, and she wanted to maintain a certain amount of friendliness with everybody, if only as an option to try and keep the peace around here and to enjoy her time. It really was a unique experience, and for three weeks, four weeks, or however long she ended up being here, she was totally okay to maximize that experience.

It would be a memory for later and possibly a good one. She was storing those up. She'd learned throughout this process that time was fleeting. Although she'd initially wasted time—waiting and hoping Whalen would show up again—she wasn't prepared to do that anymore and hadn't made that mistake in the last couple years now, maybe even longer. It was just such a funny thing how life could change your perspective in a heartbeat. In her case, she'd been on a truck delivering supplies to a FOB station in Afghanistan, when they'd driven over an IED.

Luckily for her, she'd survived basically unharmed, and yet she'd lost everybody who had been in the vehicle with her. It was something she was constantly reminded of, as she looked around and saw the friendships forming and the joking that went on in bases such as this because it was really true that every day could be your last. She just wanted to ensure that every day here was one she enjoyed, so that, whenever she did draw her last breath, it wasn't full of regret.

DAY 1 AFTERNOON

W HALEN HUNG THE last harness and turned around and surveyed the room with a feeling of satisfaction. He'd managed to install and hide two cameras successfully. He had completed the inventory and had personally checked all the gear to confirm everything was solid and functioning. He'd found one strap that was dangerously cut and had taken several pictures of it and had it well documented. He didn't know whether it was accidental or deliberate, but, with nobody checking equipment, it was also certainly possible that it was just plain negligence.

These things did happen with regular wear and tear, which was why everything had to be maintained at a very high level. The fact that it hadn't been was a bit of a concern, but that's also why Whalen was here right now—to prevent anything untoward from happening. With so many other accidents occurring, he'd put his head together with Egan and had determined where some weaknesses were in this facility—that other people could also see and could potentially take advantage of—and that was the last thing they wanted.

As Whalen grabbed his clipboard, he checked once again to confirm nothing else needed doing, and then he checked his watch.

It was dinnertime, and that made him wince because,

well, dinnertime meant having to go deal with Chrissy. Funny how her nickname rolled off his lips now, when, all the time that he had been going out with her, he wanted to call her Crystal because he absolutely loved the name, but she wasn't having anything to do with it. Even though he hadn't seen her in five years, it was almost instinctive to still call her Crystal, which would probably piss her off to no end. But he was a completely different person these days, just not fast enough for her. Groaning to himself, he walked to the door of the equipment room and hung up the clipboard, having marked and signed all the paperwork, clearing the gear.

Normally it would be a two-person job, but, with everybody both short-staffed, rations being low already, and no other people coming in, it was a case of doing what needed to be done, then carry on, which Whalen understood. Still, as he looked at the gear, he wondered if somebody else was likely to see something he had missed.

When the door suddenly opened, and Magnus walked in, he stopped and eyed Whalen intently. "Find any problems?"

Whalen shrugged. "One cut strap but, other than that, the gear is holding up pretty decently. It was a big mess, which I'm not happy about."

"No, I'm not either," Magnus agreed, "and we'll have to stop that now. Was it deliberate?"

"I don't think it was deliberate, as much as people just didn't want to be here anymore. Plus, we lost the full-time assignment to oversee all this. So, with temporary help in here, as soon as one person slacks off and allows the mess to start, then it snowballs."

"That's the end of allowing it to snowball," Magnus stated. "We have to maintain this gear. Out here in these Arctic elements, the wear and tear becomes deadly. I can't believe it was allowed to get into such a mess to begin with." He shook his head.

Whalen brought the clipboard back down and showed it to him. "I've checked all this gear, and I've signed it. So, if anything does go wrong, … we know at this moment in time everything was fine."

"Right." Magnus nodded. "However, then people also might look at *you* as being the one who did something wrong."

Whalen gave him a wry look.

Magnus continued. "Signing anything puts your name on a chopping block in cases such as this, but, as far as I know, we don't have any other issues here, do we?"

Whalen shook his head.

"But," Magnus pointed out, "I also notice that we don't have any sled gear in here."

"No, that's all over with Joe and the dogs."

Magnus nodded, adding his signature to the sheet as well. "Good."

Whalen added, "Tomorrow I'll go over there and do a full accounting and inspection."

Magnus raised an eyebrow. "Joe may not take too kindly to that."

"I don't really care," Whalen stated. "If the guys are out there, Joe can't watch everything, particularly when he is out on a lot of these training sessions himself. So it's pretty easy for anybody to go in and sabotage gear."

"*Shh.* Keep your voice down," Magnus warned. "We want to be thinking along those lines, but watch what you say out here … and who you say it to."

"Yeah, well, you and I both know that it doesn't take

much for that kind of thinking to spread to other people."

"I know, but we've been doing pretty well for the last little bit."

"Really?" Whalen asked. "I don't think Avalon would agree with you. Or even Sydney for that matter, from what I've heard."

"No, I hear you there," Magnus conceded. "Anyway, it's dinnertime. Come on in, if you're ready."

"Yeah, sure. What are you doing, checking up on me?" Whalen asked, with a note of humor.

"No, but I heard Chrissy came in."

Whalen froze and turned to Magnus. "You know about that?"

"Sure, I heard about it. The grapevine around here is pretty effective," Magnus stated. "Anything new and remotely interesting is bound to run rampant. Therefore, I'm pretty sure you'll find yourself the center of attention."

He groaned and shook his head at that. "Jesus, really? People need to get a life."

"If they weren't stuck here, they would surely have more of a life of their own," Magnus pointed out, "but they *are* stuck here, and so are you. So getting a life isn't exactly on their agenda."

"Meaning, everybody'll be watching to see how we handle life in this fishbowl."

"Exactly, and you know that any entertainment that they can get out of this, the better they like it."

Whalen didn't say anything to that. What Magnus said was true, but it sucked, big-time. The last thing Whalen wanted was to be anybody's entertainment.

When they walked into the dining area, nobody seemed to notice that they were here for a minute. As soon as they got up to the front of the buffet line, Whalen saw no sign of Chrissy at all. Everyone else, though, just stared and stared at him. He grabbed his food, smiled at Avalon, and asked, "Still here, *huh?*"

She nodded. "I am, at least for now, and we'll be switching off."

"Good." He nodded. "It was an absolutely gorgeous day outside today."

"And yet you were stuck inside," she noted in a teasing voice.

"I was, but, hey, there's always tomorrow … maybe."

Although he quickly noted he would be inside tomorrow too, checking out the dog barn and the gear there. Plus he himself needed to ensure that the gear room on base remained clear and that there was no need to worry about any other incidents on his watch—but no one needed to know that.

As he took his food over to a table, he saw several people looking behind him and knew, without even looking, that Chrissy was here.

As he sat down, Magnus sat beside him, and they were quickly joined by the rest of what had become their group, although it wasn't so much their group as just people who hung out together. Whalen was supposed to start mingling more with this group now, apparently. That's what he'd been told anyway. He wasn't sure today was the best day to do that because, no matter what he did, somebody would be watching him.

He raced through his meal, got up, grabbed a coffee, and went to sit back down again, but Samson called Whalen over. Chrissy was at the same table.

"How'd you make out with all that equipment today?"

Samson asked, as he patted the seat beside him.

Not sure how to take his friend being the new investigator flown in to replace Jerry, Whalen sat down and shrugged. "It was a real mess, but then you knew that."

"Yeah, and I was really glad you were in there for the day and not me," he stated, chortling. "I, on the other hand, was out working with the dogs."

"The inventory work isn't quite the same thing as taking the dogs out for a run," Whalen noted.

"I got the better deal. I love those animals," he replied. "I'm a dog lover. Always have been."

"I know," Whalen agreed. "You've always been good-hearted around animals."

"You used to be too."

"Not *used* to," Whalen corrected, with an eye roll. "I still am. Love all animals."

"Except humans," Chrissy replied immediately.

He shot her a surprised look and then shrugged. "Never physically hurt a human in my life—at least not one who didn't deserve it." And, with that parting shot, he patted his buddy on the shoulder and got up and walked out, without looking back.

He didn't know what she was playing at, but, if she wanted to play with fire, then that was her choice. He wouldn't sit there and take it though. As far as he was concerned, anything between them needed to be discussed privately. However, if she wanted to air dirty laundry, well, that just wasn't his style. As he walked out, he heard her calling him, but he ignored her and kept on walking.

When she grabbed his arm a few minutes later and went to spin him around, he looked down at her hand on his arm with fire in his eyes. "Take your hand off me," he uttered, his voice low but hard.

She dropped it immediately and stared up at him. "Wow, I didn't expect hostility."

"If you'll play with fire," he said through gritted teeth, "and shoot off shitty comments, that's what you'll get back in return." And giving her that same hard stare he'd used earlier, he turned and walked off again.

"I came to apologize," she replied in a low tone behind him. "I didn't mean to bring all that shit back up again."

He stopped, then turned and looked at her. "Well, obviously it's still shit that really bothers you if you went on the offensive as soon as you saw me. And in public too."

She winced. "I … I'm sorry for that too."

"Too bad that you did that in front of the others," he added, "because now everybody knows we're on the warpath." He was so mad at her. "You just made us entertainment number one for the rest of the week at least, or until something else happens to take the pressure off us and put it onto somebody else."

She stared at him in shock and then shook her head. "You know that's not what I want."

"No, I don't know that. All I know is that's what you just did," he declared in exasperation. "People here are bored. They don't want to be here, and they don't like what's happening around here. So, anything such as the volley you just shot off will get the speculation running high and all kinds of attitude coming at us," he explained. "So, you may want to just button up whatever reactionary mess you've got going on in that head of yours and keep it to yourself." And, with that, he went to turn away again.

She called out, "Stop walking away."

He put his hands on his hips in frustration and glared at

her. "Why? There's nothing between us. I don't have to sit here and talk to you if I don't want to." He was reaching a point where he couldn't control his temper, and he really needed to table it for now, before more damage was done. "So far, I can't see anything at all that would make me want to stay here and talk to you, so what difference does it make?"

She opened her mouth as if to say something, then snapped it shut and glared at him in fury.

He shrugged. "If you do want to talk to me, let's do it in private, not here, not in the middle of the hallway, where anybody can see us and hear us," he suggested in a low voice. "Other than that, I'm not interested in anything you have to say." And, with that, he made his escape.

DAY 1 LATE AFTERNOON

CHRISSY STARED DOWN the hallway in frustration. She had seen the temper on his face, but, of course, she hadn't seen it up until she had taken that cheap shot. She shouldn't have brought up anything between them. Nobody would have known, and any curiosity would have died down quickly if she hadn't mentioned anything, but now, of course, he was right. It would be something that everybody else would be watching for. Keeping them under a magnifying glass, which was not how she liked to live her life.

She was friendly with everybody, but she preferred peace and quiet, also valued her privacy, so why the hell had she brought it up? She knew exactly why, and that's because she hated the fact that he'd ignored her presence here. He could have smiled and said hi when he was called over to their table. He didn't even come over to them until Samson urged him, and that made it awkward for him not to.

She was still having a hard time getting a handle on the names of everybody here, but she'd also felt a little bit lost and even half expected Whalen to step up and to make her feel welcome. Looking back, why the hell she'd thought that would happen she didn't know. Particularly after their initial meeting. She winced and rotated her neck slowly, as she wondered what her options were.

She couldn't keep living like this, and it would only get

worse the longer that they had any obvious difficulty between them. Groaning and chastising herself, she headed in the direction he had gone, looking for his room, but she had missed him and hadn't followed him in time to see what room he'd gone into. Standing here and looking lost, she wasn't sure what to do. She didn't want to call out to him, but neither did she want to wait to solve this problem.

She watched somebody come around the hallway toward her. She recognized him from dinner but couldn't remember his name. She smiled at him and asked, "Hey, do you know which room is Whalen's?"

He pointed at the door just behind her.

She nodded her thanks, then turned and knocked on the door.

When Whalen opened the door, she said, "I want to speak with you … privately."

He glared at her but relented and opened the door to let her in. He tossed a glance behind him at Steven, who stood in the hallway staring, then shut the door in his face. Whalen turned and leaned against his door. "Okay. What is it?"

She took a deep breath and apologized. "I'm sorry. It was a cheap shot. I shouldn't have said anything to you, and I am sincerely sorry for that. I guess I was feeling uncomfortable being new, and, for whatever reason, I thought maybe you would have acknowledged my presence and said hi or something to me," she admitted. "In retrospect, it was a foolish thought on my part that you would go out of your way to be nice to somebody, but there it is. I forgot just what an ass you could be."

His eyebrows continued to climb as she vented, and then, when she finally fell silent, he just looked at her and snapped, "The door is unlocked. You can leave anytime." He stepped away from the door and popped it open.

She stared at him. "That's it? That's all you've got to say?"

He nodded. "Yeah, that's it. That's all I've got to say."

"How about an explanation of why you didn't call me? Why you didn't say anything? Why you just walked away and left me to wonder whether you were alive or dead?"

At that, Whalen looked startled.

"What did you think I thought happened? You were supposed to come home at the end of work. I made a million phone calls, trying to find out where you were, and, yeah, I even phoned the hospital to see if you'd been brought in as a John Doe or something from an accident," she explained, trying to keep the pain out of her voice.

He stared at her, and then his shoulders slumped. "That's a surprise. It never occurred to me. One of my friends told you that I'd gone out on a mission and told me that you were pretty-well okay with it."

"I was told you went out on a mission, but not before I'd already been frantic for hours, made multiple calls, and laid awake, wondering what had happened to you," she snapped, with a waspish tone. "You could have texted me and mentioned that you were on a mission, that you didn't know when you would be back, and that you didn't know if you would contact me when you did."

He stared at her. "That's hardly a nice way to break up."

"You really think what you did was a nice thing?" she asked in astonishment. "Are you really that much of an ass?"

"No," he replied, choosing his words carefully. "I'm not, and I'm sorry if you took that the wrong way. It's just, we'd been having a lot of problems anyway, and I just wasn't up for it."

"*Problems?*" she repeated. "I thought we were moving toward the next step."

"Maybe, but I wasn't ready."

"Oh, I got that message, but unfortunately not until after I'd panicked and got completely upset and distressed because, instead of being nice and adult about the whole thing," she snapped, "you decided to just disappear without a word. Ghosting somebody like that is one thing if you've gone out a few times, *then* you ghost them, but I thought we had something much more than a fling."

A muscle in the bottom of his jaw started to flicker.

"And don't tell me that you didn't think the same thing."

"Doesn't matter," he said. "I obviously chose something different."

"Yeah, and I was wondering about that too," she noted curiously, "because, according to the rumors, you didn't have another partner."

"No, I didn't. One at a time," he stated. "That's my motto."

"Same for me, so that wasn't the problem." She eyed him intently. "I just want to know what I did wrong, or what it was that you couldn't possibly talk to me about, so I don't make that mistake again." She added, "You really affected my ability to have another relationship, and I—well, I want to find a way to move past it."

He stared at her in astonishment. "There again, that's something I hadn't considered," he admitted, staring at a point over her head. Then he shrugged. "I guess maybe this is a good chance for you to find closure and to move on then."

"I'd like to, but, as I told you, I need a little more information so I can," she snapped. "Otherwise this is just a repeat of everything else."

"Maybe, but I'm not sure what you want from me."

"How about an answer?"

"I gave you my answer," he said. "You didn't like the way I delivered it, but I gave you the answer."

She sucked in her breath and inclined her head, almost in a formal way, as she tried to deal with the painful words shooting in her direction. If it weren't for the tic in the muscle of his jaw, she would have thought he was as cold as his words, but something else was going on here. Something that didn't play out quite right, that didn't sound right, that didn't feel right. But, for the moment, that's all he was willing to give her.

"I can see that you aren't capable of talking about it at this point," she muttered. "So, I'll shelve the conversation for tonight." And, with that, she turned to leave. At the door, she looked up at him and added, "But, Whalen, this conversation isn't over."

"Yes, it is," he argued, looking at her narrowly. "Just like it was five years ago."

As evenings went, his had been pretty shitty. Alternating between feeling guilty, feeling justified, and then back to feeling guilty again didn't do much for Whalen's peace of mind throughout the night.

DAY 2 MORNING

WHALEN GOT UP the next morning and marched to the kitchen, knowing that Chrissy would likely be there. He knew in his heart of hearts that he wouldn't be lucky enough to miss her. The fact that she wanted to have it out with him had surprised him, as he had had no time to prepare for that. Still, he wondered why it did surprise him.

Way back when, she'd always been fairly outspoken and called a spade a spade. He'd always liked that about her too. He just hadn't been able to speak about things the same way that she did. He didn't have any sisters, didn't even have a mother for many, many years, and his relationships with women had not included intensely personal talks, and yet Chrissy had been all about them. He'd found it quite uncomfortable when she'd pushed and pushed. However, only after he left had he come to appreciate just how much of an open communicator and a free spirit she was. That realization had also pointed out how much of those things he was not and what a difference that made in a relationship.

Not that he had too much personal experience in that regard, but he'd had several relationships, albeit short-lived, and afterward it was obvious that communication hadn't been big in those either. Only as time and distance had settled in did he realize just how different he was and how different Chrissy was and how he had come to realize the enormity of what he'd done to her. Still, he wasn't going backward; that was never a part of his world.

Obviously he had another chance to make up for it now, but her pushing was getting to him, just as it had before— pushing him when he wasn't ready to talk, pushing him when he wasn't ready to deal with issues. And yet he'd never had anybody flat-out say, "It's okay, take your time. We'll talk when you're ready" either. It was always a case of *now*, and that had never gone over very well with him. He couldn't imagine that it would go over very well with anybody else like him, and yet he'd changed a bit over the last five years too.

Maybe not enough to handle somebody like Chrissy, yet, on the other hand, maybe he could deal with it this time around. At least enough to get it to the point where they could be cordial. So far, every time they got together it was more of an explosion than anything.

As he poured himself a cup of coffee, he sensed the silence around him. He looked around to see Chef Elijah smiling at him and beside him was Crystal—Chrissy. Whalen nodded and said, "Good morning, all."

They both said, "Good morning," in return, and Whalen walked over to a table and sat down, pulling out his notebook. He would spend the day over with the dogs and Joe. Whalen didn't know whether Joe was heading out on training or not, but any discussion time that Whalen could have with Joe would be better, even if Joe didn't know that Whalen was on the way. He had to stay focused on his whole purpose for being here, which was tracking equipment and seeing if somebody was out to sabotage the equipment, causing more injuries and accidents, and whether that had anything to do with the missing Teegan, who had been out in the tundra for weeks now, with a dismal chance of surviving.

Whalen also hoped to talk to Mountain about this Amelia, the scientist who was missing, yet apparently not missing. She was missing in the sense that nobody had seen her, but not missing in that nobody appeared to be terribly worried about her anymore and that the inhabitants of the local villagers, which he also hadn't had a chance to see yet, didn't appear to be worried about her at all.

Whalen found that odd and surprising, but apparently Amelia's survival-skill level was something that they all respected. Plus, she was considered a good hunter in her own right, if need be—which was something else that he thought was fascinating, given their location and the harsh Arctic conditions. It was not an easy place to live, and it would take a lot of mental preparation to deal with the isolation on top of everything else. He had no doubt that somebody was helping this woman, and the question remained whether she in turn was helping somebody else?

With all the injuries and accidents on and around this base, it was obvious why the local villagers didn't want to have very much to do with the people from the military base. Bad voodoo or some such thing, which, considering the simplicity of the locals' lives, Whalen could almost understand. Regardless it wasn't his job to convince them otherwise. Whalen's job was to ensure there were no more accidents, at least none that were related to equipment losses or equipment damage. Of course, in these harsh conditions, equipment could legitimately fail under use, but that should be an incredibly rare occurrence.

The men and women here were highly trained in their respective military organizations. Everybody took knives with them, and everybody here was certainly capable of killing. Most of them were capable of killing silently and efficiently. That was always a concern when that was the caliber of the people you were dealing with. Whalen knew the Russians were keeping the pressure on about their dead and missing, and that just didn't help anybody.

However, Yegorahn's death was on one of his own teammates, Raffi. Still, the Russians wouldn't accept anyone's word. The Russian brass was investigating already, back when the first Russian died suspiciously. Now the Russians stationed here at the training base also wanted to start a probe of their own. It was hard to consider just how much was going wrong up here, when things would lapse into a lull, but then something else would happen— seemingly completely unrelated to the original incidents— making everybody wonder how much of it was due to intentional bad acts and how much of this was just bad luck.

When Whalen looked up to see Mountain getting coffee and walking toward him, Whalen smiled. "Hey, I didn't realize you were back."

"I came in late last night," he replied, his voice growly and deep.

"How's the village?"

He nodded. "Same as always."

"I wanted to get in to see them."

"Not happening."

"Too bad," Whalen muttered. "I gather the trust level is pretty low."

"Yeah, you're not kidding. And the more I push about our missing scientist, the more they clam up."

"Are we presuming she's not missing?"

"Presuming, but I still want to talk to her, and they

aren't interested in facilitating that meeting," he shared, with half a smile.

"I'm sorry to hear that. If she could answer any questions, it would help."

"She could if she would, but, so far, she's avoiding us," Mountain declared, "like the plague."

"And that's not suspicious?"

"It doesn't matter whether it's suspicious or not. She hasn't done anything wrong, and, as much as I want to talk to her, that doesn't mean I can, at least not yet," Mountain noted. "I did find somebody sympathetic to my cause, so I'm continuing to work that angle, hoping I can open up the lines of communication around here soon."

"I hope so," Whalen replied. "I know we have months more up here in theory, but, if we don't get answers, no telling what will happen."

Mountain nodded. "If we don't get answers soon, the brass may cave to the pressure, shut this down, and call it a bad deal all around."

"And yet if somebody is actively involved …"

"Oh, I hear you. I hear you loud and clear," Mountain agreed, "and therein lies the problem." He looked down at his watch and nodded. "I'm skiing out to the scientists' camp."

"You think Amelia's going back there?" Whalen asked curiously.

"I've got information from the scientists' group, and the brass asked me to go search for some documents they were looking for."

"Why would they have any documents still there?" Whalen asked, shaking his head.

"They left in a rush, and I know that somebody came in

and made some more changes to the place."

"But why would they have left paperwork, when every-thing is digital now?"

"That is a good question, but these cold conditions are hard on all kinds of equipment, so keep that in mind," he pointed out. "We took out quite a few boxes of materials after the generator disaster, when Myles was here, but the scientists have all that now. I understand that they need all their research and stuff, and I'll do what I can. I'm trying to keep a good relationship going with them too. I'm just not guaranteeing that I'll find these notes or records that they're talking about." Mountain shook his head. "They are willing to bring a team back up, if they have to, but we're trying to avoid that."

"God no," Whalen replied. "That doesn't exactly help our cause in trying to narrow down the number of suspects or victims. And didn't I hear that Magnus spent no small amount of time trying to keep their generator going?"

"Sure, but the scientists are not terribly concerned with us, and they are free to do their own thing. So, if we can't find this stuff that they're desperately looking for, that will be a different story."

"Yeah, but maybe Amelia has it," Whalen suggested.

"I did mention that to them, but their position has changed where she is concerned. In their minds, she's not alive, not out there, and not somebody they are willing to put any trust, hope, or faith in at this point in time. I guess that can be chalked up to professional rivalry at this point."

"Which is also confusing to me," Whalen noted, "be-cause we know she's got an awful lot of survival skills, not to mention respect in her field. So how is it they don't know that?"

"They do know it, better than anyone, but I just think they may not understand what it means to this situation," Mountain guessed. "Based on the interviews with that group, I think most were too desperate to get out, and Amelia was too stubborn to leave with them. When you think about it, I understand that too. The problem is, they have a very narrow and specific body of records they are after, and nothing else will really satisfy them but getting this information."

"And they'll really bring a team back up here, if they have to?"

"I don't think it would be a whole team, probably a couple people coming to make a final check on the place and collecting the last of whatever they need."

"Which should have been collected time and time again, especially after the last of them were out of there."

"Should have been, yep," Mountain agreed, with a nod. "So, you tell me. Why hasn't it been done?"

"I can't answer that," Whalen admitted, with a wry look. "But, as far as I'm concerned, it should have been done a while ago." Whalen frowned. "And what if they're looking for something else?" Whalen asked, curious now.

"Meaning?"

"I don't know. What if something else is up there? As far as information goes, they need it collected, so somebody knows something. Exactly who is requesting this?"

"One of the people who was in the camp when the generator exhaust was routed through the system," Mountain replied. "One of the scientists we rescued. I don't know if you know about it, but we had several who ended up going to a nearby naval ship and being shipped out. Some were doing fine, but the others were not doing so fine at last report and may never do fine."

"Right, and that's not something we really want to con-template either."

"No, it was a mess, and lack of oxygen to the brain is a pretty severe injury to the body," Mountain pointed out. "I don't know what other information they could possibly want at this point. Seems they should just be counting their lucky stars that anybody made it out of there. I don't know why this is even being supported financially at this point, not after losing good people to this curse."

"I don't know. It just seems very strange that they would go to all this effort."

"It may be data accumulated by one of the scientists who died, one of whom they sent up here, and they've spent thousands of dollars already, so it's a minor thing to ask me to go over and look for it. I'm already here, and I'm certainly capable. Plus we're out scouting all the time," he said, "so I'll just make a trip there today."

Whalen hesitated and then told him, "I will spend my day sorting through the sledding equipment."

"Oh, Joe will love you for that."

"No, probably not," Whalen argued, "but one of the things I did come specifically to double-check was that all gear had been safety-checked and was in good working order, so that we don't have any more of these *accidents*."

"I hear you and appreciate that, as somebody who goes out on a regular basis, but I check my equipment before I go out every time."

"You do, but not everybody does, and not everybody has the ability or the knowledge of what that'll look like," Whalen shared. "However, if you're up for it, I really want the chance to go with you to that camp."

Mountain stared at him for a long moment. "Any particular reason why?"

"Instincts, I guess," he finally replied, after a long moment of silence. "Not sure if it's something you don't need to be doing alone or something I need to go see, because this nudge inside me tells me that I need to go."

"Never let it be said that I interfered with somebody's instincts," Mountain stated, with a chuckle. "Grab some skis, and we'll be out of here in an hour." And, with that, Mountain added, "Make sure you tank up good and get those carbs in."

"No problem there. I've done a lot of triathlons, *winter* triathlons," he clarified, with a smile. "When it comes to Arctic skiing, I'm your guy."

"Glad to hear it." Mountain studied him. "That experience is invaluable."

"I know, and it's one of the reasons why I'm focusing on equipment. On one of the trips I was on, we lost somebody because of an equipment failure. I don't want to see it happen again, and I sure don't want to see it happen again here."

Mountain stared at him, then smiled. "Good. You'll enjoy seeing the camp then. It's not much, but it's a good place up there, and I know it's been very popular over the years. They've kept it running for a long time."

"And is this the first year they've had any issues?" Whalen asked.

Mountain nodded. "As far as I know, yes. Of course they won't tell me otherwise."

"No, but you would think that other people would refuse to go, if there had been a problem."

"Maybe, but then some problems are kept pretty quiet,

and not everybody will have access to that information in order to know what the problem was," he suggested.

There wasn't a whole lot to say to that but Whalen nodded and said, "I'll be ready."

He ate a hearty bowl of oatmeal, grabbing several of the sausages available, and then quickly headed to the equipment room, where he grabbed his preferred skis and boots. He strapped in, then quickly called Mountain and asked if they were taking the sled or not.

"No, we don't need to haul any equipment back."

Whalen hesitated, then said, "I hear you, but …"

Mountain went quiet, hearing Whalen's hesitation over the phone. "What is it you're not telling me?"

"I don't know," he admitted. "I just feel as if I need to come, that whatever is happening out there right now is something I need to see, to be a part of, to understand, or something."

"Then grab something light and portable that we can pack up and drag if need be." Mountain nodded. "We've got a couple of those collapsible harnesses. It's fine if you want to grab one of those. I don't mind."

"Good enough," Whalen agreed, "and hopefully we won't need it."

"Hopefully, because, if we do need it, we'll have bigger problems than anything we're expecting to find on this trip."

With that, Whalen set to work and gathered what they needed. As he waited outside, he heard a shout in his direction. He turned to see Mountain standing there, skis in his hands.

He nodded and called out, "I'm ready." And together they headed out.

It took the first mile to get Whalen's muscles loosened

up enough. It was cold. It was crisp, and the sun was up but had no heat to it yet. As he watched, the world around him slowly opened up, exposing the wonders of being out in these below-freezing temperatures, in a winter wonderland that few got to experience. He smiled, feeling his body settle into a rhythm and kick into a normal pace that was easy to maintain. It wasn't long before they got up to the scientists' camp.

As they took off on their skis, Whalen looked over at Mountain. "It's not that far, is it?"

"No, it's not," he confirmed, "and it's one of the reasons why I believe Amelia is alive and doing well."

It was the most definitive statement Whalen had heard about her from Mountain, but it didn't take a lot of brains to realize that he'd spoken freely because they were out in the open, where nobody was listening in. "You're really paranoid about somebody knowing or overhearing you, aren't you?"

"I'm just careful," Mountain clarified, with a nod. "If she's hiding, she's hiding for good reason. She has the skills to do it, and I think the village is helping her. Then again she must have a reason for it, and I won't intrude on that—not until I can come up with some of the solutions everybody needs in order to regain their trust in our base," he explained. "It's sad that this is where we've gotten to, but I won't nullify their concerns by not explaining and by not understanding just how bad it is," he shared.

He walked over to the front door on the first building and pointed. "See? The lock's been disturbed, and it's been unlocked recently."

And even Whalen could see that no snow was on the lock or the hinges, as if the door had been opened recently, whereas the rest of the area was pretty surrounded with snow. "Yet minimal tracks."

"Minimal tracks, yes," Mountain agreed. "A light dusting of snow came overnight but from a different angle, so this area was spared. … We can still see the hardpack underneath this dusting."

"Which there should be because you've been here multiple times," Whalen pointed out.

"Yes, but not in the last what? Three days I guess?" he noted, as he thought about it. But looking down at the tracks, he nodded. "Could be either, so again, nothing definitive. She's just sitting on that side of possible, without confirming that she's alive and well."

"And again, as you said, she must have a compelling reason."

"Exactly, and that is my primary concern," Mountain shared.

"Why are you so concerned about her?"

Mountain hesitated, then looked at him and shrugged. "We're still missing my brother. Alive or dead, I want to find him."

At that, Whalen slowly nodded. "And you think he could be alive?"

"I'm hopeful, not necessarily very hopeful," Mountain admitted, "but, until I find his body, … you can bet I'll continue to search."

That made more sense than anything as to why Mountain was out every day, looking around the tundra. "And that's what you're doing here, isn't it?" Whalen asked casually.

"I'm doing that in hope, sure. I'm checking up on all the training grounds. I'm watching all the training, and I am out here checking on this scientists' camp, the village, the local hunters, and anybody else," he stated, his voice harsh. "This place has been too much of a shit show this time around, and, if it takes somebody like me to keep an eye out from a distance so nobody knows where I am, that's fine," Mountain declared. "Sooner or later, somebody'll make enough of a mistake that we'll catch them, and I want to be sure that I'm there for it."

"Got it. That makes sense," Whalen muttered, "but what a very strange set of circumstances too."

"Yeah, and part of that has been because we've had such a tight lockdown and really bad weather, so we couldn't get outside. Some people have not handled it well, you know—short-term relationships, drugs, the whole nine yards," Mountain said, with a headshake. "Once you start packing people in and not letting them leave, mixing in a few mishaps, it's just a bad deal for everyone."

"I heard about some of it," Whalen replied.

"Yeah, well, keep an eye on your back because, while all those incidents are great distractions, whoever started this nightmare is still here and is still laughing."

"Unless he's one of the ones who died," Whalen pointed out.

"I don't think so," Mountain disagreed, as he frowned at Whalen. "Which is why I'm warning you to watch your back."

"Got it, and it's definitely not a nice thing to think about."

"None of it is, but, if you want to stay alive, you can't make the same mistakes a lot of people here already have," he pointed out.

"No, I don't plan on it," Whalen stated.

As they walked into the vacant facility, he was surprised

at just how cozy it was. "You don't really think about this as a place you would want to come to," he shared, "but, with this view and this layout, it's quite cozy, isn't it?"

"It's very central, and, with all the bedrooms tucked up on the inside and heavily insulated, the generator was causing them all kinds of problems."

"Right. That's why Magnus was back and forth all the time, wasn't it?"

"Magnus, Rogan, we all spent quite a bit of time up here, helping with the generator, and we did get it started for them time and time again. However, we weren't aware of the other issues going on. So, once the whole carbon monoxide scenario happened, the camp was evacuated—and most of them had to be airlifted out—things just went from bad to worse."

"Absolutely. I heard about that."

Mountain continued. "However, that was a completed scenario, with a known culprit, not the same person instigating these other issues we are dealing with at the base."

"At least you hope not," Whalen pointed out.

"It wasn't," Mountain declared, his voice hard.

Whalen didn't refute that, knowing that Mountain wouldn't take kindly to any argument regarding his logic. And maybe he was right. Whalen hadn't been here at the same time, so it was much harder to sort through all the information, without having all of it right in front of him. "I guess I need to see the case files," he added.

"And you can," Mountain stated, "as long as you're cleared."

"You know that Mason sent me."

Mountain nodded. "Of course I know that Mason sent you, and that's why you're here, so we can talk freely."

"Ha, and if I hadn't asked to come along today?"

"I wouldn't have talked with you," Mountain stated, with a half smile. "Only so many people I deal with on base. You have orders, and you can follow them through, and I'll be keeping an eye on you from a distance."

"*Great*," Whalen noted, "like that all-seeing eye you can't ever be sure about."

"Exactly." Mountain nodded. "You'd be surprised how much that keeps people in line, just to know that something, someone, may be out there watching you. It's enough to keep people on their best behavior because they don't know when and where I'll pop up."

"And what if somebody decides to take you out, rather than deal with that uncertainty?"

"They haven't tried yet," Mountain stated, "and they're welcome to watch me because, just as I'm watching everybody else, I'm sure some are watching me."

At that, Whalen stopped, looked back, and frowned at Mountain, as they walked through the camp. "Have you felt it?"

Mountain stopped and nodded. "You bet I have, and, if I thought I could pinpoint who it was, I would have already, so don't bother asking."

"No, but how frustrating is that?"

"It's damn frustrating, and I don't like it. I don't like anything about it," he said. "But again, until I get confirmation of who's tracking me, not to mention figuring out why, I can't really do anything about it but keep hunting whatever asshole is behind this mess."

"It sounds as if you're onto them, but they're just a step ahead of you."

"They are at the moment," Mountain agreed, with a

nod. "That's because they're trying to stay hidden and to keep an edge on the game. So, until I can get more proof as to who and what is going on, they'll have the advantage."

"Did you ever consider it could be more than one person?"

Mountain nodded. "I considered it and summarily dismissed it at this point. Only so many people are on base and only so many share connections between them."

"Yes, but what if there's a connection we *don't* know about, perhaps from before, a connection that nobody's talking about, a connection that maybe isn't something we would expect to be a negative?"

At that, Mountain smiled. "I hear you. The problem with that thought process is the fact that trying to get all that information isn't easy."

"No, but it should be something we can get."

"It's been requested. Mason's supposed to be getting it all."

"Ah, he probably put Tesla on that," Whalen noted, with a knowing smile.

"No doubt, and I'm hoping the files will be in today," Mountain said. "I'm looking forward to seeing them when I get back tonight."

"I sure hope you share because I think the bottom line here will be hidden connections."

"You don't just think we have a psychopath on board?"

Whalen winced. "Nobody ever thinks we have a psychopath around," he replied. "The trouble is, the military does seek a certain personality to some degree and gives them license to a certain level of brutality."

"It does, but not always for very long. That behavior can be caught fairly quickly."

"And yet if they're any good," Whalen pointed out, "it can go on for decades."

Mountain stared at him. "You're thinking about a certain general, aren't you? What was that? Thirty, maybe forty years ago?"

Whalen nodded. "That man got away with killing people out on missions almost indiscriminately, including killing off his own team in an accident that was quite clearly blamed on somebody else."

"I know, and all kinds of hell erupted over that one. Even now I don't think anybody truly realizes the damage that man did."

"Because he got away with it. He got away with it for years, and, the more he got away with, the more other people couldn't believe that he'd had the opportunity to get away with so much. I think it hurt a lot of people in this world just to know something like that could even happen."

"Not only *could* happen, *did* happen, and without any way of getting back all those lives. It was really heartbreaking to the service to find out they had had a psychopath in the ranks—and worse to find out he'd been promoted multiple times, often as a way to deal with the complaints against him."

"And yet the complaints weren't necessarily clear-cut, were they?" Whalen asked.

"No, and that's why they were always hard to deal with, plus he just kept getting promoted. There was never any proof. He wasn't somebody who got along well with everybody else, but he was great for command because he gave orders and expected them to be followed. Most often those commands were really good decisions. Only when it came to his little hobby, nobody believed he was guilty."

"What was the deal with the Canadian one, where … wasn't he raping women?"

"It was a long time ago, as far as years go, at least ten, I think. I'm not sure. But again, nobody could believe it was him because of his rank and the power that he wielded in his job, which also gave him a lot of leeway to cause all kinds of hell."

"Exactly." Whalen nodded. "And, once they start and get away with it, it's tantalizingly obvious that it becomes addicting, like a drug. Plus it already sounds as if we've had enough drugs on this place to last for a long time," Whalen added.

"And yet there isn't supposed to be any at all, outside of the medical clinic."

"But you know perfectly well that, no matter where you are, there are always drugs to a certain extent. It's just a fact of life."

"I know," Mountain acknowledged. "Anyway, back to the task at hand. We are looking for a brown notebook, eight and a half by eleven inches—supposed to be in the main room and supposed to already be packed up. And I don't know who missed it or why, but the request has been made for us to look for it."

"Got it."

They hunted high and low for it, and then finally Mountain turned around and shook his head. "I'm not sure that they got the right intel here because no notebook is here."

Whalen suggested, "Unless Amelia has it."

"And it's certainly possible that Amelia might have it, but why would she?"

Whalen hesitated before answering. "What are the

chances something else is in this notebook, other than general data collection? Whose notebook is it?"

Reluctantly Mountain replied, "I couldn't get a straight answer on that. I'm wondering if it belonged to the doctor who tried to kill everybody."

"Jesus, so that would be Anna," Whalen noted. "So maybe they want that notebook back just for peace of mind, you know, to make sure nothing will get anybody else in trouble or sued."

"I don't know why they want it back because I don't know what's in it," Mountain stated, as he frowned at Whalen. "But what I can say right now is that there doesn't appear to be any sign of it in here."

"And was it actually Anna's or Amelia's? I guess that is the next question," Whalen noted, as he walked over and bent down, even looking under the seats around the table, checking to see if anything was secured underneath. As he did so, he whistled. "Something's here all right." And he pulled out a small notebook that had been taped to the underside of the seat. He held it up and asked, "This isn't what they were looking for, is it?"

"It's not the size they told me that they were looking for, but …" Mountain held out his hand.

Whalen handed it over and asked, "The question is, what is this, and why was it taped underneath?"

As Mountain read the first page, he whistled and then read out loud the beginning passage, "*To whom it may concern. Please note, this scientists' camp is a big mess, and I highly suspect we've got a couple people with some major illness going on, but we've also met several people from the local military base, and I swear to God something sinister is going on there too.*"

He flipped through several of the pages and said, "This looks to have been written by a guy who's still in a coma. His colleague requested that we find the book, so maybe they both knew about it."

"Great. Anything indicating who or what may be a problem?"

"No, not from what I've read so far. They never put that in writing," Mountain stated. "He mentions that something's wrong at our base but also something is wrong with two scientists here. Now the two mentioned were killed, so, yes, he was right to be concerned. Unfortunately this writer didn't know enough to do something about it before he became a victim himself. Yet this comment about something wrong at our military base is interesting," he added.

"We'll need to go over this notebook closely," Whalen suggested.

"Let's take another look around and make sure we haven't missed anything else." Mountain frowned. "I wasn't thinking of something secreted away. We'll need to search this center again and go at it from that point of view. We also don't know whether the scientists or their university or their overseers or whoever knows about this particular whistleblower notebook or not. It does appear that more secrets were here than anybody understood."

DAY 2 NOON

CHRISSY HAD WORKED steadily in the kitchen that morning, knowing that she needed to shift her schedule so she could be outside the next day. So this would be her chance to build up a little more on the baking side. She was working alongside Avalon with Chef Elijah to make sure she could ask for some time on her own.

Taking a bit of a break, Chef dozed in the corner. Avalon turned to Chrissy. "You seem to fit right in."

"I came in for the wrong reasons, but I very quickly made the best of it," she shared. "I won't be signing back up again when my tour is complete, opening my bakery when I'm done. Maybe expand the business more than what I'd been thinking before. I've spent the last five years setting aside as much money as I could in order to make it happen."

"Running your own business is a big undertaking, isn't it?" Avalon asked.

"It is, but I've also got a girlfriend involved. We've been friends since primary school," she said, with a laugh. "She's been out scouting for the best location. She currently works for a high-end restaurant in California. So, it'll be the two of us, you know? And, although I know partnerships can be a problem at times, some things are much easier when there are two of you."

"Absolutely," Avalon agreed, with a smile. "Being up

here is easier too with a partner. I've had my trials since I've come," she said, "but it's been a blessing to be here, and I know that, when I leave, I'll take home a lot of lessons about both human nature and Mother Nature," she stated, with an eye roll.

"Yeah, I can see the burns on the wall near the stove from what looks to have been a fire here in the kitchen."

"Yes." Avalon nodded. "That's something we still keep an eye on. So, just a warning to you, if you ever come in *super*early, you need to be very careful. Don't light the stove yourself, if you can't confirm the proper adjustments. You need to know that the burners were adjusted one time at the very beginning of this session. One day I turned it on, as always, and the gas came out too fast, too hard, and we ended up with shooting flames. The kitchen caught fire, and, yeah, it singed me," she explained, with a bitter tone. "So, that is something that Elijah personally shuts down and checks every night, then double-checks every morning, just to make sure all the jets are fine."

"Jesus," Chrissy muttered, feeling sick to her core at the thought of raging flames. "That's not exactly something you want to think about at four o'clock in the morning." She glanced around the kitchen.

"No, it isn't, and it's not something I would normally think about, outside of the safety factor, but it's always there now, in the back of my mind."

"Sorry about that. It sucks."

"Not as much as everything else. We've had dogs shot. We've had people messing with our backup generators. We've had people locked out and dying of hypothermia. Scott, who used to work in the kitchen, went outside, pissed off and angry, and, just like that, he was gone. Getting locked out happened to me too," she added, taking a step back, looking at Chrissy's freaked-out face. "So that's another point. Watch that back door to the kitchen. When it shuts, sometimes it shuts a little too hard, and, if you're outside in these cold temperatures, it can close and stick, for whatever reason, one we couldn't reliably replicate, but I couldn't get it open from the outside," she warned Chrissy. "I was lucky that my pounding on the door was heard, and Chef opened the door for me, but his other kitchen worker wasn't so lucky. Scott ended up curled on the ground next to the building, pulling his knees to his chest, and dying outside."

Feeling sick to her stomach, Chrissy stared at the door in question, frowning. "We can't ever forget that Mother Nature rules, can we?"

"Nope, she absolutely does," Avalon agreed. "Other than some of the guys with their bets on dating the women here, I don't know that we have any other issues right now. Just take it easy. Remember. You've come to a base that has some weird stuff going on, so be *extra* careful."

"I know. It's one of the reasons why I was surprised to get the request for a transfer, looking for somebody with kitchen experience," she explained, with a nod toward where Chef Elijah was sleeping. "Anyway, if you're done there, I'll get ready to start serving breakfast, and you might as well go get started on your day." When Avalon frowned, Chrissy asked her, "Aren't you out today?"

"No, I'm out for tomorrow's training."

"Oh, I thought it was today."

Walking over to the schedule, Avalon said, "I'm on kitchen duty here today, but you're not."

Surprised, Chrissy shook her head. "In that case, I'd better double-check where I am supposed to be." And she booked it down to the master schedule for everybody and found that she was supposed to be outside, training.

"Shit, shit, shit," she muttered to herself. "I've already missed four hours." She quickly changed into her gear, raced back to the kitchen, and, with a nod to Avalon, confirmed, "Yeah, I'm out today."

"Make sure you grab some bars and eat," Avalon offered, "plus pack a lunch. I don't have instructions for lunches for everybody today, so presumably they're all coming in to make their own." She pointed to the side table, already prepped for sandwiches.

Chrissy nodded, her heart pounding, knowing that she was already behind. So she quickly packed up a lunch and raced out to join the rest of the team. As a belated start to the training day, it sucked, big-time. However, when she stepped up to her squad, the others stared at her.

One of them said, "Hey, there you are. Your name was just called, but we saw no sign of you."

"Yeah, I thought I was in the kitchen today," she replied, with a headshake. "I just put cinnamon buns in the oven too."

The others smiled and rubbed their stomachs.

She nodded. "But, if you're unlucky, they'll forget to take them out."

And that's how her day evolved.

WHALEN AND MOUNTAIN spent another hour searching the scientists' camp and finally shared a look.

Whalen spoke first. "If something else is hidden here, it's

well hidden and passed a pretty thorough check."

"We're not destroying beds. We're not destroying walls," Mountain declared. "So what do you think? Are you comfortable that a thorough check was done?"

At that, Whalen nodded. "I am. What about you?"

Mountain nodded. "Absolutely." He walked toward the entrance.

"We'll lock up after us, right?" Whalen asked, catching Mountain's nod.

At the front door, they took their time to lock up securely. Mountain added, "I'll set a couple hairs here, so I can tell if this door gets opened. It's pretty tight, and the wind won't dislodge it on its own."

With that complete, they quickly buckled into their skis.

Whalen pointed off to the distance. "Look. We've got a storm coming in."

Mountain frowned and nodded and assessed the distance. "We could sprint some of the return trip."

"We could," Whalen noted, "but, if we raise our body temperature too high, you know what the end result of that will be."

Mountain groaned and nodded. "All too well. Slow and steady it is."

"How about fast and steady?" Then Whalen took off at a good pace, with Mountain roaring behind him to catch up.

With the two of them side by side, following their own tracks back, Whalen knew they would come in just before dinnertime, and they would be more than appreciative for a break from the cold and the wind. They were facing the wind the whole way back, and it felt more brutal than he'd expected.

When Mountain came in closer at one point, he motioned to Whalen to stop, then spoke, "I can't see anything, but, dammit, it sure feels as if we're being watched."

Whalen looked around a bit and nodded. "I've had a weird feeling for the last while, but there are miles between us and our teams out doing training today. Surely at this point in time, they should be back at base again, right?"

Mountain nodded. "They should be, but they often run behind. So anyway, whatever it is, keep alert." And, with that, he took off.

They reached the base and got inside and quickly unbundled and hung up all their gear. As Whalen grabbed his skis, he told Mountain, "I'll take yours over too."

"Nope," Mountain countered. "I handle my own equipment."

"Good enough."

And together they made their way to the equipment room, where they strung up their skis. Whalen checked for damage and whistled a couple times. "You tend to forget just how hard ice can be. He pointed to some of the scratches in the wax.

"Yeah, they'll need to be resurfaced tomorrow," Mountain muttered.

"Ongoing maintenance regardless," Whalen noted.

Mountain nodded, checked out his own skis, and confirmed that they were solid.

With the rest of their gear returned to its proper spot, and everything else looking the way he'd left it, Whalen turned to Mountain and asked, "Dinner?"

"Yeah, absolutely. If we're lucky, there might even be dessert."

Rolling his eyes at what he knew was an obvious reference to Chrissy, Whalen nodded. "Maybe so, but I think she was slated to go out on training today."

Mountain groaned. "I sure hope Avalon managed to get something done then. Even just a cookie makes a huge difference."

"Yet that's ridiculous, and you know it."

"Sure, I know it." Mountain flashed him a big grin. "Still, it's the truth."

As they walked in, cold and tired, their faces red and purple from the wind, Whalen noted that the first wave of people at dinner were already seated and eating. As he and Mountain walked up, he was thrilled to see big slabs of roast beef, gravy, Yorkshire puddings, mashed potatoes, and a bunch of veggies. He loaded up. As he was about to walk off to the side, he nudged Mountain and pointed out a pan of cinnamon buns that appeared to be almost gone.

At that, Avalon came around and saw them. "Hey, you guys almost missed out."

"Considering it was almost a missed-out scenario," Whalen suggested, "grab us a couple of those cinnamon buns, before there aren't any more, would you?"

She chuckled, brought over a plate with two big ones, and added, "If you're still hungry, one apple pie is left."

His eyebrows shot up, as Mountain leaned closer. "Grab us two slabs of that too, will ya?"

And, with Whalen carrying the cinnamon buns in one hand and his tray in the other, Mountain snagged the plate of apple pie in addition to his heaping tray, and the two of them found a table in the corner.

As they sat down and unloaded their trays, Whalen eyed it all and chuckled. "Most people wouldn't get through this amount of food in a day."

"Yep," Mountain agreed, as he sat down, "but most

people don't burn the calories we did today, and even fewer people use up the calories that I do."

"That's because few people are your size, and fewer still maintain your level of fitness," Whalen added, still chuckling.

When he looked up, Chrissy stood in the middle of the room, frowning, a tray in her hand. Knowing it was probably a bad idea, he groaned, pulled an empty chair back, and motioned at it for her. When she hesitated, he just shrugged.

She walked over, put her tray down with a little more force than necessary, and glared at him.

He chuckled. "See? Even when I am nice, you aren't."

"That's not fair," she cried out in a hoarse whisper. She looked at Mountain, and her eyes widened.

He nodded to her reaction. "Yep." He gave a casual flick of his hands. "The name's Mountain. If you don't finish your dinner, it's not a problem. I'll finish it for you."

CHRISSY WASN'T EVEN sure what to say to that. She stared blankly at Mountain for a minute, and then, for whatever reason, his words caught her quirky sense of humor, and she started to laugh. But it wasn't just a simple laugh, it was a huge release-of-tension laugh. By the time she wiped away the tears from her eyes, Mountain studied her, bewildered.

Still in between giggles, she waved her hand at him. "Whether you intended it or not, I really needed that."

"Apparently." Mountain still stared at her. "Glad I could help."

"Me too." She smiled and picked up her fork. "This looks decent."

"More than decent, it's awesome," Whalen said.

She glanced at him and nodded. "You always did like your groceries."

"Still do," he agreed. "I think most of us here do."

"I sure do," Mountain confirmed, with a big fat grin, as he sliced off a big chunk of roast beef. "Never did understand why anybody wouldn't."

"I'd never been a big eater," she replied, "until I joined up, and now it seems as if I'm always fighting for food these days."

"You shouldn't be," Mountain noted, looking at her.

"Generally there's enough for everyone, unless we run into shortages of course. And then," he added, with distasteful expression on his face, as if he'd had a bite of kale instead of roast beef, "rations will get cut but not at a horrific level. At least I hope not."

She nodded and smiled. "I know. I think the constant work is building my appetite in a way I hadn't expected, speeding up my metabolism, so to speak."

He nodded. "Yep, that makes sense. Plus, if you had a more sedentary lifestyle before this, you will burn a lot of calories on these training missions."

"And I sleep like a rock, so that is something," she confessed.

"Which is a good thing," Whalen pointed out. "You didn't use to sleep well."

"No, I've been working on that," she said, with a nod. "Now with fresh air, exercise, and lots of food, … I pretty-well crash at night."

"Does it take a lot to wake you?" Mountain asked suddenly, giving her an intense look.

Surprised, she gave him an odd look. "I don't know. … I've never slept through a fire, if that's what you're asking."

"I'm not sure what I'm asking, just want to make sure that, in case of an emergency, they know that you're a sound sleeper."

"It's never been an issue before, so I don't know how to answer that question," she said, "but I would hope not." Mountain just nodded and continued to eat, but it gave her an odd feeling. "Speaking of fires, I heard there was a kitchen fire." She stared at Mountain.

At that, Whalen nodded. "And it was investigated, but no definitive answers have been found, as far we know."

"And yet, how is it there are no definitive answers?" she asked. "Particularly if somebody was fooling around with the jets?"

"Which is one of the problems of course," Mountain replied, as he studied her. "So make sure that you are careful around that stove."

"I've already been told that I'm not supposed to light it and that Chef will be the one to check it every morning before he does. It's a little sad to think that's even necessary."

"It's beyond sad," Whalen noted, "but we're all about safety right now and making sure there are no more *accidents*."

With his emphasis on the word *accidents*, she winced. She ate, while she contemplated the thought of a deliberate attempt at arson or a gas fire misadventure. "I guess there's no hope that it was accidental?"

At that, Mountain shook his head slowly. "But that's not for public information, and I'm just warning you because that's where you'll be working."

She winced and nodded. "Right. So, everybody else is a little confused and are drawing their own conclusions."

"You mean, the fact that they were slack in the kitchen? Yes. But then Avalon took a lot of the heat coming out of the kitchen, so, in a way, you're coming in at a much easier time."

"I'm sorry for her," Chrissy muttered. "That couldn't have been easy."

"No, it wasn't, but she handled it fairly well," Whalen noted, with a grin. "I'm sure that Barret helped in that regard," he added, with a twinkle in his gaze.

Chrissy frowned. "Seriously? Relationships are working out here?"

"There are the inevitable quick meetings in the dark, I suppose," replied Mountain. "And I'm not sure that those are any more than what they're intended to be, so *working out* maybe be an overstatement in that case." He gave her a smile. "But definitely a few have come to bear over these past few weeks, and they appear to be quite successful, at least at the moment."

She frowned as she thought about who she knew who was in a steady relationship. "I'll probably find out the others as I go along. Since not very many people are here, it's hard to keep secrets."

"I don't think they are even attempting to," Whalen said. "You'll quickly see that Sydney, our doctor, and Magnus are together, while Egan and Berry are also partners. Rogan and Lisa are together too."

"I have to admit I thought I noticed sparks between Avalon and … I'm still learning names. Barret, is it? So, that takes away eight, and what have we got left for kitchen-fire suspects? Thirty-four other people are here roughly?"

Mountain nodded.

"So, excluding us, that only leaves a couple dozen," she said, with a smirk. "Presuming that these are solid relationships and not prone to murderous intentions, that should narrow the field as to who's causing the chaos."

"You would think so," Mountain replied lightly, "but please do not presume so. Because, as we found out the hard way, … there have been more than a few sideline problems happening here."

"*Sideline?*" she repeated.

At that, Mountain got up, nodded at her, and quickly left.

She looked over at Whalen. "He's an interesting character."

"That he is. And he'll come and go, so you'll never really know when he'll turn up."

"Oh? Is he not part of the regular team here?"

"No. He's in his own world."

She laughed. "It must be a big world, whatever world it is that he's in."

He gave her a smirk. "Yeah, he's a big man, though that's been probably more of a disadvantage for him than an advantage."

"Oh, I can imagine," she noted, "particularly around a military base, such as this. There will always be a certain type person who wants to take him on just because of his size."

He looked at her and then slowly nodded. "I think there's always one or two, but they're usually young and stupid. Mountain's not somebody you take on in a challenge."

"He also doesn't look as if he has much of a sense of humor." When he turned to stare at her, she flushed. "You're right. That's a judgment. I don't know him, don't know anything about him." She gave a wave of her hand. "Forget I said that, please."

"Not to mention that the circumstances here have hardly been conducive to having a viable sense of humor," he pointed out.

"No, you're right," she agreed, feeling like an idiot. "Sorry."

She had to wonder why she had even opened her mouth. It had taken her a while to learn to keep her mouth shut and to just smile at everybody in these situations, but something about seeing Whalen all over again seemed to have loosened her tongue somehow. She didn't know it was nerves or trying to find a level of naturalness, but it was something that she needed to get control of and then button up her mouth again. Determined to not be quite so open about life, she reverted back to the silent treatment and continued to eat.

Almost as if he understood, his lips quirked. "And being quiet was never your thing either." She glared at him, and he just laughed. "I'm not saying you did anything wrong, so don't even think about it."

She relaxed ever-so-slightly. "It's one of those lessons that you have to learn, I guess, that not everything here is quite so easy to deal with," she murmured.

"A lot of competition is here, so it can be an aggressive environment," he shared. "Also a lot of camaraderie, depending on the groups that you end up connected with. So, it will probably come down to what cliques you socialize with and what teams you work with. Just keep that in mind too."

"Normally I would, but I find myself doing so many things differently, just because you are here."

"Have you found it difficult here?"

She nodded. "Actually I have. I regretted my choice almost immediately." He stared at her, and she shrugged. "I joined up for the wrong reason. I have since found peace with that and a sense of understanding of what I was doing and why, and I've come to really enjoy it," she admitted. "But I'll leave when my years are up, which is coming fairly quick," she added, with a smile, "and I'll finally open up that bakery with Elaine." The look on his face was priceless. She chuckled. "I know. You always thought I was just messing around with it."

"No, I'm surprised that you didn't do it right off the bat. It's where your heart was at."

"It is where my heart was," she confirmed, "but I needed to make more money. Elaine has been working. I've been working, and we've been putting money into the same pot for a while now. She's looking for a location, so pretty quickly I'm about to start a whole new world." She gave him a fat smile of satisfaction, almost as if to say, *So there.*

And yet he hadn't been in any way responsible for her *not* setting up that bakery before. He'd been very supportive of it, but she hadn't been ready, emotionally or financially. "It's taken a while to get that financial nest egg up to what we needed to do it right," Chrissy pointed out, "but we're there now."

"Good for you," Whalen said. "It's really nice to see that you're making your dreams come true."

"Oh, I need to," she replied, with an eye roll. "I spent enough time trying to figure out what was wrong with me and what this military life had that I couldn't offer you," she explained, with half a smile. "And I'm not doing that anymore."

"Good." Whalen nodded. "It was never about that."

"Sure it was," she argued. "You made it very clear that it was one or the other and that it couldn't be both."

"No." Whalen shook his head. "I made it very clear that it couldn't be *you* at that time. Obviously I didn't do it in a very good way. I didn't do it in a very nice way, and, for that, I'm sorry. I didn't mean to send you on a crazy life path, not when I know this is not what you wanted to be doing all this time."

"No, but maybe I needed to," she declared, looking at him silently for a moment. "Sometimes we take a little longer to grow up." And, with that, she got up a bit too quickly. "Now I'll head to my room and grab some quiet me-time."

She took her dishes back to the kitchen, quickly washed them, and, with a wave at Elijah and Avalon, headed to her room. She needed to think and to clear her head for good.

WHALEN WATCHED CHRISSY leave with an odd sense of disquiet. To even consider that she was here was simply … flabbergasting. Military service had been something so completely opposite to everything that she had ever wanted to do, plus a challenging environment on this survival training base. Now the bakery was another thing. That was definitely where she belonged, and Whalen was glad she was finally going in that direction. He'd tried to convince her when they were together that she should do that, but, as she admitted, she hadn't been ready mentally or financially.

He didn't know how she would go about getting ready mentally for pursuing her dream for a bakery shop, but maybe she did. He remembered her friend Elaine as also being incredibly driven; and both of them were very gifted bakers. To see Chrissy here in this military base just blew him away, and the fact that she had enlisted because of him was also very disconcerting.

He never wanted to impact her life in such a way. It would be good if she had found a certain amount of peace with the years that she spent doing this, but it certainly wasn't the life for her. Although it might make it easier for her to understand why it was the career he had chosen.

And maybe not. Maybe that was just foolishness all around. He hadn't shared anything with her yet as to why he'd left back then and wasn't even sure he wanted to get into that conversation. Yet it might not be a bad idea to clear the air. While it had been a shock seeing her again—and here of all places—but, more than that, it had been a shock to realize he was still affected by her presence.

He'd always known she had a special ability to hit him where it counted, and still he had never been ready back then for what he knew she wanted. That had always been part of the problem for him. And yet, even as he watched her walk away, just something about her movements, her attitude, her everything, still attracted him in a big way. But as that ship had already sailed, and he'd messed up the ending of that story, he knew there was no way that he would go back, and, by rights, that time had come and gone.

When somebody spoke to him, he jerked his head out of his reverie and twisted around to see Magnus, just staring at Whalen with a quizzical gaze. He smiled at Magnus. "Hey."

"Hey is right," Magnus murmured. "You doing okay?"

"Yeah, I'm fine." He nodded toward the exit. "Just an odd trip down memory lane."

Magnus looked at him for a long moment and nodded. "Is it a problem?"

"Nope, no problem," he stated, as he got up. "However, after the day I had, you can bet I'm heading to bed," he replied, with a smile.

"I guess there was nothing to report after today, was there?"

Not knowing where Magnus was involved in this whole deal, Whalen just shook his head and left it at that. "No, not really, although Mountain may have something to say about whatever he deems appropriate."

At that, Magnus stared at him, his eyebrows up.

Whalen repeated, "I'm hitting the sack." Then he turned

and headed down the hallway.

In his room, he pulled out the notebook found at the scientists' camp and started taking pictures of it. He would send copies of every page to Mason. Whalen wasn't sure it would be of much value but didn't want to take the chance that something was here that could be helpful. Thus Whalen kept at it. By the time he was done, and he'd flipped through the whole notebook, he had some idea of what was in it. Yet the fact that it was hidden underneath the chair was still a bit disconcerting.

When Mason phoned him a little later, he asked, "Where did you find this exactly?" When Whalen explained, Mason went quiet for a moment. "What the hell do you think it means?"

"I'm not sure," he said, "but what I do know is that somebody didn't want it found, and now we're trying to find out who was sitting in that spot. Why that actual chair was utilized, I don't know," he added.

"I'm not sure how you'll ever find that out, considering what's going on there."

"No," Whalen agreed, "and it's not this notebook that they were asking us for. However, we can do some handwriting analysis. We may end up with a better idea of who wrote the note. Plus there is definitely some code here and there, so definitely more to this notebook than meets my quick review of it."

"But are we sure about that?" Mason asked. "What are the chances that whoever was looking for this thought it would be available, ready to just pick up, and thought that most of it would be hidden on the inside and that nobody would know or care what was in it?"

"Potentially. Though it's a lot smaller than what we were

asked to look for."

"Yet maybe the request is coming via other people, so that the details in the request were slightly diluted by the number of people involved in that link."

"It's possible," Whalen murmured.

Mason continued. "I'll talk to a few of the people who were at the scientists' camp and have recovered. Maybe this notebook belongs to a scientist who won't recover," he pointed out, "which will just compound the issue."

"Take a look at the pages I sent you and see if you can make heads or tails out of it," Whalen noted.

"It does seem to be some code. If it is, I'll get Tesla on it," he said, with a note of humor. "She would never forgive me if I didn't."

"Right. That's fun for her, isn't it?"

"It absolutely is fun for her. Now, get it to the other members of the team and see if they have any idea about it too and let me know."

"Obviously the chances of anybody here knowing anything about it aren't great."

"No, but it might help to clarify why Amelia won't come in."

"I think at this point, … she probably thinks we're all suspect. I thought Mountain mentioned that somebody at the village was helping her."

"Maybe," Mason hedged. "Maybe he's right about that." After a brief hesitation, he shared, "I've met her, you know?"

"Amelia?" Whalen asked in astonishment.

"Yes, Dr. Morrison," he confirmed. "That's Dr. Amelia Morrison."

"Okay, so Dr. Morrison, it is. Everybody's been calling her Amelia."

"I know." Mason laughed. "She would probably be totally okay with that too but … not under the circumstances."

"It seems this has been more of a shit show than any of us were expecting," Whalen muttered.

"Correct. So, keep me posted and be careful."

Whalen disconnected from Mason, pulled out his own notebook, and started writing down as much as he could remember. He had a little bit of the recent history of these base accidents, but it was scant, and that's because there just wasn't a whole lot of information on the earlier cases, involving the military base, like those first two MPs who had been killed, which got more suspicious when trainees went missing too.

There had been multiple searches for the missing men and then nothing. Whalen frowned at that, wondering how hard it would be to disappear this close to the base. However, after taking a good look at the world around him out there today, while he'd been out with Mountain, Whalen realized it would be damn easy to go missing and to not be discovered. Maybe in spring things would show up again but, even then, maybe not.

It's quite possible that any missing persons were done for, just because the world here offered little forgiveness. Whalen pondered the idea of somebody willingly going out there. There had been talk about jokes and dares and all kinds of stupidity along those lines, yet nobody had fessed up to such a thing when questioned. That didn't mean it wasn't happening though.

Whalen had certainly seen it happen in various bases at various places all around the world. He'd hoped that they wouldn't be doing anything quite so stupid when they were in this Arctic winter environment, but it would explain the missing persons, especially since nobody was talking about these stupid games of dare.

Nobody wanted to get in trouble, and nobody wanted to pay the price for somebody else's death. Whalen wasn't sure it was a criminal act anyway. Lots of times people signed up to do stupid shit and wished later that they hadn't, but that didn't make anybody else responsible. Yet they needed to stop it here, and it did appear that it had stopped, but Whalen couldn't really figure out why. What he wanted to do was listen in on conversations, yet not too obviously. And, with that in mind, he headed back to the kitchen.

As soon as he walked in, silence fell. He glanced over at the others and smiled to dissipate the attention. "Hey, I wondered where everybody was."

"Most people are in their rooms at this hour," noted one of the men.

"Considering I've been out on skis all day," Whalen explained, "I was going to turn in myself but thought another hot drink might help chase away the chill."

"Don't get cold out here," warned one of the men, his tone serious. "It really can set you back for days."

"And yet, how do you not get cold?" Whalen asked in a half-joking manner. "Did you look outside?"

The other guy cracked a smile and nodded. "Yep, I sure did," he muttered. "Doesn't mean that Mother Nature will spare any of us here." He got up with that comment and looked over at the people at his table. "See you in the morning." And, with that, he was gone.

Taking a chance, Whalen made a hot chocolate, walked over, and motioned at the empty place at their table. "Mind if I join you?"

"Sure," one of the men replied, with an open smile.

"We're just playing cards."

"Yeah, what's your game?" Whalen asked, a bit excited to have something going. "It sure as hell better not be strip poker in this weather."

That cracked a smile, and the others just laughed. "No, we're not that stupid," the same guy replied. "Although there was talk of that early on, but it's definitely not something to try in these conditions."

"I hope you're kidding about the stripping part too," Whalen added, with a smile. "Even inside I can't imagine it would be terribly fun."

"Nope, I don't imagine it would be," one of the guys noted. He got up and looked at the others, half lifted a hand and walked away.

"Something I said?" Whalen asked.

"No, everybody's just a little on edge. And the fact that new people are arriving, when we're not allowed to leave is, … well, it's causing some issues and adding to the frustration." This remaining guy sounded a bit too grim.

"I came by special request," Whalen noted, with a shrug.

"I'm Ralph. And I know the new woman in the kitchen did too, mostly because she's a baker."

Whalen nodded. "In my case, I'm not technically new. I've been here for a while already."

"Have you?" The Ralph guy studied him.

Whalen nodded. "A couple weeks."

Ralph frowned. "Sorry, I'm not even sure I saw you."

"I was here. I'm the one doing all the equipment checks and safety checks all around the place."

"Ah, well, I'm glad to have you in that case," he stated, giving Whalen a haunted look, "because something stinks in this place."

"I haven't found anything out of sorts, besides house-keeping type stuff," Whalen shared, "but, if you know of anything or see anything, let me know, would you?"

"Will do," Ralph said, "but I sure wouldn't want anybody to know about it."

Whalen's eyebrows shot up at that. "Even if it's a safety issue?"

"Yeah, even if it is," he confirmed. "Things aren't all that easy around here. We've also had some people pull some shitty-ass stunts, and that's made everybody even warier."

"Sorry to hear about that," Whalen replied sincerely. "None of us need that. I'm just trying to ensure that there are no more accidents." He took a moment to stress his point again. "We'll know for certain that the equipment was solid beforehand."

Ralph looked at him for a long moment and then slowly nodded. "I have to admit. I feel a little better myself knowing that you're doing that. ... I didn't tell anybody, but I was on a trip out, on one of these training missions," he explained, "and shots were fired. I knew that we weren't doing work or any shooting off to the side, yet something plucked at my jacket awful damn hard." He looked around, as if to confirm that no one could hear him. "I booked it out of there and never said a word to anybody."

Whalen stared at him. "Why not?"

"Because there was no reason for anything to come my way," he said. "As far as I was concerned, that was a targeted shot, and somebody came damn close to making it a good one. I won't give them a chance for a repeat."

"Well, damn," Whalen muttered. "I'm really not happy to hear that."

"No, and believe me. If I could have gotten out on any

of these airlifts that you guys seem to magically get in and out on, I would be long gone myself."

"I'm sorry. If we had known about it, we would have been able to investigate and maybe get some leads on the shooter."

Ralph shook his head at that and lowered his voice, as he again looked around the empty room. "And, if I had told, I could have gotten another bullet while I'm out. Even now, talking to you, I'm taking one hell of a chance."

"Got it," Whalen said, "yet live rounds are supposedly counted."

"Sure they are." Ralph shrugged. "It didn't seem they were doing a mission on the side," he repeated. "And I've always been a little suspicious about these *accidents*, especially with Teegan being missing."

"Why is that?" Whalen asked.

"Because Teegan, who went missing early on, … he was looking into the accidents," Ralph declared. "He didn't like what was going on around here, and he told me that he was looking into a couple incidents. I told him not to be an idiot, but he was the hero type." Ralph gave a mocking smile. "I'm the survival type," he pointed out, with a raised eyebrow. "I just want to make sure my sorry ass gets home."

"How many days has it been since the shots were fired? Can you place a date and time on it?" Whalen asked him.

"Teegan went missing soon afterward." Ralph paused. "And, just to add to the confusion, on that same day, I was wearing Teegan's jacket," he added a bit hesitantly. Then he stood and snapped, "But, if you send anybody to talk to me about it, I'll deny it all." And, with that, he was gone.

Whalen sat here alone, wishing he knew more about Ralph.

DAY 3 MORNING

I T WAS CHRISSY'S day in the kitchen, as per the schedule. As she dove right in to help out and to do some of the baking, she looked over at Chef and smiled. "Everything okay?"

He gave her a curt nod. "So far, yes."

She winced at that. "Be nice if you'd just said *yes*, without a caveat."

He snorted. "Be nice if you didn't even have to ask."

"Okay, point to you for that one," she muttered. "What's on the menu for baking today?"

He suggested, "If you're up for it, I need bars. I need cookies. I need …" He stopped. "I need muffins, and maybe something that will keep the guys happy, without using up too much of my supplies."

She laughed and nodded. "Do you care what order?"

"No, I just need lots," he replied. "Fill up my freezer, and that'll give us a few days again."

"Sure thing."

And, with that decided, she got to work. They were a little short on some of the supplies, so she had to make a few modifications. By the time lunch rolled around, she had several items in the oven and more ready to go. Some of it was cooling on racks already.

Chef grabbed the muffins and put them out to go with

the lunch and nodded appreciatively at the rest. "I do enjoy being able to just say, *I need something*, and then turn around and find it happening," he noted, with a big grin.

"It's what's supposed to happen," she claimed.

He nodded. "I hope you end up getting that bakery you're talking about," he muttered. "I think you'll be really good at it."

"It's still a gamble."

"Sure, but following your heart is always a gamble," Chef Elijah pointed out. "Look at what brought you here." She flushed at that and then glared, as he shrugged. "Doesn't take much to see how things are with the two of you." Chef nodded to where Whalen was pouring coffee.

She frowned at Chef in astonishment. "Wow, I wouldn't have thought anybody would care enough to notice."

"It's a small place, and people are bored," Chef explained with a smile. "Relationships, drama, and, well, the fuss you made, … is big news around here."

"And yet it shouldn't be," she muttered. "There isn't any relationship to gossip about."

"No, but it sounds as if you guys have a history."

"We *had* a history," she pointed out. "Not anything between us now."

"Yep, I hear you. I hear the words, but I'm not sure I'm hearing the actual meaning of them." She stared at him, and he shrugged. "Sometimes people say things, but they mean something completely different." Chef smirked. "Sure seems to be what I'm hearing now."

"Oh, wow," Chrissy said. "Can't say I expected to have that thrown at me."

He frowned at her and asked, "Did I throw it at you?"

"Let's just say that you startled me with it."

"Oh, … well." Chef gave her a stern look. "You'll get over it."

She burst out laughing. "Not so sure I will. It was honestly a shock to hear you say that."

"It shouldn't be, though," he argued, with a smile, "if you think about it."

She didn't know what to make of that and got back to work, baking more things designated to fill up his freezer. Still, the whole time she pondered Chef's words and how he meant them.

When dinner was served, and, with her thankfully not on the serving line, she grabbed a plate and headed out, looking for a place to sit. Once again it seemed all the tables were full. She frowned as she looked around, and the only empty place was beside Whalen. She groaned as she walked over, lifted an eyebrow, and asked, "Please?"

He nodded immediately. "No please required. This is all a common space, and, as it is, … everybody should be sharing."

"Yeah, well, not so much."

As he looked around the room, it seemed everybody had closed ranks, or at least had their own cliquey little groups. He frowned as he pulled her chair back. "Don't worry about it," he noted, with a smile.

She shrugged. "It's such a weird feeling. It's almost as if I'm unwelcome, yet nobody even knows me."

"I don't think it's that you're unwelcome, as much as the fact that you're a new arrival, when none of them can get out. That's what's giving everybody the attitude problem," he muttered. "And it sucks, I know, but even though it probably seems directed at you, I don't think it is."

"It feels directed at me," she muttered. Regardless she sat

down, picked up her fork, and asked, "How was your day?"

"It was okay," he muttered. "Another long day out on skis."

He did look tired and worn out. She eyed him closer to see the wind-burnt cheeks and his chapped lips. He glanced around, his gaze ever searching. She noticed that he never seemed to relax. "You seem more tense these days."

He glanced at her, and his lips quirked. "Generally, when I was with you before, I wasn't on duty."

She nodded. "I'm sorry."

"Sorry for what?" he asked, astonished.

"For not understanding."

He shook his head. "How would you understand, if you weren't actively involved in any of the stuff that I was dealing with?" he asked, with half a smile.

At that, she had to laugh. "I have to admit that being here has opened my eyes to what I didn't understand before. Not that it would have changed anything, but it certainly has made me a more mature person."

"Nothing wrong with you before," Whalen stated firmly. "I'm sorry that I didn't talk to you before I left, but the bottom line is that it wasn't you. It was me."

She snorted at that. "And that is a cop-out," she muttered. "If it wasn't me on some level, … you would have been comfortable talking to me." She spoke in a harsh tone, maybe more so than she intended. "The fact that you *didn't* talk to me, purposely avoided talking to me, means that it was exactly about me." He looked at her, bemused, and she nodded. "You can say whatever you want, but it doesn't change the facts, Whalen."

The use of his name seemed to startle him or maybe it was her tone of voice.

"If you say so." He shrugged. "I'm not trying to bring on a fight, but the fact that you now understand where I was at regarding missions does make it an interesting prospect for you—especially since you have another future lined up for yourself."

"One that you were always pushing me toward," she noted, after a moment.

He shrugged. "I knew it's what you really wanted to do, and I wanted you to be happy."

"What if I wanted to be happy but be with you too?"

"If we could have made both of those things work, that would have been fine," he shared, "but we couldn't seem to do it." She opened her mouth and then slammed it shut again, and he nodded. "I appreciate that," he said, with a nod. "And, yeah, we do have some talking to do. I'm not quite there yet, but I'll get there."

At that, she frowned at him.

He shrugged. "I guess I could say a few things about that time between us, if you're up for that. I'm not sure that the discussion will be all that easy, so I'm not quite there yet. I'm still working my way through it."

"I always wondered what your mind-set was, when you just walked away," she admitted. "I get that that's not what you want to talk about right now, but, … to just walk away without a word?" She shook her head. "I would have been so worried about what the other person thought."

"I also knew that you'd contacted Mark and that he had told you how I was out on a mission and that I was no longer interested."

She winced. "Yeah, that was *lovely* to hear."

"For the record, I didn't ask him to say that. However, since I had waited too long to get back to you afterward, there wasn't a whole lot I could say that didn't make me sound more idiotic than I already was."

She didn't know what to make of that statement, and she wanted to ask even more questions, but, as she looked around, several people were getting up to leave. It was about time to change the subject because they were moving in circles. "What do they do in the evenings?"

He shrugged. "I haven't been invited to anything. They've closed ranks. Those of us who came in afterward, when they weren't allowed to leave, have been seen as negative. Thus we don't really get that break that we're supposed to have or the camaraderie that generally develops when you're involved in training or a mission," he explained, with a lip quirk. "It's very much a *them against us* thing."

"Which really sucks," she admitted, "because, although I knew about all the other issues, … I was really hoping to have this training opportunity—prior to finishing up my tour—so I was pretty excited when I heard I was coming up here."

"And you were also requested, I understand."

She nodded. "They were giving special access to those who were willing to do cooking time, even though they had some people lined up. Apparently Elijah took note of my application."

"Which is also interesting." Whalen turned, facing her.

"I know. I'm not exactly sure I understand how that worked or whether he stomped on other people to do that, which could also be why nobody's been particularly open and friendly."

"Don't you worry about everybody else," Whalen said. "Just remember that some shitty things are still happening around this place and that we don't want you getting involved in any of it."

"That's nice," she muttered. "The thing is, I don't think I'll recognize who the enemy is from anybody else, when nobody is willing to open up and talk to me."

Whalen gave her a one-arm shrug. "That is always an issue when we have these kinds of problems."

"And yet it shouldn't be," she stated, studying him. "None of this should be an issue."

He smiled. "Yeah? And, until you find a way to get around all these people, that's a different story. What about the rest of the women? Have they been nice?" he asked, looking over at her.

Chrissy shrugged. "I've met Sydney a couple times and Avalon, of course. Both of them are pretty friendly."

At that, a woman behind them chipped in pleasantly, "Well, that's good to know."

Startled, Chrissy looked back, and, sure enough, there was Sydney. Chrissy smiled at the base's only doctor. "I was just telling him how hard it is to get to know anybody here."

Sydney nodded. "Particularly when you're new."

"Yet since when is *new* in a place like this a negative?" Chrissy asked, with a wry smile. "It used to be that everybody was happy to see new faces and to have somebody new to talk to, you know?"

Sydney nodded and smiled. "Under different circumstances it would be exactly like that," she declared. "However, here, *new* also means that transportation came to drop you off, *without* picking them up. Every time that happens, it's another reminder that they are stuck here and can't leave," she explained.

"That's what Whalen was just telling me." She shrugged, turning to him, asking a bit too lightly, "And you're working on all that stuff, aren't you?" He gave her half a smile, but it didn't reach his eyes. "Your gaze never stops searching your surroundings," she pointed out. "It's disconcerting." He just raised his eyebrows, and she shrugged again. "I know. It doesn't make a whole lot of sense."

"Stop knocking yourself," Whalen stated. "You're doing just fine."

Surprised, but feeling an odd sense of joy, she laughed. "Good to know. Especially when I'm not even trying."

Sydney spoke up. "When you're not even trying is generally when you get the best results."

"I've heard that too," Chrissy muttered. "I hate the fact that I feel as if I need to try, but I wasn't really expecting to feel as isolated as I am."

"What about in the kitchen?"

"No, you're right. It's all good there. When I think about it, plenty of people have been quite friendly. I don't know why everybody else is hitting me the wrong way, but it feels very much as if there's this divider between *them and us.*"

"Because there is," Whalen confirmed, yet with a smile. "And you know why that is, now that we've explained it."

She nodded. "So, is it even worth trying to get friendly with everybody?"

"If you feel like being friendly, then be friendly," Sydney advised. "Other than that, don't go out of your way. Definitely some issues are here, but most of the teams are dealing with it. I appreciate the fact that they are trying," she shared. "It makes our job a whole lot easier."

"It's such a weird thing to think that something on that level is going on here," Chrissy muttered. "And yet you would think there would be so much security that it wouldn't be possible for these things to happen."

"Which is part of our problem." Whalen gave a nod in Sydney's direction. "But Sydney here has seen an awful lot more than I have, since I've only been here a little longer than you, Chrissy. Sydney's been here through a lot more of the trouble."

At that, Chrissy looked over at Sydney and asked, "And you couldn't leave either?"

"I could have, since I was cleared for the later incidents," she added cheerfully, "but I decided I didn't want to."

At that, Whalen laughed. "Did Magnus have something to do with that?"

She nodded. "Yep, he absolutely did. Plus, when you're in a situation like this, it really helps to have somebody to watch your back."

"Exactly, and that's why you're still here because you know that he'll stay, and you want to make sure that, if anything happens, you're there for him."

The doc's eyes twinkled, as she looked around at the rest of the people in the room. "It's not just me and Magnus in that regard," she noted. "A few other pairs have happened."

"I noticed that," Chrissy said, with a smile. "I am used to seeing relationships on missions. Generally a lot of them don't continue beyond the duration of the assignment, … but I can imagine how it would be a great way to get through a time, especially where you're locked up in an unpleasant situation—as long as," she emphasized the point by rolling her eyes, "you find somebody of your ilk."

"And doing that is a whole different ball game," Sydney agreed. "I don't come on missions looking for somebody," she admitted. "Yet, when somebody special suddenly appeared right in front of me, I didn't walk away from it either. And now? … Well, I don't think I could ever do that."

"Of course not," Chrissy agreed. "I'm happy for you. I really am."

"Yet you don't think it'll happen to you?"

Chrissy flushed and deliberately avoided looking at Whalen. She shook her head. "Nope, I'm a whole lot more … Well, I choose my partners a whole lot differently now," she shared in a dry tone. And, with that, she hopped up and looked at them both steadily. "I'll head back and spend some time by myself," she muttered. "At times, nothing is better than your own company." And, with that, she turned and walked away.

"THAT WAS AN interesting response," Sydney muttered, her gaze intent on Whalen's face.

He shrugged, willing his face not to flush, as he knew it wanted to. "We had a relationship, some five years ago, and I walked away, … and I probably didn't do it in the best manner," he admitted, chewing on his own words. "I *definitely* didn't do it in the best way. The fact that she's even speaking to me says something about her level of forgiveness."

"And the fact that you did something needing forgiveness, when I know you're a really nice guy, also says something about how you either couldn't talk to her or weren't ready to discuss whatever was going on in your head at the time."

"Exactly," he muttered, "though I can't say I'm all that ready now either."

"But it's right in front of you, so how do you get out of it?"

"Yeah, I was trying to figure that one out," he said, with a chuckle, "but, so far, no luck."

"I'm not at all surprised." Sydney gave him a droll look. "I didn't come here looking for a partner, and I don't think Chrissy's here looking for a partner either. No matter what her reasons were for joining up or for coming here, that's a very different story than looking for that relationship at this point in time in her life. It seems she's got big plans of her own, you know? Places to go and things to do," she noted, "and that's really cool."

"It absolutely is, and I'm really glad. Her bakery was a dream I was trying to get her to follow through on when we were together," Whalen added, "but she wasn't ready, at least that's how she put it."

"And, you know, that's valuable too. We're not always ready in the time frame that everybody else thinks we should be. It's not easy to follow other people's schedules either," she noted. "Maybe Chrissy thought she needed to not be alone for that. Maybe she needed a partner in order to make her bakery dream happen."

"She has a business partner," he replied, "an old girlfriend of hers, who I really like."

"That's good. Friendship, being the backbone of all relationships," she noted, with an eye roll.

Whalen waited until Magnus joined them, then leaned forward and told him what he'd heard from the other guy.

At that, Magnus sat back and stared, a slow-building fury on his face.

Whalen continued. "He also warned me that, if I sent anybody to talk to him about it, this conversation never happened, and he would call me a flat-out liar."

"Jesus Christ," Magnus muttered. "So, he gets shot at, doesn't tell anybody, and he was wearing Teegan's jacket at the time? How can someone be so dense as to keep it from the brass?"

Whalen nodded. "I know, and I might get more information out of him on the sly. I didn't get much of a chance to even process what he was saying before he booked it, and I'm sure it was because he was feeling horribly guilty."

"He should be," Magnus declared. "Teegan is Mountain's brother, you know."

Whalen sighed. "Jesus Christ, what a mess."

"Have you told Mountain?" Magnus asked.

"Not yet, I haven't had a chance." Whalen looked around the dining room. "I wasn't sure whether he'd come in or not."

"That's a good point," Sydney agreed, now frowning. "I'm pretty sure he was going to the village and likely staying there overnight this time."

"Does he have a place to stay there overnight?" Whalen asked cautiously. "I'm not saying he has a special friend, but when he disappears all the time …"

"I believe he's made an arrangement regarding his visits," Magnus noted. "He's trying to be a little more friendly because the locals' relationship with us isn't that great. They have a seriously flawed idea of how we operate. As Mountain's mentioned over and over, he suspects they might know more than they're telling us."

"I would think so," Whalen agreed, "though I can also understand their not wanting to share."

"And yet, if people don't open up, we'll never get to the bottom of this. Mountain's still hoping that his brother's alive."

Sydney winced at that.

Magnus reached across, laced his fingers with hers, and nodded. "He's not a fool, and he can take care of himself and his feelings. At the moment, he's definitely focusing his efforts on soothing things between the village and the base and everything in between. The bottom line is that Teegan *is* his brother, and to know that something happened just prior to his disappearance is really important to this overall investigation."

"I understand," Whalen agreed. "This guy knew that Teegan was investigating too, and also my informant seemed to have some idea about these accidents and disappearances after Teegan went missing, but the guy wouldn't give me any more information."

Magnus leaned forward, his gaze narrow and hard, as he declared, "That's your next mission then. You need to get whatever information he's got. Whoever this guy is, he needs to be more forthcoming."

"If he'll talk," Whalen noted. "I think he's running scared, and he's also quite pissed off that he can't get out of here. Plus he's very wary that he might not make it out. He did mention that he's more concerned about saving his butt and surviving than getting justice over being shot at."

"What makes you think that it couldn't have been friendly fire?" Sydney asked, then winced. "I guess when it comes to that, you're keeping track of all the firearms though, aren't you?"

Magnus nodded. "Right now, we're specifically working on keeping ammunition low, and people are required to keep track of how many shots are fired, to pick up their casings and any other garbage that they have out here." He shook his head. "That's not something that we'll let slide easily. But to get a record of any shots fired back at that time? … I'm not sure that's even possible."

"Damn," Whalen muttered, "if that isn't right."

"Listen. I'll tell Mountain when I see him, but you can expect him to come to you," Magnus noted.

"This guy won't cooperate at all, and I can tell you that he won't really cooperate with me after sharing that either."

"Got it." Magnus rapped his fingers in a staccato pattern on the tabletop. "Don't you think that we can just force it out of him?"

"I think if you even try, you'll stop him from talking at all."

"Well, shit." Magnus seemed deep in thought. "He's that scared, *huh*?"

"Yeah, he's that scared," Whalen confirmed. "Terrified. I think, based on everything else that we've seen around here, he's fully justified in that fear."

Sydney immediately nodded. "Nothing like fear to cripple somebody," she murmured. "We've already seen that here." She looked back at Magnus. "We can't do anything to alienate him. Not as long as he has information that you need to collect."

"And we do need him to cooperate." Magnus glared at Whalen. "So, you need to stay in his good graces and talk to him. I guess I'll hold off on telling Mountain, so that we can try and stop him from going all berserk on the poor guy. Guess it's all on you then, Whalen."

"Thanks. You do know that he may not talk to me further and probably regrets what he shared already, right?"

"I know, but give it your best shot. If he doesn't want anybody else talking to him, then he definitely needs to talk to you."

"I can try," Whalen noted. And, with that, he got up and smiled over at Sydney. "Thanks for the advice earlier." And, with that, he was gone.

DAY 4 EARLY MORNING

C HRISSY WOKE THE next morning and groaned at her first note of consciousness. The wind had picked up even more than usual, and it seemed to be ripping through her bedroom. She shuddered and curled up deeper into the blankets, but still she had an odd sense of something being off. She hated that, dammit. She'd only ever had that instinct since she started her five-year tour. Since then there was just something about it, almost an inner sense that something was wrong, and she had never been able to ignore it.

Knowing that she was not on kitchen duty but that she would never get back to sleep, she got up, quickly dressed, and raced to the kitchen, hoping there'd be at least coffee for her. Everybody else knew that there wouldn't be coffee for a while, but she thought her coworkers might already have a little on for themselves.

As she stumbled into the kitchen, Whalen and Magnus stood there in an angry confab. She cleared her throat noisily, so they would know she was here and not trying to sneak up on them.

Whalen turned to her and asked, "Are you on kitchen duty this morning?"

She shook her head. "Actually, no, but I woke up with that, I don't know, that *off* feeling that something was wrong. So I decided to come in search of coffee, instead of tossing and turning because I couldn't go back to sleep." As she studied the men, she knew something was up. "What's going on?"

Magnus frowned and didn't say anything.

She looked over at Whalen. "Something I need to know about?"

He shook his head. "No. Not yet anyway."

At that, Chef Elijah stepped through and glared at her. "We could have another man missing."

"Christ, no," she wailed, her heart sinking. "And here I was really hoping that all that shitty stuff was over with, before my arrival."

"Wouldn't that be nice." Chef snorted. "And you're not on shift, so what are you doing here?"

She sighed. "Nice to know that everybody really wants me here, since everybody's been shooing me away, but," she added, taking a deep breath, "I woke up feeling a sense of wrongness and decided to come and grab some coffee, if there was any."

"And you know there isn't," Chef grumbled, "so you had better come in and put some on."

Immediately she stepped inside and grabbed the pot and started making coffee. She heard the other two still talking angrily around the corner. "When you say, *missing,*" she began delicately, speaking to Chef.

Chef shrugged. "Let's just say somebody's not in his bed."

She nodded. "Anybody check the women's beds?"

"Yeah, I'm not sure how close they are to doing that. Magnus went to knock on somebody's door this morning, only to find the room empty."

"That doesn't necessarily mean anything," she hedged,

frowning at him.

"I know, and that's what the current argument is about."

"You mean, whether he's really missing or not?"

"Yes. And, of course, if he's not, they don't want to stir everyone up by going door to door and waking them all. Yet, if it *is* a case of missing a man, well, that's a different story."

She looked over at Whalen, and he stared at her. He hesitated and then walked over and in a low voice asked, "Have you seen Ralph?"

She frowned and shook her head. "Not that I know exactly who that is," she murmured. "However, if I think I know who it is, then no. Honestly, I ... haven't seen anybody yet this morning."

He nodded and stared around distractedly.

"But seriously," Chrissy added, "an awful lot of nighttime activity happens across the corridors."

"And I would be more than happy if that were the case," Whalen acknowledged, "but I'm afraid it isn't."

She shook her head. "Let's stay positive." He shot her a look, and she winced. "I'm not trying to sound naïve in this case," she murmured. "Yet I don't, ... I don't know when I would have last seen him."

"I saw him last night," Whalen noted. "I talked to him." At that, his frown deepened.

She realized that Whalen was quite possibly the last person to see Ralph. "Would he have left?"

"Not at that hour and not alone. I would hope not, at least."

"Maybe Joe has seen him though," she suggested, with a shrug. "If Ralph needed to leave, he would have definitely visited him."

"Possibly. I'll head over and talk to him in a minute," he

murmured. "If you see Ralph …"

She nodded. "I'll let you know."

"And do it quietly," he ordered. "Better yet, text me."

She looked at him and pulled out her phone. "What's your number?" He quickly gave it to her, and she nodded. "Will do." And, with that, she headed back to grab a coffee. When she turned around, Whalen was gone. She looked over at Chef. "That could be bad news."

"It would be, indeed," he muttered, "but it's also early yet."

"I know. I know," she muttered. "Let's hope that he's just, you know, sleeping in somebody else's bed."

He shot her a cheeky grin and asked, "Sure it wasn't yours?'

"No, it definitely wasn't mine," she stated. "Really not looking to hook up on this trip."

"And here I thought you'd already made a choice," Chef teased, now laughing.

She groaned and muttered, "That's not even funny."

"No, but it's already pretty obvious."

She stared at him in shock, shook her head, and declared, "Hell no." With that, she picked up her coffee and announced, "And now I'm going back to bed because it isn't my shift, so I don't need to be taking shit from you." With that, and a smile on her face, she walked back down the hallways, silent, except for the sound of the wind rustling outside, and curled back up in her bed, but sleep was the last thing on her mind.

IT DIDN'T TAKE long to set up a head count, once everybody

approached for breakfast. As soon as everyone's name was checked in, Whalen noted no sign of Ralph. Whalen called out to the crowded dining room area and asked, "Anybody seen Ralph this morning?"

There was a muffled round of *no, nope, nada* and all, but he didn't hear a yes. "Anybody seen Ralph put up a hand, please," he added, just to be sure of it, but no one raised their hand. Whalen nodded. "I'll go check his room."

He'd already been there once, but right now it was important to keep checking, just in case. As he headed toward the area of Ralph's room, he passed Chrissy, stumbling back out again. "Did you fall asleep?" he asked, looking at her curiously.

She shook her head. "No, and I wish I had. Definitely feeling on the groggy side now." She paused and asked, "Any sign of Ralph?"

Whalen shook his head. "I'm heading to his room right now for another check, just in case he was off on a nighttime prowl."

She nodded. "Honestly, as I have found to my detriment, that's a fairly common occurrence."

"Not that many women in this place though," he pointed out gently.

She nodded. "That doesn't mean there isn't some pretty interesting activity going on."

He gave her a sideways look, as she fell into step beside him. "Any that you'd care to divulge?"

She looked at him and then quickly shook her head. "Hell, no," she muttered. "No way I'm getting involved in that."

He just smiled knowingly and didn't say anything.

She glanced at him and asked, "Is that your type of romance now?"

"No, it's sure not, never was."

"Maybe," she muttered. "Not at all sure about that."

He looked at her and frowned. "I was always faithful."

"Yeah, when you were there. But, as I found out, you weren't there for a very long."

He winced at that and didn't say anything.

She groaned. "Sorry, I'm not here to try and ruin your life."

"I'm sure glad to hear that," he replied in a brisk tone, "because I sure as hell wouldn't let you."

"Right. I'm part of your past, aren't I?"

"You are," he agreed, looking at her. "And that's where you want to be, isn't it?" And, with that, he turned a corner, leaving her in the main hallway.

He didn't check behind to see if she was following, but, when he didn't hear her footsteps, he realized she was heading off on her own. As she needed to go to the kitchen and to grab food before whatever she had on tap today, it was better that she got there and had a chance to settle in. It was also one hell of a cold and windy day outside, and he wasn't sure just how many of the training sessions would even be offered. It was one thing to push a training session in ugly weather; it was another thing to push a training session in fatally stormy weather.

But he wasn't part of that, and, as soon as he was done looking for Ralph, Whalen would go back to keeping track of equipment again. A constant niggling in the back of his mind said that things were just a little too accessible, that people were just a little too available for various shenanigans. And, of course, just being available meant temptation was always there too. It made him seem panicky, an overcautious worrywart, but the fact of the matter was, they had plenty to be worried about here on base, much less outside, and Whalen didn't like it one bit.

At Ralph's door, Whalen knocked again, and, when no answer came, he pushed open the door and announced his presence. When he found no sign of anybody inside, he shook the bed and realized that it was empty but it did look as if maybe he'd either not made his bed, which would be unusual, or had slept in it and had left a bit too quickly. Frowning at that option as well, Whalen quickly backtracked to the kitchen area. As soon as Magnus saw him, Whalen shook his head.

Swearing at that, Magnus stood up and announced to all in the dining room, "Okay, before anybody's heading off on their day, we are looking for Ralph. Nobody leaves or heads out on any training until we find him. I don't know if he's sleeping off a drunk that nobody invited me to," he added, injecting a note of laughter into the place, "or if he's still asleep in somebody else's bed, but you've got five minutes to wake that guy up and to get his ass out here." Magnus paused. "Now, if that doesn't happen, … we'll go room by room," he declared, his voice cool and calm, but there was absolutely no give in it.

Several people looked around at each other, but nobody moved.

"So, I take your silence to mean that nobody here had some assignation, appointment, or rendezvous with him last night?" After posing the question, he looked pointedly at all the women.

Each and every one of them shook their heads, and the answer was unanimous.

At that, he turned and looked back at Whalen. "In that

case, everybody is on full alert. This is an all-hands-on-deck, top-to-bottom search for a missing man." The words were like a crack of the whip. "Everybody, fall in." No need to say much more, and, within minutes, they were assigned to go room by room, looking for Ralph.

That underway, Whalen headed to the equipment room to see if everything there was as it should be. When he stepped inside, he definitely noticed disturbed equipment from where he had seen it all the previous night. Swearing at that, he quickly checked everything over—only one set of skis was missing. He quickly phoned Magnus. "I've got a set of skis missing," he muttered.

"I'm on my way," he replied, equally quietly. When he arrived, he looked at Whalen hard and asked, "You're sure?"

"Yes, I'm sure, but I haven't been over to see Joe yet though."

"I did check in with him earlier. He's always up early."

"Yeah, he is always up early," Whalen confirmed.

"I'll head back over there right now and double-check," Magnus stated.

Whalen nodded and waited in the equipment room to ensure nobody else came through. When Magnus returned, his face was grim.

"Joe hasn't seen him. So nobody has seen any sign of Ralph since last night."

"I'm probably the last one to have seen him then," Whalen pointed out.

"Right. Not exactly something we want to make note of."

"We may want to keep it quiet, but I sure as hell didn't do anything to him," Whalen noted. "I've got nothing to hide, but I hear you. He was also fairly upset and potentially mad at himself."

At that, Magnus slowly turned and asked, "Ralph is the one who had something to say?"

"Yep, and now I'm wondering if he didn't decide to up and disappear, before the questions started coming back at him."

"Which means he would have headed for the village."

"I'm already halfway geared up. I thought I'd head out on skis to see if I could find him."

"We really need to finish the search of the base to confirm no sign of him here," Magnus suggested.

"You can always contact me while I'm out there," Whalen pointed out. "We're well behind schedule. If he left when I thought he was missing earlier, we might have had a chance to catch him. Right now I'm not so sure we'll have a chance to find him in time at all."

"All right," Magnus agreed. "If he's gone to the village, Mountain is likely on his way back by now if he's not already home. I'll contact him and have him keep an eye out."

"Good," Whalen said. "I'll let you know what I find." And, with that, Whalen quickly dressed, having already pulled his gear together, and slipped out the door before anybody could stop him.

The wind slammed into his face as soon as he got outside, and he swore. If these were the conditions that Ralph had left in, or if he hadn't checked the barometer to see what was happening to the air pressure around him, then it would be a sad find. Honestly, in his heart of hearts, Whalen knew it would be a sad find anyway.

Hours later, he did find Ralph. He was curled up in a ball sideways, the snow piling up around him. Whalen put in a call to Magnus. "Hey, I found him."

There was a short silence on the other end. "I gather there's no rush?"

"No rush," Whalen confirmed. "Unfortunately it seems he just curled up and went to sleep."

"Shit," Magnus muttered. "I can see that happening."

"If I hadn't talked to him last night, I probably wouldn't have seen it happening, but the fact of the matter is, … I did, and he was pretty upset."

"Sure, but would he have really taken his life over it? He had survived this long."

"But what if somebody broached him about it? What if somebody talked to him or saw that he had spoken to me?" Whalen asked.

"I'm not sure we have any other issues to bring forward, but don't worry. There'll be a full investigation," Magnus stated, his tone firm. "Still not what anybody here needs. We were just starting to settle into life without that added drama."

Whalen sighed. "The fact of the matter is that, at least on the surface, it seems he took his own life."

"Meaning?"

"All I'm saying is that anybody who headed out at that time of night, with a storm of this magnitude looming, had a death wish. To get out there and see how bad it was, then keep going? … It was folly," Whalen declared. "Surely he would have known better."

"So, in that case, what would have sent somebody out in this weather?" Magnus asked.

"The only thing I can think of that would make me do it is absolute panic."

"Yeah, but you still wouldn't have gone out blind, would you?"

"No. He came out in skis, and he's wearing winter gear," Whalen noted, as he crouched down beside Ralph's body. "Yet he didn't make it very far. I'm only a couple miles from the military base."

"Tell me where you are, and I'll head that way."

Almost before he knew it, both Magnus and Mountain were there, dragging a sled behind them. Whalen hadn't touched the body, outside of checking that Ralph was gone, and, when the two men approached, they both checked him over carefully.

Even Mountain swore and said, "He just curled up and didn't give a shit."

"Which goes along with how we found Jerry," Magnus added.

"Yes, and Scott," Mountain replied.

Whalen frowned. "I thought it was decided that Scott's death was accidental."

"I know we figured that, but, at the same time, I'm keeping an open mind. And I know that sounds terrible, but I don't want to find out after the fact that somebody got away with murder because we were all too happy to accept the *accidental deaths*."

Whalen didn't say anything. He stared down at the man he had hoped to talk to a second time. He looked over at Mountain cautiously. "Did Magnus tell you about the conversation I had with him?"

"He did," he replied, his tone of voice hard, as he looked down at the dead man. "What do you want to bet his death is connected to that?"

"Oh, I think it's connected all right," Whalen agreed. "What I don't know is whether he did this to himself or if somebody suggested it to him."

At that, both men looked at him in surprise. "Meaning?"

He shrugged. "Meaning that this way he gets a chance to get to the village on his own, potentially getting picked up and catching a ride out, still caught perhaps, but alive, versus staying at the base and not knowing when and where somebody might have taken him out. I don't know. Everybody there is …" He hesitated but thought it better be said. "Everybody there is trained to kill." Whalen threw caution to the wind because no one could listen in out here. "We all are trained in many things, and we came here for winter survival training. Lots of people are very green when it comes to that, but even Ralph had to know not to be out in the face of that storm."

"You think so?" Magnus asked, looking around. "I'm not sure how the training's been going, but I know there's been a whole lot less of it accomplished than was planned."

"That's because of the weather," Whalen noted.

"Exactly," Magnus pointed out, "so Ralph had every opportunity to know that there were times when you just don't go out in this, not without a plan. The weather has been a bitch, but he was supposedly fully aware of the dangers *before* making this move to head to the village. So, yes, the storm was a factor, but he never should have been out here in the first place. Even still, he didn't get that far. Why did he stop here?"

"We might never know the answer to that. And I don't disagree with you," Whalen replied, "but maybe we need to look at his schedule and see how much training he's been through. After having that shot almost take him out, what are the chances that he's backed out of most of the training, just so that he wouldn't be a sitting duck out here?"

"Good question. We'll find out when we get back,"

Mountain noted, his face grim. He looked down at the sorry scene and added, "I don't know about you guys, but I came here to find my brother and to stop this BS from happening. Right now, it seems we haven't had a chance to stop anything. This entire time somebody has been pulling our chain and doing whatever the hell he wants, making us look like idiots."

"Oh, I agree with that," Magnus confirmed, staring down at the body in front of them. "And this just pisses me off even more. If Ralph knew something, he should have told us, and, if he didn't know something, why the hell would he have run?"

"That'll be the question," Whalen noted, "unless he had something to do with it because innocent men don't run."

Mountain looked at him and shook his head. "You're wrong there. Innocent men do run, but only when they're terrified. Ralph had plenty of chances to talk. Everybody on base has been interviewed over and over. I'm willing to bet something loosened his tongue last night, and just knowing that he'd spoken out loud to somebody and would have to face the consequences is what, one way or another, made him terrified enough to run."

DAY 4 LATE MORNING

CHRISSY STOOD AT the doorway to the medical clinic, talking to Sydney in a subdued tone, when the men arrived with the stretcher. They carried Ralph straight into the clinic, at which time Sydney motioned for Chrissy to leave. She quickly stepped out into the hallway to see a group gathered around. She frowned, hearing and seeing just how upset everybody was at yet another death. She looked over to see Whalen—standing there, surveying the crowd, as if looking to see if anybody was guilty. She walked over to him. "I think you're terrifying them," she murmured.

He turned to her and shrugged. "If it makes somebody open up and talk, I'm okay with that," he stated, his tone hard, as fury radiated off his body.

She winced. "You really think it was on purpose?"

"Oh, it was on purpose all right," he declared. "He was fully dressed and seemed to be doing fine, so I'm not sure at what point in time he decided to give up and just curl up in a ball. I also don't have any idea how long he was out there. Just because I didn't see him in his room doesn't mean that he wasn't somewhere else overnight."

She winced at that. "So, I presume then that you'll talk to all the women?"

He studied her, as if sensing something in her voice. "You got a better idea?"

"Let me talk to them," she suggested. "I'm not sure there's any way for you to say it so it doesn't come across as if they're all hiding something."

He looked at her and laughed, but nothing humorous filled his tone. "I'm far less concerned about them hiding or being accused than finding out the truth as to what happened to Ralph in his last few hours."

Avalon joined them and asked in a hushed whisper, "Is it true?"

He looked over at her and winced. "Yes, it's true."

Chrissy watched the interaction with interest. She motioned at Avalon and asked, "Did you know him?"

"Yeah, he gave me no small amount of grief several times," she shared, "and he wasn't always the nicest person."

"Maybe the reason for that is because he was struggling over some of the issues here," Whalen noted. "He was withholding information," he murmured. "Information that might have helped with Teegan."

Avalon stared at him and swallowed. "God, it's happening all over again, isn't it?"

"Depends on what you mean by *all over again*," he said, with a wry look. "Seems to me this BS has never stopped." And, with that, he turned and strode off.

The rest of the crowd hung around for a little while and then slowly dispersed, as if they realized nobody could do anything for Ralph. Chrissy didn't know why she remained here, but, when Sydney came out, Chrissy nodded and said, "Hey, seems it was a pretty rough day again."

"It's always rough when we have a death," Sydney confirmed, "particularly such as this one."

"I won't ask what that is," Chrissy replied, "because I'm sure I'm not the person you're allowed to talk to, but I sure as hell hope it isn't more bad news."

Sydney sighed, nodded, and in a grim voice said, "It absolutely is more bad news. Do you know where the guys are?"

Not sure who exactly she was referring to, Chrissy answered as best she could. "If you're looking for Magnus or Mountain or one of the others," she began, "chances are they're probably in the cafeteria. They looked pretty upset when they left."

Sydney didn't say anything more but nodded her thanks, then quickly headed to the dining room.

Afraid that it would seem she was prying, yet desperate to know what the hell was going on, Chrissy followed the doc to the cafeteria.

Sure enough, at the far table, voices muted, Magnus and Mountain sat together. Sydney walked over and plunked herself down beside Magnus, who immediately opened his arms and gave her a hug.

She settled back and apparently had a muted conversation that nobody else could hear.

As much as Chrissy wanted to hear it, she hadn't been invited into the conversation and knew that she definitely wasn't part of the in-crowd. So she poured herself a cup of coffee and leaned against the wall, wondering just what the hell was going on in this place and why somebody would want to take out Ralph. Of course that possibility didn't even make any sense to her, but neither did it make any sense that Ralph would head off for the village on his own in this ugly weather. Surely there was better timing to pull a stunt such as that.

When Whalen walked in and saw the conversation on the far side, his gaze swept the room and landed on Chrissy.

He frowned, walked closer, and muttered, "Hey."

"Hey," she said, with a nod.

"So, back to your point earlier about the women," he asked, "are you still willing to talk to them?"

"Sure. It's not as if I'm on friendly terms with anybody anyway."

"You should know that doing this may not put you on friendlier terms either," he pointed out, "and may have the opposite effect."

"That won't matter," Chrissy stated. "At this point, the only thing that matters is getting some answers." And with that, she asked, "Have you got anybody ready for me to talk to?"

He smiled and nodded. "They're as ready as they ever will be. I don't know that they'll be terribly cooperative."

"I really don't give a crap if they're cooperative or not," she muttered. "We just want answers."

"I'll let you talk to them, and we'll see if that makes them any more amiable to being questioned," he explained. "Just be aware that some of them may immediately go silent and may not say anything."

"I know, and I get it. Nobody would want a private relationship to become public in this instance, but it could also very well be that none of them have had anything to do with Ralph too."

"Let's go find out then. Normally Helen is here, but she got sick again and had to be evacuated to a nearby naval ship with a working hospital. She shipped out before you arrived, so she's not a suspect here. We don't know if she will return. That helps you with the headcount issue. Plus I asked Sydney and Berry directly, just to confirm. Avalon's on kitchen duty. I can speak to her later. So the rest of the women I've got lined up for this *conversation*, if you want to come down this way. And thank you, by the way."

He led her to a small room that was completely empty. Chrissy noted the three women leaning up against the wall in the hallway, their arms across their chests.

Chrissy lowered her voice and added, "You might want to also consider the fact that, for all we know, Ralph could have been gay."

Whalen snorted and nodded. "In that case, it'll be even harder to get anybody to talk."

"I know, but let me see if these women have anything to tell."

She entered the room and addressed the first woman. "Hey, come on in. You're first. It's Sally, right?"

Sally shrugged, came into the room, and sat down. "Why you?"

"Either me or one of the guys," Chrissy explained, "and I thought maybe it would be easier somehow if I handled this."

Sally shrugged. "We still won't talk to you," she stated bluntly.

"Got it." Chrissy stood, with a casual dismissal. "In that case I'll go tell Whalen to come in, and he can record your refusal."

"Why record anything?" she asked warily.

"Because if anybody will talk willingly, then they'll have to record it, so that they can match up your statements at a later date," Chrissy explained, with a hard gaze. "And then, of course, if you've lied or didn't give them the complete truth, well, you know how that'll go over with the military. I'm just here to facilitate the questions, but you rejected that offer."

There was a visible tic in Sally's jaw.

"These are the questions I've been requested to ask." Chrissy passed over a clipboard Whalen had given her. "I'm hoping you will at least give me the truth, considering we have a dead man, and we're just trying to find out where he was and what happened in his last few hours."

Sally stared at Chrissy. "I wasn't … He wasn't with me."

"Okay, so can you tell me where you were?"

She nodded. "Sure, in my room."

"With anybody?"

"Yes, with my roommate, Alicia."

At that Chrissy smiled and nodded. "Okay, now we're getting somewhere." And, with that, they quickly ran through the questions. When she was done, she motioned to the door. "Thank you."

Sally shrugged. "It probably was easier to talk to you than to those men," she muttered. "So, whatever." She got up and walked to the door.

From behind her, Chrissy said, "Send Alicia in next, will you?"

Alicia came in, without saying a word to Chrissy, then just sat down and glared.

"I know. You don't want to talk to me, so you have a choice. You can talk to me, or you can talk to the men, who will record every word," she spelled out. "I'm just trying to find out if anybody may have interacted with Ralph in his last few hours."

"You might also want to check in with a few men." An odd note in Alicia's voice stood out.

"Was he gay?" Chrissy asked bluntly.

Alicia hesitated before responding. "I don't know, but he sure wasn't interested in me, and, yes, I did try," she admitted bluntly. "He made it clear that it was a *hell no*, so I just went from there."

"That's interesting. What about any other women? Do you know if anybody else tried?"

"I don't know, other than he was really hassling Avalon at one point in time," she stated, "but I really don't know what the answer is. … I can't even believe that he's gone. I didn't like the man, but I sure as hell wouldn't wish death on anybody."

"Any idea why or where he would have taken off to?"

She snorted. "God no. In this weather, you could be dead in no time, and everyone knows that all too well to have messed up this big."

"He was bundled up, and he should have gotten farther than he did," Chrissy shared, "but, when they found him, he was curled up in a ball."

"He probably got exhausted from the panic of running away, and then just dropped and died," she whispered, as the tears started to run down her cheeks. She didn't seem to be the hard-ass she had projected when she'd initially entered the room. As she tried to brush them back, she muttered, "God, I just want to go home."

"I'm sorry," Chrissy said quietly. "You and me both, but until this is settled—"

"It'll never get settled, and, one by one, people are dying. This resembles too much an Agatha Christie movie of *Ten Little Indians* or something."

Very familiar with the story, Chrissy nodded.

"But *you* just got here," Alicia stated bluntly. "What the hell do you care?"

"Yeah, well, for one thing, nobody told me what I was walking into," she shared. "Now here I am, finding myself in this nightmare."

Alicia stared at her. "They didn't tell you?"

Chrissy shook her head. "No, they sure didn't. *Need to know* and all that."

"God, somebody must really have it in for you."

"That is something I might have to take another look at," Chrissy added. "It's not exactly something I would have signed up for."

"No," Alicia murmured. "Anyway I don't … I don't know where Ralph was or who he was with, if he was with anybody. I suspect he was probably in his room until time to book it, and he made a quick trip outside … and never came back." With that, she scrubbed at her face, then got up and walked out of the room.

Then Chrissy finished with the final woman, Emily, and none of the women admitted to having had anything to do with Ralph the night before.

She reported back to Whalen. "None of them were with him, though one did say she had come on to him at some point, but he wasn't at all interested."

"So … gay?" Whalen asked. "Or did he have somebody else in mind?"

"Apparently he had made life difficult for Avalon at one point."

Whalen nodded at that. "Yeah, I know a little about that, and I will talk to her about it."

"It's too bad cameras aren't all over around here, like in the rest of the world."

He raised both eyebrows. "I installed some cameras."

"Seriously? For monitoring the equipment?"

He nodded, and then he gave a half laugh. "And I completely forgot about it. Jesus." And, with that, he turned and raced to the equipment room.

She followed along, almost as fast as he was moving, catching the attention of several other people, but nobody else joined them. She and Whalen were probably considered bad luck at this point in time. As she walked in the room not far behind him, she asked, "Anything?"

"I'll let you know in a minute." He quickly pulled down a camera, removed an SD card, and then motioned to her. "I need to go check this." She wanted to come, and he eyed her intently. "You can come. I just can't guarantee that I can tell you anything."

"Right. I want to come, if it's okay."

He nodded but didn't say anything, so she followed. As they headed back to his room at a normal pace, several other people asked him, "I guess it was nothing, *huh?*"

He shook his head. "No, false alarm."

As they got to his room, he looked down the hallway and then back at her. "If anybody sees you …"

"Oh, to hell with that." She glared at him in disgust. "Several people have already commented that it's so obvious we have a relationship, so what the hell does it matter?"

He frowned at her, as they walked inside, and he closed the door behind him. "I'm sure you were very quick to clarify the matter." She didn't say anything, while he pulled out his laptop and sat down. So he looked over at her and asked, "Didn't you?"

"I didn't think it was worth clarifying because people will believe whatever they want to believe."

He gave a bark of laughter. "Isn't that the truth?" As soon as he downloaded the file, he looked at her and whistled.

"What are you whistling at?"

He frowned, pulled out his phone, and called Mountain. "Can you come see this? I pulled the camera I'd put in the equipment room."

Within minutes, Mountain arrived at the door. He looked at him and asked, "What's up?"

Whalen turned around the laptop and started the feed again. She hadn't had a chance to see it. She looked over at Mountain and asked, "Can I see it, please or should I go?"

"You can stay, but you're safer if you don't see what's on this. Do you understand that? Just give us some time to see what's going on."

A MAN WITH a hoodie over his head was talking with Ralph, who was in plain view. Their voices were hushed, so most of it wasn't audible.

But still Whalen did manage to hear bits and pieces.

"Look. Just get down to the village, and get yourself out of here. You'll be out of trouble in no time."

"Yeah, sure, as long as I can convince them to get me off this godforsaken place," Ralph muttered.

"It'll be fine. Just don't do anything stupid."

"Yeah, stupid like what?"

"Stupid like *stop*. Remember? This is killing weather. But you're only about forty minutes from the village, and I know that these guys are doing it all the time, going back and forth," the hooded guy explained. "So you know you can do it. You're in great shape."

Ralph nodded. "I am in great shape and I'm just as good as the rest of these guys here." Ralph snorted.

"Exactly," agreed the other man. "So just take it easy,

stay steady and strong, and find a way to send me a message to let me know you're okay."

"All right."

The two had a bro-hug, and then Ralph headed out into the storm. The other man disappeared into the shadows, and at no point in time was his face visible, and even his voice was indistinct.

Mountain sat back. "Somebody on this goddamn base knows who the hell that was. And we will go one by one to find out who helped Ralph get out of here." He looked over at Whalen. "I had no idea you put in cameras."

"I did a few days ago," he muttered. "I brought them up with me."

"I'm glad you did." Mountain seemed impressed at the initiative. "Although this isn't terribly helpful, it does give us an idea and confirms that Ralph went out there on his own. As much as I don't like to hear it and don't want to think anybody doing this survival training and living through the alerts and the warnings about how dangerous it is out there still went out on his own, but at least we know that's exactly what happened."

"But he was heading to the village, so he had a reachable destination in mind, and was well geared up for the weather. Why did he stop?"

"He might have gotten too cold," Mountain suggested. "That's a constant here too."

"But if you're cold, don't you want to keep running, keep working?" Whalen asked. He hesitated and then murmured, "I guess I'm just concerned that there's a reason why he stopped."

"Of course there's a reason why he stopped." And then Mountain added, "You mean, *another* reason."

"Yeah, another reason. Did we find a phone with him?"

Mountain shook his head. "I never found a phone. Were there any other tracks?"

"No, not that I know of. I followed the one set, but …" And then he stopped. "I didn't go past where I found him. It was snowing, but there would have been dips. There was … It was as if … It's not likely that he just rolled over and curled up. He made a half-circle motion, as if wondering at the folly of coming back again. Maybe he was starting to feel too cold, or maybe he was having second thoughts."

"Or someone called to him. … He's in the doc's hands right now," Mountain murmured. "Not sure we'll get any answers or at least full answers. That'll piss me off all over again, but trying to get anything up here is always a challenge."

Whalen smiled. "Not only a challenge but somebody is deliberately making things difficult. Did you ever wonder if this base wasn't a combination of putting a certain number of animals in a cage and seeing how they react?"

At that, Mountain slowly straightened, then turned to look at him. "You know that you're not the first one to suggest that," he replied in a hard voice.

"I didn't mean anything personal by it," Whalen replied cautiously, astonished at the harshness in the big man's voice. "I was just thinking that, in this situation, in these circumstances, the scientists would have a heyday analyzing what went wrong."

"I'm not sure that anything went wrong," Mountain clarified, "as much as it's currently going wrong on a steady and continuing basis." And, with that, he left.

AS MOUNTAIN DISAPPEARED, Chrissy stepped forward, then whispered, "He is one scary dude."

Whalen gave her a one-arm shrug. "It's not that he's scary. He's determined. He's angry, and the one lead we had that might have offered something about his brother just died with Ralph. I don't think that's a coincidence, not in a million hells." In a voice getting harder by the minute, he glared at her and asked, "Do you?"

She winced and shook her head. "I don't know how it could be, but, of course, I would prefer to think it is. The fact that Mountain's brother is missing is intimidating already," she murmured. "I can see why Mountain's here and why he's so driven to find Teegan, though I worry it won't happen until spring."

"There is no easy task finding anybody in these temperatures, in these altitudes. As for spring, it's not what you expect," he pointed out. "It warms up, and there's some snowmelt, but nothing like what you're used to in terms of a spring thaw in the States." He gave a shake of his head. "If his brother was caught out up here or lost up here," he corrected, "he'll stay that way until some crazy fool out doing a study on some newfangled whatchamacallit trips over his body." Then he took a deep breath to add, "And I know that's the last thing Mountain wants to find."

She had to admit privately that it would definitely suck, but the reality was that so much activity was being put into searching for Teegan all this time that she wondered how Mountain was getting that help through the government. She stared at Whalen intently. "I get that they're brothers and that he cares and wants answers, but how is it that he's allowed to do all that on government time?"

WHALEN HESITATED, REALIZING that this was the crux of where their friendship would go. In a low voice, he replied, "Teegan may have had some information about all this other stuff going on." In an even lower voice, he continued. "He was actively investigating the military base when he was the one who up and disappeared."

"Oh, shit." Chrissy stared at him in shock.

He nodded. "So, it's not just about finding his brother because it's also likely the key to what happened to all the other people here," he said. "I don't think anybody will stop Mountain from trying to find answers because everybody here wants answers too. And hopefully before anybody else dies."

"Too late," she stated bluntly, "since we just lost another one."

Whalen probably shouldn't have mentioned anything to her about Teegan's involvement, and then about Mountain, yet she was right in the firing line now and needed to be very careful herself. He knew she wasn't involved, and that was good enough for him. He also knew, from before, that she was incredibly honorable. Which just brought him back to the whole reason why he'd walked instead of contacting her, back when they'd split up. And, of course, he didn't really have a decent reason.

He would have to explain it to her at some point in time. Or maybe he didn't have to. Maybe he could just walk away and not have anything to do with confessing, but somehow that felt even more wrong. She hadn't looked for an answer yet, so that was something at least.

Hearing a voice behind him, he turned to see Mountain,

walking toward him at a good clip.

Mountain lowered his voice when he reached Whalen. "Hey, just a reminder to keep all this to yourself, right?"

He nodded. "I did tell Chrissy," he murmured. "She's new, doesn't know anything about what's been going on, and she's in a position now where she could be in danger."

Mountain contemplated Whalen's expression for a long moment. "Not to mention the fact that she's special to you."

Whalen shook his head. "She *was* special, but that's been over for a long time."

Mountain snorted at that. "Dude, you might believe that, but it's only because you're full of shit. When you get real about it, the rest of us might believe it too." And, with that, Mountain was gone again.

Whalen stared after him and shook his head, thinking back to the gossip that Chrissy had mentioned and wondering how everybody was getting the wrong idea about him and her. Frowning, he headed to his room and stopped, when the conversation up ahead of him immediately went silent as he appeared. He smiled at everybody, as he walked past them. "Hey, hope all is well in your world."

"Considering that this world sucks right now," one of them said, "I can't say that it is. So, how the hell did you guys find him?"

At that odd question, Whalen turned and frowned at him. "What does that mean, Jaden?"

"It's just weird that he goes out in whatever crazy-ass attempt he made to escape this place, yet you guys find him a little too quick, you know?"

Whalen eyed Jaden for a long moment. "Are you in any way implying that we had something to do with him going missing, plus suggesting that's how we knew where to find him, not that the logical theory was he ran to the village for help?" he asked, his voice deadly soft.

Jaden flushed and shook his head.

Whalen knew Jaden was from the British team. He studied him for a long moment and added, "We spent hours looking, following tracks. You know there is such a thing out there, right?"

Jaden flushed in anger or embarrassment; it was hard to tell.

Then one of his friends said, "Come on, bud. Leave it."

"Leave it? Leave what?" Jaden asked in a flash of what was unmistakably anger. "What I'd like to do is leave this damn place. It's such a shit show, and everybody's a suspect, particularly those who conveniently go and find missing people."

"There was nothing quick or convenient about going out and finding Ralph," Whalen noted, "but I do know that somebody helped him to leave, and believe me. We're looking at that and everybody else involved."

"What do you mean, *helped him to leave*?" asked one of the guys.

But Whalen didn't say anything more, realizing he had obviously revealed too much. "You can bet that everybody will be interviewed as to their involvement."

"There was no involvement," the same guy replied, looking at him. "What are you talking about?"

But Whalen's gaze was locked on Jaden, the one man who had accused Whalen of potentially knowing where Ralph had gone and then had defiantly suggested that Whalen was involved in some way. "You got something to say about it, Jaden?" Whalen demanded, as he studied the guy's physique, wondering how it matched up to the guy caught on camera.

Jaden shrugged. "Don't know anything about it. I just know he was really upset."

"Yeah, I know he was upset." Whalen nodded. "A lot of people are upset, but that doesn't mean that they take a drastic chance like that and head off into the storm, trying to reach the village."

"The village isn't that far away," Jaden argued. "Lots of us have seen it, while we've been out doing our training."

"Of course, but distance is very deceptive in this cold and especially at nighttime," Whalen pointed out, staring at him, wondering if this was a necessary warning, in case this guy was planning on doing something dumb-ass too.

"Look. I don't know why he decided to take off. I wish he hadn't because that decision cost him his life," Jaden stated bluntly.

"But we also know for a fact that he had help, and that person is among those we want to talk to." And, with that warning, Whalen took particular note of the three people standing here and added, "As are you guys."

They immediately started to protest. "We don't know anything about it," one of them cried out in anger.

"Maybe not, but somebody does. Somebody helped Ralph prepare. Somebody got him ready, and somebody kept up the pressure, even when it looked as if Ralph was showing signs of potentially changing his mind, but they persuaded him to go ahead with it anyway, even during that storm."

At that, the group fell silent, and one by one the other two turned and looked at Jaden, standing there beside them.

Jaden flushed and cried out, "Hey, don't go looking at me."

"Why not, Jaden?" Whalen asked. "You two were always together, and you're the one who's most upset that Ralph's dead."

"Obviously we're all upset," Jaden stated, with a wave of his hand.

"But you're the one who lost a really good friend. At least we thought you guys were good friends. Did you know he was leaving?" Whalen asked Jaden, staring at him, waiting for an answer. The other guy squirmed, but Whalen wasn't ready to lose the advantage. "I suggest you rethink your actions and where you were last night."

Jaden stared at him. "You had cameras?"

"Yeah, we have cameras. What the hell do you think? All kinds of shit is going on and problems like you wouldn't believe, so, of course, there's freaking cameras," Whalen roared. "So how about the truth for a change."

Jaden looked around nervously, and the other two men instinctively took a step back, distancing themselves from him. Jaden glared at them. "I didn't convince him to go," he cried out. "He really wanted to."

"Yeah, I know he was talking about going, but a friend would have tried to talk him out of it, not encourage him to do it," one of the men said in horror. "It's a death trap out there, and you knew that."

"Yet he was still very convinced he could make it to the village, or he could get back here, if needed."

"Why was he so anxious to get out of here?" Whalen asked Jaden in a hard voice. "Why did he want to go so badly he would risk his life during a storm in the attempt?"

Jaden stared at him. "It's not what you think."

"Then you better help me out here because, right now, somebody took a chance, risking his life to escape a base, where he was safe and secure from the weather, only to become the next victim—and, in this case, not necessarily by direct foul play," he muttered, as he stared at the man in front of him. "Why the hell would you let this man go out into those temperatures?"

"Let him? He was fanatical about going," Jaden replied hotly. "You don't know what it was like for him."

"No, I don't because nobody's talking. All we ever hear is how shitty it is here. We get that. It's been a pretty rough go, but we haven't proven any serial foul play with the deaths and the missing trainees—outside of the people we've already caught and whatever the hell happened at the scientists' camp, plus what appears to have been a couple of really sad accidents," Whalen pointed out, "which is why everybody here knew to not go out in those temperatures. We have focused on that over and over …" When he heard another voice behind him, he turned to see Magnus staring at the group of them, frowning.

"What's going on?" Magnus asked in a clipped voice.

Whalen immediately pointed out Jaden. "This is the guy who helped Ralph get geared up and convinced him to go out into deadly conditions."

"I didn't convince him," Jaden snapped, but fear penetrated his tone. "He wanted to go."

"It seems he was changing his mind on the video," Magnus declared, studying the British guy intently. "So, I'm not so sure that we'll take that as gospel because it sure seemed you were pushing Ralph to go."

"Even if I was, so what? He wanted to go," Jaden cried out. "I was just trying to help out a friend."

"Help out a friend?" Magnus repeated, a bit too hot and a lot bothered. "Help out a friend to his death? Is that really what you want to say?" he asked, taking his time. "What kind of a friend does that?"

Jaden glared at him. "You don't know anything, and I don't have to answer to you." And, with that, he turned and headed back in the direction of his room.

Except that it wasn't that easy. When Whalen called out to him again, Jaden refused to turn. Whalen looked over at Magnus, who was already on his phone. Whalen turned to the other two men and pointed a finger at them. "I know both of you, and you need to go to your rooms right now, and nobody is to talk about this." They glared at him, and Whalen shook his head. "We don't know what was on Jaden's mind when he sent Ralph to his death," he declared, with a commanding tone, "but, for your sake, you need to stay out of it, unless you had something to do with it."

One of them nervously shook his head. "I didn't have anything to do with it. Jesus, if I'd known, I would have stopped Ralph." He seemed lost in his own head. "That's a death sentence out there."

"It absolutely was a death sentence, and we have to wonder why this Jaden guy was okay sending his friend out there. Have you heard that they've had any problems, any arguing, disagreements, anything?"

The two men shook their heads. "Not that we know of, and Jaden seems genuinely sad that Ralph is gone."

"Sure, but he should have known that his friend was already as good as gone, and that's the thing. That was far too much of a gamble to have it make sense. Maybe if Ralph had been highly trained and experienced, but you guys aren't, and that's why you came here, for survival training, but that sure hasn't made you bloody pros at survival in the Arctic, especially during a goddamn hell of a storm," Whalen snapped, staring at them.

By then, Magnus had caught up with Jaden and took him to a different room, while Whalen quickly asked a few more questions of the other two, then got both their room numbers and dismissed them. Afterward he raced to join Magnus.

As Whalen walked into the room, Jaden glared at him, and Whalen saw a glint of hatred. He stopped, stunned at the emotion in the other man's face. "This whole time, you've had an awful lot of anger directed at me," Whalen noted. "I'm not sure why that is because I can't think of any scenario that makes sense for you to be upset with me."

Jaden didn't say anything, just turned his gaze back toward Magnus. Whalen looked at Magnus, one eyebrow raised. He shook his head and didn't say anything.

"So I gather he's not being very cooperative," Whalen stated, as he sat down and studied Jaden. "Which is interesting, considering that he had an awful lot to say to Ralph."

"I did not," he snapped. "And you're full of BS about the cameras."

"Meaning you checked?" Whalen asked, with half a smirk.

He shifted ever-so-slightly. After a moment of silence, Jaden looked back at Magnus. "I didn't have nothing to do with this."

"Did you speak with him just prior to him leaving?" Magnus asked.

Jaden hesitated and then nodded reluctantly. "Yes, I did."

Whalen shook his head, as Jaden was suddenly too quick to be honest.

"Yeah, okay, so he was always talking about leaving,

thought he could make it to the village, and then he could get out. He was starting to panic, and he was having panic attacks. He had gotten hellish to be around, and he was pretty determined to do it. I figured if I helped him get dressed properly and set out sensibly, then he could make it just fine. He's strong. He's fit like everybody here, and there was absolutely no reason for him to not make it." And at that, he turned and glared at Whalen. "Unless somebody made sure he didn't."

Whalen's jaw dropped. "Are you seriously suggesting that we killed him out there?"

He shrugged. "Maybe you did. Maybe that's what happened. I don't have anything but your word, saying that you found him out there alone and frozen," he muttered. "I just know that he was strong, that he was fit, and that there was absolutely no way that he should have died. It was a straight run. You guys have done it multiple times."

Whalen sat back and nodded slowly. "That's true. We have, and we wondered at the same time if something else was going on, if somebody had done something to make it harder on him."

"What do you mean, *harder on him*?"

"We've already had some drug issues here."

At that, Jaden stared at him. "Jesus Christ, you can't blame that bullshit on me too," he muttered. "If anybody was drugging anybody, it was you guys."

Whalen shook his head, snorted, totally surprised at the tack this guy was taking, yet he didn't have any proof one way or another of what Jaden had just said. Whalen turned to Magnus. "Looks as if I'm just hindering things here, so I'll leave you to it."

At that, Magnus nodded. "Thanks."

Whalen got up and headed out and back to his room. There he sat down hard, wondering at the sudden turn of events. He'd only been here a few minutes, when a knock came at his door. He called out permission to enter. Nobody was more surprised than him when Chrissy opened the door and slipped inside. He frowned at her. "You're the last person I expected to see."

She flushed. "I just wanted to see what was going on," she muttered. "Did you guys capture somebody who was involved in this?" she asked curiously. He hesitated, and she glared at him. "*Now* you are telling me that you're not talking?"

"I have been warned off about talking to anybody," he replied pointedly. "However, we do have somebody who saw Ralph just before he left, but he's not saying he had anything to do with it."

"Of course," she muttered. "Since you have it on camera, you should check out what he's saying."

"We do have it on camera, but it doesn't have very good audio," he noted, "and I've never learned to lip-read, so most of it is gibberish anyway."

At that, she shrugged. "I can lip-read, you know."

He stared at her for a moment, then realization dawned. "Your sister. She was deaf."

"Yes, exactly." Chrissy nodded. "I had been speaking that way with her forever and, with that, comes a really good ability to learn to lip-read."

"I remember that," he muttered, as he stared off in the distance. "I'll have to get clearance though."

"Whatever you need. I don't want to get you in any trouble."

"Thanks, I appreciate that."

"On the other hand, if there's anything we can do to get justice for Ralph, we should."

"*If* there is justice. According to this guy, Jaden, Ralph was bound and determined to take off and to find his way to the village and to get out of here as fast as he could. Apparently he was having panic attacks and was quite unsteady by the time he left."

"And yet Jaden didn't say anything when we were all searching for Ralph, didn't get him any medical help, didn't in any way try to stop him," she argued, frowning at Whalen. "What kind of a friend does that?"

"Then the question becomes who's the friend, and what is a friend, when it comes down to these kinds of circumstances." Whalen sighed, feeling a fatigue inside that made him feel used up and tired.

"You look as if you really need a break."

"Oh, I won't catch one anytime soon," he noted, with a half laugh. "Let me talk to Magnus or Mountain and see if we can get clearance for you to see the video."

"You could see their lips moving?"

"In some of it, yes," he confirmed, "not in all of it, obviously, but definitely in some instances."

"Okay, good enough. I'll go back to my room, and you let me know."

He got up and headed back down to where he'd last seen Magnus. As soon as he approached the door, it was open, and nobody was inside. He texted Magnus at that point. **Hey, don't know if it'll help or if it's not considered necessary, but Chrissy lip-reads. Her sister was deaf, and it helped to lip-read for better communication. She could view that video and see if this guy is telling the truth or at least hopefully get a little more off it.**

It took a bit to text that much, but, seconds after he had sent it, his phone buzzed with an incoming call.

"Is she any good at it?" Magnus asked.

"I think so. I know that this is an art she's quite comfortable with, and it helped with her sister."

"Yeah, but lip-reading is not the same as speaking to the deaf," he reminded him.

"I know, but Chrissy's the one who said she lip-reads."

"We can try it, if you want."

"I'm just saying it could clarify some of our issues."

"Yes, it sure could. As far as Jaden's concerned, he claims he didn't have anything to do with Ralph's death, and he was just being supportive, knowing that his friend would go with or without his help."

"And yet that still doesn't explain why Jaden didn't inform anybody else."

"Yeah, well, he says he didn't want to get into trouble. Then he makes the point how people found out, and now he's in trouble."

"Yeah, but … it's still a shit deal."

"Oh, I agree with you. It's a shit deal, and it sure as hell is dodgy to say the least. You've got somebody who went out after dark in stormy conditions, … and, sure, he was prepped for winter in terms of gear, but he sure as hell wasn't prepped for what he would face out there," he muttered. "Anyway, bring her down to my office, and we'll see what she can do."

W HEN CHRISSY HEARD a knock on her door, she knew instinctively it would be Whalen. She opened the door and smiled at him. "Well?"

"Magnus wants to see what you can come up with," he said, speaking softly. "And again, this is all to be kept quiet, and nobody is to know anything about it."

"Got it." She followed him down the hallway. "I presume this Jaden guy didn't offer very much in the way of assistance?"

"Only that he didn't do anything to encourage his friend and that he did try to protest his leaving but decided, since he couldn't change Ralph's mind, he might as well support him the best he could and make sure he was well-dressed for being out there, at least. He seems to think there was no reason Ralph couldn't have made the trip on his own and that we must have had something to do with his death."

She stopped in her tracks and in a hoarse astonished whisper, she asked, "*You* guys?"

Whalen nodded. "Yeah, according to Jaden, we were the ones who found him after all and *so soon*," he shared, with an eye roll. "Therefore, we probably got to him while he was still alive and made sure he didn't come back that way."

"But he had to have been dead for hours."

"I don't think Jaden's in any way prepared to hear that,"

Whalen noted, with a lopsided smile in her direction. "People shift their perception of things to suit themselves. Remember?"

"You used to say things like that all the time," she muttered. "I didn't really realize, not until I had to deal with people a lot more myself, just how true it is."

"Unfortunately it's quite true, and everybody's perspective is different. You'll come up with one perspective, and somebody else will come up with another one."

"Which is okay. Different perspectives can be great," she acknowledged, "but, when everything is so seriously wrong and when those different perspectives seem so far removed from reality, you have to wonder how they reach those conclusions."

"It's frustrating when we're up against these things right now because obviously I didn't do anything to kill Ralph. He had been dead for hours before we ever found him. We went out knowing it would be a recovery mission, yet hoping he might have made it to the village. It definitely can be done, and we have people here who make that trip on a regular basis. But they are people who really know what they're doing in these conditions."

"Like Mountain. So that huge body mass, … do you think it would take him longer to die of the cold?"

"Sure, an extra what, two minutes?" he muttered.

She nodded. "I guess size doesn't save you then."

"Keep in mind Mountain also requires a certain amount of body heat to keep that mass going. It's not as if we have much in the way of easy answers to give doubters, like Jaden. It doesn't save you just to know that you're a certain size," he said pointedly.

"Right."

"And I really don't want to be thinking about somebody like Mountain dying out there. The man seems invincible, and I really don't want to be proven wrong."

She laughed. They approached a door just then, and he led her inside.

Magnus sat there, waiting for her, a video playing on the screen. "Hey, thanks for taking a look at this." She shrugged. He motioned at the chair beside him. "Sit down, have a look. Take your time, and let me know what you think."

As soon as the video played, she leaned forward, watching their lips, her mouth instinctively reading off their words.

"*Dude, now remember. Stay low, don't let anybody see you. It's the only hope of not getting caught.*"

"*I know. I know,*" Ralph said, and then he hesitated. "*Maybe we should do this on a better day, when the weather's not quite so insane.*"

Jaden snorted. "*I'm sorry, but when does the weather ever get better here? I'd go myself, but you know I've got this bum leg.*"

"*Yeah, no, no, I don't want you to go and take any chances. I'm fine to do this,*" he grumbled. "*I just wish there wasn't the need.*"

"*If there wasn't the need, then we wouldn't be doing it,*" his friend pushed. "*You and I both know our chances of getting out of here alive are pretty damn small. If you don't get out, you'll never get me help to get out, and you know I can't do much with my leg.*"

"*No, man, I know. I know. Besides, this is what friends are for. It's why we came here to do this, right? Help others.*"

"*And I appreciate it. I really do. Now you go, stick straight on the paths. You know how to get there. You've been there before.*"

"I've seen it off in the distance," he muttered.

"Right, so you know that it's not very far away then."

"No, no, and that's a good thing. I feel okay about that part."

"So, what part is bothering you?" Jaden asked, looking at his friend as if he were crazy.

Ralph flushed. *"I don't know, just … I just wish we didn't have to do this."*

There was silence, and then his buddy said, *"Look. If you're really scared about this, I'll try to do it tomorrow."*

"I'm not scared," Ralph snapped, glaring at him. *"Don't you go call me a scaredy-cat."*

"Dude, I'm not saying that." He raised both hands. *"I just don't want you to go if you're scared."*

"Of course I'm scared. You know what it's like out there. Bloody polar bears are out there."

The other man laughed, and that seemed to bring a reluctant grin on Ralph's face too.

The conversation continued in the same vein right up until she said, "He's giving him a hug here, and I can't see his lips to read them, but then there's something about *Remember to stay quiet. Otherwise we're both in deep shit."*

At that, Ralph headed out into the winter weather.

She turned to Whalen and then Magnus. "Does that sound about right?" she asked them.

Magnus stared at her, a hard look on his face.

She shrank back slightly. "I don't understand what that look means. I'm only reading what they're saying."

"How close do you think you were?" Magnus asked.

"Ninety-nine percent?"

He nodded and stared off in the distance. "It's a very different story than what he told us," he murmured. "I recorded your voice while you were doing that, so we could have it play back at the same time and consider what they're doing."

"Sounds to me as if Jaden was encouraging his friend to go. I don't understand that last bit about not telling anyone or about being in trouble."

"No, I don't either," Magnus admitted, "but, if they were involved in something they shouldn't have been, Jaden very conveniently got rid of Ralph, the weak link in his world."

She sucked back her breath. "Not something I want to contemplate."

"No," Magnus replied, "none of us would. It doesn't change the fact that what you just read off as being their conversation isn't even close to Jaden's version of what happened. But that's our problem, and we'll deal with it," he said grumpily. "Thank you very much." He hesitated, then added, "I know that you've been told some of what's going on, but please don't spread any of that around here."

She immediately shook her head and replied in a low tone, "Don't worry. I don't want to do that anyway." And, with that, she nodded to both men and said, "Good night." With that, she quickly escaped.

She returned to her quarters, not exactly sure that the information she had provided was well received. She'd done her best, and it hadn't even been hard. Anybody who could read lips would have been able to read that. But those certainly weren't the words of a man trying to hold his friend back.

It was more of a man encouraging another to go, to take the chance, and to make the steps that would eventually take this young man's life. Saddened by the turn of events and the lip-reading she had just done, she curled up in her bed, lights out, wondering at the life choices she had made that had brought her to this point.

A knock came at her door a little bit later. She knew it would be Whalen and called out for him to come in.

He stepped in and looked at her with concern. "Are you okay?"

She shrugged. "Yeah, I'm fine." She nodded. "You just don't realize what an impact doing something like that has."

"I'm sorry. I never even thought about it in those terms," he murmured.

"Neither did I," she agreed, as she sat up in bed and pulled the covers with her. "That somebody died after being actively pushed into something known to be so dangerous, and by a friend no less, is shocking," she said, truly disgusted. "That will take some getting used to."

Whalen didn't say anything, but he continued to study her.

"I'm fine," she repeated, with a wave of her hand. "Don't worry about it."

"I will worry about it. You came to help me because I asked."

"I would have done it anyway," she murmured. "I just didn't know that the need was there."

"Right, … but anyway I'm very appreciative."

She looked over at him and groaned. "You know, it would be easier if we weren't quite so formal. Wouldn't it?"

"And here I thought we were doing better," he said, with a half laugh.

She grinned. "Maybe we are at that." She shrugged. "It just still feels … *off* somehow."

"We haven't seen each other in a long time," he pointed

out, "so *off* may be pretty apropos."

She sighed. "How have you been?"

He looked over at her, shrugged, and said, "I'm fine. I stay busy, you know, on missions, out doing drills, out doing training." He sent her a smile. "I did a tour in Afghanistan." He shook his head. "All kinds of events to keep me busy."

"And to keep you from doing anything else in life?" she challenged.

He stared at her for a moment. "Maybe, and maybe that's partly why I do it. I don't know. ... I wasn't ready to stop before."

At the mention of *before*, her eyebrows went up. "Are you saying you are now?" she asked.

"I don't know. I haven't considered that yet."

She nodded. "I think that's the point I am trying to make. ... The thing is, you have to be ready. I wasn't ready to open the store before," she said. "Now that I realize what I missed out on and how much I could lose, I really want to go home and to make that happen."

He gave her the gentlest of smiles, making her heart jolt. "I hope you do make that happen," he said. "It's always been your dream."

"For the longest time, I wondered whether it was my dream or my dream or my friend's dream," she shared, with a sad smile. He looked at her, startled, and she shrugged. "When you have somebody else's dream locked into your radar, you wonder sometimes if it's you or if it's them."

"I'm not sure that anybody can help you with an easy answer," he began, "but, from what I could tell, it was always your dream."

She laughed. "Thanks for that. Not sure I believe you, but okay."

He grinned at her. "The thing is, out here, you get a chance to think. You get a chance to reassess what you really want out of life." He shook his head. "So, take the opportunity now, while you're here, and do that. If you still want that dream when you're done with your five years, then go for it."

"I'm almost done now, you know," she replied. He frowned at her, and she nodded. "Yes, that means that I joined up pretty quickly after you left."

"And that," he snorted, "is difficult for me. I didn't realize that what I did would impact you so much that you would enlist."

"I didn't understand your need for the military. I've explained that to you." She stared around the room, frowning. "I just didn't understand, and my sister passed away not long after that. I became quite confused as to what I was doing, and why I was doing it, and decided to find out what *this* was," she explained, with a wave of her hand around the room. "I wanted to know why so many people felt compelled to be a part of this, and, yeah, I, … I understand now," she muttered. "I understand so much more about military life and what it means to be a part of this. I also understand that it's not where I want to be on a long-term basis."

"It's definitely not for everybody," he stated immediately.

She smiled. "It's been good. And it's been good for me. It really has. I've grown up a lot," she admitted. "As much as I hate to consider the fact that I had so much growing up to do," she said on a half laugh, "but I definitely did. Now I'm here, and I'm feeling pretty good about where I've come from. So, as much as I didn't sign up for the right reasons, I am still very glad I enlisted and that I came on this assignment."

"I'm glad to hear that, and I'm sorry that things between us meant that you had to take such an extreme move to figure it out."

"I'm not," she said, "but it's not the path that everybody would have chosen."

He hesitated and then sat down on the side of the bed. "Look. I don't even know that I have a serious answer for you."

"Then don't give me an answer," she said. "I've been through too much over the years to even want to go in that direction. Would I like an answer to know what went wrong and why you felt as if you couldn't talk to me? Yes. But I would just as soon have the truth, so, if you can't give me that, then don't give me anything."

He nodded slowly, hesitating. "I'm not sure that I can verbalize it quite yet."

"Then wait," she replied impulsively. He looked at her, and she shrugged. "I've waited a long time. I can wait a little bit longer for you to get your head on straight." She gave a short laugh. "Am I curious? Yes, but will it break me down? No way. Been there, done that."

And such a wry tone filled her words that he winced.

She added, "Sorry, I didn't mean that quite the way it sounded."

"Oh, I think you did." Whalen smiled. "You have every right. I should have said *something* to you, but, once I'd heard from my friend that you'd already contacted him and that he'd already told you, it just seemed easier to let everything alone."

"And that was just a cop-out too."

He hesitated, then shrugged. "At the time, I was heading

off on that mission, and I was really confused," he shared, as he gave her a wry look. "You were extremely special, and the thing is, you were staying special, and I—"

She frowned at him. "What does *staying special* mean?"

"It means that I would have cheerfully walked off my job and out of my passion to stay with you," he admitted, as he looked at her almost painfully.

She found it hard to look away from the naked truth in his eyes. "So, hang on a minute. You left me without even giving me a chance to say goodbye because you cared too much?"

"And because I couldn't *not* care." He looked down because he wasn't able to look at her. "I was at the point where I either stayed and committed to a relationship, marriage," he explained bluntly, "or I continued to live the life that I had promised myself."

"And you promised yourself that or was that your brother's promise?" she asked equally bluntly.

He winced. "And that's where your words about living the dreams of others had such an impact just now," he said, "because we all have dreams we live out that are ours, and yet we are also impacted by those around us living out their dreams. I came into the military because of my brother. Losing him devastated me, and sticking to that path was also part of the plan in terms of honoring my brother, and I had absolutely no problem doing that, … until I met you." Whalen sent a sideways glance her way, then quickly jolted away again.

She didn't even know what to think because—of all the plausible excuses or reasons she had imagined over the years—*that* was never one of them. "So, you were afraid that because I didn't understand what was going on with you and your need to be in the military that I would make you quit, and, in so doing, … you could no longer honor your brother?"

He looked at her and nodded. "You put that way better than I ever could, but, yeah, that's the gist of it."

She sagged back against the bed, her head on the wall, staring at him. "Would I have understood that back then? I don't know," she muttered, wondering at how her life had changed. "Do I understand it now? Absolutely. I get it completely. I understand why you do what you do." Again she gave a wave of her hand. "And just because it's not my life or the life that I would choose in the long term, I get it. And you're right. I would have tried to get you to quit," she admitted, "because I knew that you preferred it over me."

"It was a promise I'd made that I preferred, not over you but over breaking that promise," Whalen clarified. "And I knew that, if I stayed, I would have broken that promise, and I wasn't ready to do that."

"No," she murmured. "You wouldn't have been. I wouldn't have been ready at that stage to let you have the life that you needed to live, without trying to best it."

"That was part of the problem. … You already saw it as a competition."

"Yeah, I did," she confirmed. "I don't know if I still would though."

"Maybe you would," he said, "but maybe you would also understand that it wouldn't be competition so much as something that was compatible, understanding that you can have more than one thing that you care about in life and that you don't have to give up one for the other."

"Do you finally believe that?" she asked, looking at him strangely. "Because it seems as if you are the one who had trouble with that thought."

He laughed. "I think now I would be okay with it," he murmured. "Now that we're well past that point, … but, at the time, I couldn't see myself breaking that vow."

"And now you can?"

"No, but I have served another five years with that memory in his honor," he stated, "and I know that there is a time when I need to do things for me. Do I want to continue to serve? Absolutely. I do a lot of special missions, a lot of special intensive secret ops, and I know that it provides value for people in this world, yet a lot of those things I can never talk about. That's just the nature of that type of mission, but it doesn't make it any less valuable."

"If anything," she added, "it probably makes it more so because nobody can talk about that stuff, and, therefore, very few people can know about the problem, the solution that's been decided upon, or the execution of that decision."

His smile, when it came, was intense, and she gave a happy sigh.

"I didn't think I would ever understand your reasoning," she noted, "but I have to admit. … Now I do, and I guess … I kind of agree with it." Astonished, he could only stare at her, as she nodded. "Because you're right, I did see myself in competition, … with the navy, which was stupid. I did see it coming down to your choosing one or the other, but you made the decision before I ever got there, and I knew that it would be it."

She looked at him intently. "That hurt. It hurt really badly, which is why I ended up enlisting, so I could figure it out myself. Yet, at the same time, I also admired you in a way, but …" She hesitated and then gave him a bright smile. "I'm glad for both our sakes that we've grown past it."

He stood up, with a smile. "You're not kidding, and I'm really glad I came to talk to you. I didn't think I could verbalize any of it in a way that you could even understand, much less forgive me for, and I guess you haven't said that, but, at least, if you can understand what I did, it goes a long way in my books to not feeling so damn guilty for the way I treated you."

"In a way I still want you to pay for hurting me so badly," she shared, "but I also understand why you couldn't explain it at the time and why I wouldn't have understood it." She shook her head. "We're into a whole new world now, so forward ho and all that stuff," she quipped, with a wave of her hand. "Now, if all of us can just survive this lovely mission, we—"

"You do need to be *extra* careful now," he said.

"I will." She checked her watch and winced. "I probably need to crash. I'm doing the early morning shift in the kitchen."

"Remember what I said, really."

"I will." She hesitated, and, as he walked to the door, she called out to him, "What will happen to Jaden?"

"We'll start again in the morning and go over what you said versus what he told us. We'll check it ourselves, and then talk to him again. Chances are, he won't give up anything and will just call you a liar."

She winced. "In that case it would be nice if he didn't know it was me."

"I wasn't planning on telling him, and, as I mentioned before, let's keep it quiet. Be careful out there, ... please."

She nodded, and, as soon as he closed the door, she locked it and curled back up into bed and fell right to sleep.

WHALEN WOKE THE next morning and, immediately after breakfast, searched out Magnus. "Have you talked to Jaden?"

He nodded. "Yeah, and, as soon as he was given the evidence against him, he confessed," Magnus stated, as they walked down the hallway. "I'm about to go see the colonel and talk to him about it."

"Great, so I presume Jaden's under guard?"

"We don't have very many guards left," Magnus noted, with an eye roll. "However, he will get his wish and get airlifted out of here on the next supply run."

Whalen winced at that. "Will they charge him?"

"I'm not sure. That'll be up to the brass and the MPs, should we ever get any up here. But, either way, they'll talk to him down there and decide what to do. He certainly aided and abetted in Ralph's foolish actions, but is that enough to get him in trouble? That I don't know. I want to think so, but it will be out of our hands. We have the truth of what happened to Ralph, and, as sad as that is, he still went out there willingly."

"With a little push from his friend."

"Exactly. And the real question is, to how much that friend pushed, and what was behind the meaning of the push. That's the part we don't know," he murmured. At the door to the equipment room, Magnus added, "I highly suggest you make sure all your cameras are working again and get everything reset, just in case."

"That's exactly where I was heading right now," he murmured.

And, with that, the two parted ways, and Whalen headed into the equipment area, where he would immediately set about double-checking the safety of everything. It was almost an obsession with him now. As he stepped deeper into the equipment room, he groaned because the last group in hadn't done their proper diligence. He would definitely get on that team leader's ass for the mess Whalen had to sort out again. It took him all morning to sort, to check, and to double-check that everything was returned and was in good shape.

When he showed up for lunch, Magnus looked at him and asked curiously, "Everything okay?"

Whalen nodded. "Yeah, but I'm about to go find Samson and Ted. See why they haven't solved shit here yet. And, if Samson doesn't have anything else to do, he can deal with the teams leaving the equipment room the way they did last night. Surely that's criminal."

Magnus snorted at that. "Yeah, I don't think that was the top priority for anybody yesterday."

"Maybe not," Whalen acknowledged, "but, at the same time, it seriously sucks that this continues to be an issue."

"Do you think it's an issue, or do you think it's deliberate?"'

At that, he stopped, turned, and frowned at him. "I don't know, but I'll still tell Samson because whoever the hell goes out with this equipment seems to be bringing it back just to treat it like shit. After lunch I'll go over and have a talk with Joe and check that equipment too."

At that, Magnus shook his head. "I'm sure everything over there is fine. Joe is too cautious to let his equipment go bad."

"Maybe so, but I can't get rid of the feeling that something involving the equipment just isn't right."

"Okay, I hear you," Magnus replied. "Go for it."

For now they both sat down and ate lunch. As soon as Whalen was done, he headed over to Joe and the dogs. He loved the dogs, particularly Patches, one of the big white Samoyed crosses with dark rings around both her eyes. Damn he loved having her around. He snuck over every day so that he could cuddle her, being the teddy bear that she was.

As he walked in, Patches raced over to see Whalen. He gave a boisterous laugh, as he crouched to hug her. Barking and yipping, she got the others going, until he was surrounded by canines.

When the noise calmed down, Joe looked up, popped his hat off his forehead, and asked, "What do you want?"

Whalen snorted. "I know you look after your equipment," he began, "but I wanted to go over it myself."

Joe's gaze narrowed. "Why the hell would you want to do that?"

"Because two sets of eyes are better than one," he noted carefully. "And, no, I'm not insulting you. I just don't like the stuff going on around here."

"I hear you caught the guy."

"I don't know about caught-*the*-guy, but we did get someone, and his motives are not clear yet. I guess rumors travel pretty fast."

"They sure do, especially when they're rough. Did that kid really egg on his friend to go out in those conditions?"

Whalen nodded. "Yeah, he did, and, of course, Ralph died of hypothermia. He was under the impression he could make it to the village and get help getting out."

"There's no way out of here. The village people up there aren't going anywhere either. What the hell did Ralph plan to do? Sit in the village for the next four months until winter's gone? What was he …" He let the thought hang there.

"I think his friend filled his mind with something other than logical thoughts," Whalen suggested. "And, whether it was on purpose, as a joke, or one or both of them is off their rocker, I don't know," he muttered. "Sounds as if Jaden will be flown out, when the next supply trip comes in."

"*Great,*" Joe muttered. "And what has that got to do with my equipment?"

"I'm on a mission to make sure all the equipment is sound," Whalen stated, "so just humor me, will you?"

Joe glared at him and then shrugged. "Fine. I've been working on mending some straps all day anyway."

"Why'd the straps break?"

"They didn't break. It looks as if they wore down."

"Is that normal?"

"No, it's not normal at all," he declared, "and that's the only reason I'm letting you look. Just in case you see something I didn't."

"Got it." With that, Whalen headed over to the harnesses and the sleds, the dogs on their heels, then very carefully, step by step, they went over every piece of equipment.

As Whalen stepped back, Joe asked, "Anything?"

"No, it looks good."

Just then, Patches jumped against him almost knocking him over. He bent down, but the dog was demanding more and toppled him to the floor.

Joe barked with laughter. "Before all this chaos, we had a lot of visitors. However, now, over time and with the cold and all the shit happening over there at the main building, we don't get anywhere near as much company as before." He seemed both happy and sad, with maybe a glint of anger mixed in there too. "I'm both sad for my buddies here and happy because I don't have to deal with people," he admitted, with a wry look. "There are no easy answers to this shit going on, but I keep hoping that we'll deal with the complete assholes and get some decent training in. But then you get guys like this Jaden, who sent a supposed friend out to his death." Joe shook his head. "He knew how dangerous it was. They both did."

"They all did," Whalen noted. "That's what we've been working on, you know? Extra security, extra safety lessons, reminding everybody how dangerous it is to be out there on their own."

"But Ralph still went."

"And still Ralph went. As far as we can tell at this point, nothing untoward happened, outside of the fact that he stepped out of that door in the middle of terrible conditions, then decided it was a good time to travel to the village. Ralph was cracking under the pressure a bit."

"Yet he was plenty fit, and I still don't understand why he didn't make it," Joe stated, eyeing Whalen suspiciously.

"That is one of the things we don't understand either." He should have realized that no way would Joe be mistaken as to what had gone on and wouldn't miss that point. "The problem is, we don't have any clear-cut idea of exactly what happened because we can't do an autopsy. His body will go back, an autopsy will be performed, and, if anything was used, like drugs or something," he said pointedly, "then we'll find out at that point. But, in the meantime, Jaden is under house arrest, until he'll be shipped out."

"Hopefully we get answers real fast after that, but, if you're taking him out of play here at the base, I'd like to think that would be the end of it."

"I would too," Whalen agreed, "but I can't be sure."

"No, of course not," Joe muttered. "Only so many people are in that damn base over there." Joe glared at Whalen. "How the hell can so many things be done without anybody knowing?"

"I don't know," Whalen admitted, "and that is the next thing. Some of us came up here to investigate, and we're not getting very far. Instead we keep getting more deaths."

"And yet this death was a stupid one," Joe added.

"They're all stupid," Whalen pointed out.

"No, I'll give you that," Joe said, "but it's not as if this was like one of the other murders."

"No, it isn't." Whalen dropped his head in his hands for a second. "Which just begs the question. Has the person who perpetrated those murders gone underground? Is he dead? Has he solved whatever he needed to solve, or is he just lying in wait, until something else goes on?"

"That is the question, isn't it?" Joe replied. "Either way, it would be nice if this whole scenario was over."

"Never been involved in a training session with so many deaths. We've had several where they all perished at the same time in one event, and we've had some really ugly scenarios where, you know, stupidity came into play. There'll always be some incidents that you wish you could go back in time and completely redo. But nothing like we've had this time."

Back in the main compound, Whalen walked over to a small common area room, finding Egan all by himself, sitting off to one side, paperwork in front of him. Whalen sat down, and Egan looked up, startled, and then nodded and went back to the paperwork. "Finding anything?" Whalen asked Egan.

"I just got a bunch of material from Mason," he replied

in a low voice.

At that, Whalen leaned forward and asked, "Do you want me to help?"

"Yeah, I do," he said, a bit frustrated. "I need somebody to start correlating some of this. We've got a lot of history on a lot of people."

"Everybody here?"

"Yeah, and there's a surprising amount of crossover."

At that, Whalen froze for a moment. "Are you saying crossover between the people here in times past?"

"A lot of them, yes. Not everybody, obviously, since we've got a lot of different countries here," he explained, "but, even then, a surprising number of things are becoming clearer."

"In what way?"

"Four of the Russians had already been out on missions with Jaden. They met over in Iraq and were doing joint training together."

"Oh, wow," Whalen muttered. "So Jaden knew Yegorahn and Helsky and the first Russian who died—I don't have his name."

"Yes, as well as Eric, the Russian who went missing not long after Teegan did."

"Four of the original Russian team here knew Jaden from an earlier training session? Wow."

"That's what I'm just double-checking." He handed over a sheaf of papers and said, "Check and see if Jaden was on any of these missions, will you?"

"Not a common name. A nickname or just his name is spelled differently maybe?"

"Oh, shit, that could happen. Try something else. … *Jayden* with a *Y* maybe?"

At that, Whalen moved his finger swiftly down the line, and he nodded. "Yep, four years ago in Iraq."

"There you go, so we have a connection between them."

"Does that connection mean anything yet though?"

"Not yet, but I was trying to figure out if anybody had any history that they brought forward."

"That's a good point," Whalen noted, eyeing Egan, excitement in his voice. "We've been completely blank so far. What about any overlap for Teegan?"

Egan winced at that. "I don't think so. If anything happened along that line, I think it's purely because he started sticking his nose where somebody else didn't want it."

"And yet what would he have seen that nobody else saw, and who did he tell?"

"I don't know," Egan replied, "and that's what we have to figure out because, whoever he told, whatever he shared, they have something to do with this base right now."

"Do you think he went to the colonel about it?"

At that, he looked up, startled, then he shook his head. "No, I don't. I don't even want to think about him being involved."

"I didn't mean that," Whalen clarified. "I just wondered if Teegan went to any authority at all, and, if so, which one would he go to?"

"His brother," Egan stated bluntly.

"And yet communications would have been cut off, and so Teegan wouldn't have had a chance to do that."

"I know, which is also why Mountain is so pissed."

"At what point in time is this a done deal?"

Magnus joined them a few minutes later. "Mason said you have the material."

"Yeah, and I've got it printed off," Egan stated, "but a

lot is here, and we're still just tracking the players."

He looked over it at Whalen. "You okay to stay and help out?"

"Absolutely. How's Jaden doing?"

"I let him stew for a while in the back under guard, playing a hunch," Magnus explained. "I was hoping that this would happen."

"What's it say?" he asked, as Magnus hopped to his feet.

"He wants to talk."

At that, Whalen nodded. "What do you think he wants to talk about?"

"I don't know, but you can bet it'll be important."

Just then the colonel walked in, looked around, saw Magnus and frowned.

Magnus immediately walked over. "Sir? Can I help you?"

"Looking for Mountain," he said.

"He's at the village, I believe," he replied respectfully. At the colonel's deepening frown, Magnus nodded. "I know, but he's trying to improve relations with them."

"Not happening as long as people keep dying on the way over. They must think we're fools to still even be here," he barked.

"I do think that their impression is less than positive," Magnus stated.

The colonel nodded. "Tell Mountain that I want to see him when he comes in." As he went to walk out, he stopped and looked back. "What about the prisoner?"

"I'll talk to him now, sir."

"Good, report afterward." And, with that, the colonel was gone.

Whalen hopped up and asked, "You want me to come?"

Magnus turned to Egan. "Do you need him right now?"

"No, he can come back in half an hour and bring an update with him," Egan replied.

Just then several more people walked in, and Egan waved Whalen away. "Go. Come help me with this afterward."

And, with that, Magnus and Whalen slowly headed toward where the security guard was holding Jaden.

Whalen asked, "Why do you think he's decided to talk? What could he possibly have to say?"

"Maybe a reason for his actions. I don't know," Magnus admitted. "However, I was hoping, if we gave him enough time to sit there and to stew on his thoughts, maybe he would figure out that he could be in deep shit and then decide to come clean. Even if it doesn't make a whole lot of sense, we need some sort of logical reason for Ralph doing what he did."

"You mean, his panic attacks and growing panic about being here and surviving wasn't enough?" Whalen asked in a dry tone.

"It's not. Ralph was safe here, and, if you ask me, … he didn't need to go out there. It was akin to committing suicide."

"I agree," Whalen noted, "and that is something that a lot of people are talking about, quietly of course. Plus, morale is at an all-time low. We can't afford any more of this shit. … You'll have fun talking to the colonel afterward."

"No, *fun* and *the colonel* do not go together. Apparently he doesn't have a good rep with anybody at the moment. Something about his last tour. He just wants to complete this and to get his pension."

At that, Whalen winced. "Won't make him popular with

anybody that way."

"No, but he's done a lot of years, so, of course, he wants to go out in glory, though at this point he'd settle for something better than shame. He mostly doesn't want anything to affect that all-important pension."

"He's worked his whole adult life in the military. So, you would think, at the end of the day, there would at least be that for him."

"Not if he screwed up anywhere, not if there are some major wrongdoings," Magnus pointed out, as they approached the storage area, serving as their jail.

As they approached the storeroom where Jaden was being held, the guard stepped out to see who was arriving and nodded. "Hey, finally. He's been getting really antsy."

"I just got his text," Magnus replied, looking at him in astonishment.

"He's been talking back and forth about wanting to see somebody, but I couldn't reach anyone," he muttered. "Anyway," as he backed up into the room, he said, "he's in here now."

When they stepped forward, Jaden hopped up and grabbed the security guard around the neck and whipped his handgun from his holster, holding it against the guard's head.

"Jesus," Whalen muttered, staring at him. "Why the hell do you want to make that dumb move?"

But Jaden wasn't looking very normal. He was beyond panicked. His eyes were wild. His hair was standing on end, as if he'd been running his fingers through it nonstop. He looked as if his world had come crashing down on him.

Magnus held up his hand. "Jaden, take it easy, just calm down."

But Jaden wasn't listening either. He kept shaking his head, saying, "I ain't doing this. I ain't doing this."

"Ain't doing what?" Magnus asked.

The security guard looked stunned at the recent turn of events and not in very good shape himself mentally. He kept staring at Whalen and Magnus, as if telling them to fix it.

Whalen stepped forward and looked at Jaden. "Come on. Just tell us what's going on, buddy. You weren't in any trouble, up until now."

He snorted. "I'm in bigger trouble than you can imagine, and somehow somebody found out."

"Found out what?" Magnus asked, stepping forward.

"Found out what the hell was going on," Jaden snapped. "I don't know how. I don't know how he knew. I came to tell you … I would tell you everything, and then I got that warning," he said, "and the warning is basically something I'm not prepared to live with."

"Whoa, whoa, whoa. Hang on. You're going too fast. What are you talking about?" Magnus asked, trying to take another step forward, but then Jaden pushed the gun harder into the security guard's head.

"Don't come any closer, or I'll blow this guy's head right off."

"What will that do for you?" Whalen asked, staring at him in shock. "Then you've got a murder on your hands, instead of just really poor decision-making, which is what you have right now."

Jaden looked at him, and then he started to laugh, almost hysterically. "Poor decision-making? You're not kidding. But the minute anything goes wrong in this place, you better believe it's not about decision-making. It's a whole lot about screwing up your whole life." He was on the verge of tears, too desperate for the situation at hand. "You screw up once here, and you're in deep shit," he muttered. "You think I haven't learned that? And now this? I was fine earlier. I would have told you everything, until I got that message."

"How did you get the message?"

Jaden stared at him and shook his head. "No, no, no, no, no, they've got eyes and ears everywhere."

"They?" Whalen pounced.

Jaden nodded slowly. "*They*," he repeated, shaking his head from side to side. "You can't trust anybody in this base," he cried out. Then came this look of almost fatalistic realization. "I'll never get free of it." He looked at the guard, pushed him away, and instantly turned the gun on himself.

Whalen, seeing the intent in his eyes, rushed to him, but Jaden still got off the shot, a chest wound.

Magnus roared at the guard, "Go get Sydney."

The guard took off at a run, as Whalen looked over at Magnus. "What the hell precipitated that?"

"I don't know. Something about a message. He would have told us everything, and now, after that message, he knows he'll never get free."

"Of what?" Whalen asked, shaking his head, as he tried to slow the bleeding.

"Of them. *Them*. That's the concern. … Them. As if there's more than one person playing some sick game in this place, with some retribution or something for those who tell."

"Yes, I heard that loud and clear." Whalen looked down at the dying man, still trying to staunch the blood flow, but knowing it would be too little, too late. "He's … He's a goner. You know that."

"He will be in seconds, dammit," muttered Magnus.

"Check his pockets," Whalen suggested urgently, "before anybody comes."

Magnus did a full body search and shook his head. "Nothing, absolutely nothing."

"So, what message and how did he get it?" Whalen asked.

They looked at each other.

Magnus asked, "Where's his phone? We took away his phone, but did he get it somehow? … And, from the look of him, I hate to say it, but what are the chances he's got drugs in him?"

"It's possible," Whalen noted. "I thought we had that under control here."

"I sure as hell thought so too," Magnus muttered, "but it could explain Ralph, as well. I don't know. Maybe, … maybe Jaden's got another source somewhere."

Sydney rushed in, gasped, then dropped at Whalen's side, as she quickly ripped open Jaden's shirt and took a look. She looked back at the two men, shaking her head. "Nothing I can do. This is directly into the heart. I can't medivac him out anywhere, even if he could survive that long."

As she spoke, Jaden took one last gurgling breath and passed away right in front of them.

"Shit." Whalen sat back on his heels, staring down at the dead man, his hands covered in blood.

Magnus looked over at Sydney. "You won't believe what just happened."

"I'll need a full report of what just happened," she stated crisply, as she studied the dead man, doing a full check on everything else. "I need to know what happened, so I can figure out what the hell is going on here."

"He took the guard hostage," Whalen noted. "Then, almost as if realizing he was doomed and couldn't get out of this with any kind of decent life, he turned the gun on himself."

She stared at him, as she sat back on her heels. "Seriously? Why though?"

"I don't know. That's the thing. He seemed convinced that somebody was after him. He said that he'd gotten a message from somebody and that the message hadn't been good, but, whatever it was, he didn't tell us. He had called us down here to tell us everything, then ended up telling us nothing—except that *they* had found out he would talk and had warned him not to."

She just shook her head again. "Magnus …"

"I know. I know," he said. "We need to solve this and fast. We've lost too many men at this point in time."

"Short on men and short on suspects too," she noted in an aggrieved tone. She looked down at the dead man. "So damn young too. Plus so depressed about the questioning …" She turned to the two of them. "I trust that the questioning was aboveboard, not hard-pressed, and you certainly weren't torturing the poor man?"

Magnus stared at her, trying to decide whether he should be insulted, and shook his head vehemently. "You can see for yourself. No wounds, no signs of torture, nothing."

"I know," she stated. "I already looked." She gave him a gentle smile. "Hey, I have to do my job too."

"I know, but we didn't do anything. We sure didn't do this." He turned around to see the security guard standing there, still looking pale. "Simon, tell her."

Simon immediately nodded. "Doc, it's just as he said. I

brought them in here to talk to Jaden. He'd been ranting and raving all day about needing to talk, and then I gave him my phone, so he could call Magnus here. Jaden really wanted to talk to Magnus in private, nobody else. Next thing I know, we're just standing here, and Jaden jumps me, grabs my gun, and holds it against my head. They talk for a few minutes, and he gets more and more spun up. I'm thinking I'm a goner. The next thing I know, Jaden pulls the trigger on himself." Simon looked down at Jaden's body. "And I'm … I'm sad about that, but I am not upset that he didn't take me with him." Simon looked around at the others. "He was not talking normally or rationally, was he?"

"No, he wasn't. He was panicked, and I even wondered if he was high on drugs," Whalen suggested. "And, if not, he was just seriously afraid. Like to the point of being hysterical."

At that, the guard nodded. "Since being in here, he had been *off* and getting more and more off as time went by. Then he just … He had to talk to somebody, but I was under orders to keep him separated and alone, so that you guys could talk to him later."

"Yes, I wanted him isolated, so he could consider his options," Magnus confirmed, as he stared down at the dead man. "But never in my dreams did I think that this would be one of his options."

"None of us did," Whalen agreed. "It certainly isn't your fault."

"No." He stared at Whalen and asked, "But what do you want to bet that other people won't agree with you?"

Whalen winced. "Yeah, I'm sure there'll be a lot of people around here who will wonder what we did to him."

"And not just you, me," Magnus added, "or Simon here

too, for that matter."

"Me?" the guard asked. "What the hell?"

"It's just that you were with him since we detained him. When he told you that he wanted to talk to somebody, did he talk to anybody else?"

"No," Simon declared. "I swear. He had no visitors, nothing. Now, I did go get him a cup of coffee and a sandwich, but I had Bruce come and relieve me for that twenty minutes while I was gone."

"Bruce?" Magnus repeated, frowning at Simon. "We need to talk to him too."

"Yeah, he's my relief whenever shit hits the fan, and apparently shit hits the fan at this place more than you would expect." He shook his head. "Man, I don't, … I don't know. I just want to go home to my wife and kids now."

"Take off and go grab yourself a coffee, but please don't talk to anyone, do not spread tales at all. We have to notify the colonel about this and write up reports. Not to mention we'll have to move the body."

"Shit, shit, shit," Simon muttered. "Put him in the store-room."

"Yeah, and Chef will love that."

Simon nodded. "I know. I, I don't even know what to say." And, indeed, Simon definitely seemed on the weary side.

Sydney looked at him and nodded. "Go on to your room, grab a coffee or a cup of tea if you need to, and, if you want to talk, you come down to the clinic, okay? And, if you're having trouble sleeping, just give me a shout."

"Thanks, Doc." Simon looked relieved to be getting out of there and quickly disappeared.

Whalen looked over at Sydney. "So, what's the procedure now?"

"I do a full exam of the body, including taking samples of his blood, and I write up a full report. And then we'll put the body in the storeroom." She winced and added, "I'll have to order more body bags. *Again.* Jesus, who would have thought?"

"I know," Magnus said, looking at her sideways. "Not exactly what any of us thought we were signing up for."

She winced and shook her head. "No, we sure as hell didn't, but I feel worse knowing Jaden felt this was his only option. How the hell does a young man in his prime come to this?"

"Pressure," Whalen stated instantly. "Pressure from somebody else, and the only other person I would have thought he could have gotten that pressure from is Ralph, the man he helped walk out to his death. Now with the both of them dead, I have to admit we need to reassess whether that first death, Ralph's, involved just the two of them, or was there somebody else."

Sydney looked at him and frowned. "But you have the recordings, right?"

"Yes, and Jaden did admit to saying all that, to pressuring Ralph," Magnus noted. "But then why do this?" he asked, with a motion toward the body in front of him. "That was not in any way, shape, or form the reason for doing something as extreme as this. Even if Jaden were discharged from the military, he still would have had his whole life ahead of him."

"Unless he was a lifer," Whalen suggested. "Some guys just can't stand the thought of not being in the military or not in some service, after having signed up. It's everything to them."

"Maybe," Magnus acknowledged, "but, at the same time, … I don't think Jaden was a lifer. I could be wrong, but he also seemed to be handling all the problems here relatively well."

"I wouldn't say so," Sydney disagreed. "Look at how he was with his supposed friend. Jaden was more than willing to encourage him to go out to his death. I'm not sure that is somebody who was handling his time here all that well."

"Yeah, but maybe that was psychologically something Jaden was having some fun with. He was well-known for gaslighting people, making digs about abilities, and he's already had several relationships on both sides of the sexes," Whalen shared, looking over at the body. "I wouldn't be at all surprised to hear that Ralph and Jaden may have had a couple nights together."

Magnus looked at him in surprise.

Whalen shrugged and went on. "Just the way a couple people have talked. I don't have any proof, and I was hoping to ask him but never really could find a reason *why* to ask that question. After all, it didn't matter if they had a romantic liaison. It was just another of those boxes to check, and I didn't want it to be something that was held against him."

"No, of course not, but on the other hand," Magnus suggested, "if they were in a romantic relationship, what are the chances Jaden's in a relationship with somebody else, and that someone else didn't want that to come out, especially now that Jaden was being held for questioning."

"I don't know," Whalen replied. "Would somebody kill over a same-sex relationship in the military?"

"Hell yes," Magnus declared. "Particularly depending on what the association is and who it's with."

"*Great*," Whalen muttered. "Now I wish to hell I had

asked."

"Chances are, Jaden wouldn't have told you, and the question would have been crossing the line, so you probably would have heard about it somewhere, somehow, down the road."

"Maybe, but Jaden and even Ralph might still be alive."

At that, Magnus winced and nodded.

Whalen stood up and asked, "What do you need first, Sydney?"

She groaned and said, "I'll need a gurney."

"I'll go get one for you." And, with that, Whalen turned, walked out, and headed to the medical clinic.

DAY 5 EARLY MORNING

THE RUMORS WERE rampant. Yet Chrissy hadn't heard anything directly, so she didn't want to believe it. People were saying that somehow Jaden, who had been in custody, had committed suicide, and now everybody was looking at each other sideways, wondering why he would do such a thing. It made no sense to her either, but rumors being rumors, she knew it may or may not be true. She walked into the kitchen to get a cup of coffee early this morning to start her shift.

Chef Elijah stood here, a morose look on his face, just glaring around his kitchen.

"You okay?" she asked.

He nodded. "Sure am, but you're locked out of the storeroom."

"Why is that?" she asked.

He hesitated but then explained, "If you haven't heard by now, Jaden shot himself using his guard's gun. He attacked the guard, took his gun. ... So, a body is housed in my storeroom ... *again*."

"Wow, so your refrigerator is the morgue, is that it?"

"Yeah, and unfortunately it's been in heavy use lately."

"Is that normal?"

"Sure, to a degree, although in a place like this, the generator room would suit me better."

"I guess it's a little warmer but not much, *huh*?"

"Not much, I think in this case it's more that Sydney still likely needs access. I don't know." Chef raised his hands. "I guess it's just convenient."

"Maybe, but, if it bothers you, and you don't want it close to the food, you could just ask them to move the body elsewhere."

He stared at her. "I don't give a shit really," he stated bluntly. "Meat is meat, but don't worry. I certainly won't mistake it for a roast."

She winced at the callousness in his tone and added, "Let's not have anybody else hear you be quite so blunt about it, *huh*?"

He shrugged. "Can't really be anything but, when you think about it. Too damn many dead bodies this time around," he muttered. "Just too many." And, with that, he slowly walked back to his table and sat down.

She nodded. "I'm with you there. Look. Do you want me to take over breakfast this morning?"

He looked up at her, then shrugged. "It ain't going to stop me from doing my job," he muttered, "but it sure as hell isn't the way I wanted to start my shift this morning."

"No, and I'm sorry," she said. "The rumors are flying around that he shot himself. I didn't realize what had happened though."

"No, nobody ever does. Unfortunately the rumor mill is often the first source of information, whether it's right or wrong," he noted.

She nodded. "And, in this case, it sounds as if they got it right."

"Not that many people here anymore, so it's harder for them to get it very wrong," he muttered, as he stared at her.

"Anyway, here's the menu I had brought up. If you can whip up some of these today, that would help a lot."

She looked down at it absentmindedly, noting the cinnamon buns, which she had to start on right now in order to have them for breakfast. Normally he would tell her about it ahead of time, but she also noticed his printing was on the illegible side as well. She groaned softly, realizing just how much this death had affected him. "Did you know Jaden well?" she asked gently.

He shook his head. "Nope, I didn't."

"Ah." She wanted to say more but then decided that her best move, the best thing she could do, would be to just get to work and to forget about trying to help Chef deal with his grief or whatever this was. Maybe it was anger. He'd been in the service for a very long time, after all, and he'd seen a lot. Maybe this was something new, and he didn't want to see it ever again, or maybe it was just one more body in a long line of bodies, and the cumulative reality was something he didn't want to deal with.

Regardless, she focused and quickly had cinnamon bun dough rising, cookie dough in her mixing bowl, while she started a fresh batch of pastries. He smiled when he came to see her industrious work.

"It's nice to have somebody with your skills in a base such as this," he stated. "We tend to use cheap packaged stuff, as much as we can, instead of making everything from scratch, simply because we can't count on having the staff to support it."

"Cheap packaged goods are one thing," she noted, "but making it from scratch is often less expensive, and it uses ingredients that we currently have and don't really need for anything else, so it just makes sense."

"It does. Sorry about the short notice on the menu," he said. "Normally I would give that to you ahead of time."

She looked at him and nodded. "You do, but things seem far from normal right now."

"No, not only are they *not* normal," he declared, "I don't have much hope that they'll ever be normal again." And, with that, he shut up and got to work.

WITH A CUP of coffee in his hand, Whalen headed over to find Egan.

As Whalen entered his buddy's private bunk space, Egan looked up from the paperwork on his desk, frowned at him, and noted, "You look like shit."

Whalen nodded. "Standing over a corpse before you go to sleep at night doesn't exactly give you the best night's rest."

Egan winced. "Yeah, I heard about that. I'm sorry, and, yeah, it sucks."

"Not only does it suck," Whalen noted, "it makes no sense. I was contemplating what reasons anybody would have to shoot himself like that, given the investigation we're looking at, but it just doesn't add up."

"No. Did you also realize that he was under the same CO and, therefore, the same chef a few years ago too?"

Whalen studied Egan and then shrugged. "It does make sense that our CO and our chef would have been to the same postings along the way. They've both been in the service for a long time."

"Yeah, I know," Egan muttered. "All I'm finding so far is a lot of situations where it does make sense that they would have seen each other," he muttered. "That just makes me even more frustrated because I expected to have some answers, and I'm just not finding them."

"No, and, at this point in time, none of us are getting the answers we want," Whalen noted, "just to add to everybody's frustration."

"What about Sydney? Has she come up with anything from Jaden's body?"

"Nothing definitive as far as I know, but I haven't talked to her yet this morning. There was nothing on him last night—no drugs, no phone, no message, no nothing."

"And he used Simon's phone to call you?"

"Yeah, but only after a lot of persuading," he muttered. "It wasn't me who Jaden called. It was Magnus. Simon called Magnus, saying that Jaden wanted to talk."

Egan nodded. "Which also makes sense because Magnus is the one who technically set him up in solitary confinement to sweat it out."

"Yeah, and, right about now, Magnus is feeling pretty shitty. It's normal to feel that way, but it's not his fault. It's not my fault. The only person at fault is the one who pulled the trigger and the one who sent the message."

"I want to hear more about that," Egan said, sitting back. "Talk to me about this message."

"There's only so much I can tell you. Jaden was rambling on about somebody having given him a message. He told us that he was planning on telling us everything, but then he realized, after getting that message, that his life was worthless and that they would find out and that he wouldn't play that game. He rambled on for a little bit more, but that's the gist of it."

"But it was plural?"

"That was the one thing that both Magnus and I really locked on to was the fact that it was clearly *them*. Jaden repeated that *they* sent him a message and that *they* wouldn't let him go or wouldn't let him say what he wanted to say. *They* would have something to say about everything he did for the rest of his life, if he didn't watch it. How *they* were listening. *They* had eyes and ears everywhere," he shared, trying to remember all the bits and pieces that he'd heard last night, over and over again heading back to that same scene.

"How much of that was fear or panic in this case, or how much of that was drugs? And, man, I want to know where anybody's getting those damn drugs," he muttered. "Or how much of it was more gaslighting by somebody else in the group?"

At that, Whalen stopped. "I hadn't considered that last one."

"We have to because an awful lot of talking is going on around here. No way Jaden should have convinced that kid Ralph to go out in the middle of that storm under normal circumstances."

"Yet nothing that we're in would qualify as normal circumstances, and nothing that we're doing is getting us any further ahead."

"I know," Egan agreed.

Whalen shook his head. "Just another one of those weird things happening right now."

"I don't know about *weird* things happening, but I think there's something, some insidious group behind all this," Egan suggested.

"Jesus, I hope you're wrong," Whalen replied, feeling a little shocked. "That's the last thing we need."

"It might be the last thing we need," Egan agreed, "but

I'm not so sure that there isn't something much bigger than we're expecting here."

"Yet who, how, where, when, and why this guy Jaden, why these guys, Ralph and Jaden?" Whalen pointed out. "That makes no sense."

"It will," Egan stated. "It will. We're just not to the point of finding out what or how yet—but don't forget. It's early yet."

"No, it's not early," Whalen snapped. "It's not early at all, and it's been going on for far too long already."

"Oh, I agree with you there, but this is the first time that we've had anybody scared enough to give us any details to go on."

"So, I guess it's because you just weren't there," Whalen replied, with a note of humor in his voice. "Maybe that's why you can be so positive about having some information about this because believe me, I don't see that we have a thing."

"We do. Honestly we do. Sure, we don't have enough yet. We don't have the answers that we really need, but I have faith that now that we have a start and that we have some idea of how to roust into this, that we will find exactly what we're looking for."

"So, how do you keep yourself sane while you're at it?" Whalen asked. "Because, from what I'm seeing, as soon as anybody involved does something to get on our radar, they are taken out, and they're taken out well before anybody has a chance to find out even the basics of this nightmare. A safety issue is here even bigger than what we considered it to be."

"That's the next problem," Egan agreed. "Trying to make sure that nobody else dies while we're here."

"And that seems to be pretty-damn impossible because we've all said, *Enough is enough*, but we're not getting to the end of it because we haven't even got to the beginning."

Egan nodded. "Which is why I need your help and why we have to keep this incredibly quiet. We know those of us who came in after the fact are clear."

"But do we?" Whalen asked immediately. "Think about it. Do we really, or did somebody manage to finagle somebody inside, somebody who they wanted and somebody who's a part of this?"

At that, Egan sat back and studied Whalen. "Jesus, I don't like the way your mind works."

He snorted. "Hey, I'm the one who came in with a cup of coffee, hoping that you had some news or maybe no news and had decided this was all BS."

"Yeah, well, not only do I not have news, I haven't cleared anybody of anything yet," Egan admitted. "It's not all BS. If anything, I'm more concerned that it's way more than we had expected. So sorry … but no. It won't be that simple." Egan sounded frustrated right now, but added, "Surprised you didn't get a cinnamon bun."

Whalen repeated, "Cinnamon bun?"

"Yeah, apparently your girlfriend made fresh cinnamon buns this morning," Egan said, with a smile. "When I asked her what the special occasion was, she told me that, whenever she gets upset, she bakes, and Elijah had put them on the menu."

Whalen considered Egan's words, as memories flashed through Whalen's mind, and he nodded slowly. "Actually that's very true. Whenever Chrissy did get upset, she'd go whip up a storm in the kitchen," he said, with a gentle smile. "She's a hell of a cook too."

"So, she's not just a baker?"

"No, she's a really good cook." He shook his head. "Sometimes I wonder if I made the right choice."

"As somebody who absolutely adores fresh baked goods, you may want to rethink your life decisions," Egan suggested, with a smirk. "But, if you want to go grab cinnamon buns for yourself, grab me a coffee while you're there."

"I think I will," Whalen said.

And, with that, he left his coffee behind and headed back to the kitchen, hoping that a cinnamon bun would help improve his mood. However, he also knew that one other thing would improve his mood for sure, and that was to see Chrissy's sweet face once again.

It was a hell of a nectar in these dark times, and he wasn't stupid enough to turn it down, not when he knew that she could help him get through this rough day. And it would be rough; no way it couldn't be. The moods were already dark. People were already looking at everybody sideways, but, more than that, they were looking at Magnus and at him that way too.

Whalen expected fights would break out soon. As a matter of fact, it was looking to be a shitty day all around. So, he would take whatever he could to make it a little easier, even if it was just for a moment. He was starting to realize that the same attraction that he'd had for Chrissy before was still there, even more so. He was just as attracted now as he was back then, and, if he wasn't careful, he'd end up right back in the situation he had been in before.

Although his mind immediately argued that it would be different this time. It would be a lot different, and maybe it would be okay now. Maybe the two of them could work it out. But immediately he told his mind to shut up and to not go in that direction. Yet in the background he heard his mind whispering, *You're just scared. You're scared that you'll screw up. Again.*

And stomping those thoughts down tight in his mind, he headed into the kitchen, and that hope of seeing Chrissy reared its head.

DAY 5 BREAKFAST

TO SAY THE attitude among everyone on base was dark and ugly was to put it mildly, and Chrissy watched as they all came through the buffet line, most of them either not talking or anything they had to say was not in a good light. Lots of furtive looks were cast around, as if to see who might be listening. As soon as any of Whalen's group walked in, silence was the immediate response. It even applied to her, as apparently she'd been pegged as the enemy, although most people tended to ignore her when she was working behind the counter.

Gee, wasn't that a surprise? Everybody ignored most kitchen staff as if they were invisible. But, when she came out—looking for her own breakfast and hoping to sit down and to visit with somebody, instead of just sitting in the back room of the kitchen—the eating area had been completely cleaned out, except for Whalen and Egan, sitting in one of the back corners, secluded.

She walked over and asked, "Is this a private conversation or can anyone join in?"

Egan frowned up at her.

She took that to mean it was private, and she nodded. "In that case I'll just go into the back and eat."

"No," Whalen said. "You have to get out of the kitchen sometimes too." He stood up and explained, "Egan is working on something private, but I can join you over here, while you eat."

She frowned at Whalen, then nodded slowly. "You don't have to, you know? I'm a big girl."

He shrugged. "I know. And I also know that, in some ways, I'm sure you've been painted by the same brush that the rest of us have," he noted. "And that can get lonely very quickly here, if nobody talks to anybody."

"They're talking, just not to me and likely not to you," she replied, with a nod.

"No, and the fact that we have another dead body has cast a fresh pall on everyone."

"Jaden was also fairly well-known, as was Ralph," she shared, "at least from what I'm hearing. I was talking to Avalon about it, and, of course, being in the kitchen, she's heard an awful lot of the conversations going on. Plus Ralph seemed to have one hell of an ax to grind with Avalon."

"Yeah, again it's a unique spot where you are. I'm surprised you don't eat in the back more often."

"I do, and I eat back there with Chef and Avalon a lot of the time. Sometimes they prefer to stay back there, so that they're not involved in whatever's going on out here," she explained, "but that can get to be a bit much too." She gave him a knowing smile. "I'm also trying to do training with people here, and I don't want it to be something that, when I show up, they all give me that closed-rank feeling—in which case I won't go out and get any valuable education anyway."

He nodded, and she hoped he understood. She sat down anyway, hoping that he would stay and visit for a few minutes, and, when he did, she smiled at him. "Did you get any sleep?" she asked.

He shook his head. "Not a whole lot. I should have

though. It's not as if we pressured him into doing it or anything. I'm pretty sure Simon, the guard, is pretty messed up over it."

"With good reason," she agreed. "Nobody wants to see their life flash before their eyes, particularly in that scenario."

"Simon's also wondering what he could have done differently, what he didn't see. Everybody hashes it over, trying to figure out just what it was that they were supposed to have done differently in those circumstances." Whalen shook his head. "Honestly there wasn't a whole lot anybody could have done. Jaden made a decision. Whether it was a panicked decision or not, once he'd taken that step, ... things changed."

"I feel bad for him," Chrissy said, "for Jaden. I don't ... I don't know what made him take that step, and I'm sorry that he felt it was the only step available to him."

"And that's what the rest of us are trying to figure out. Why suicide? What else is going on here that we don't know about?"

She winced. "Yeah, I was wondering that myself. ... For Jaden to take that step is pretty, ... pretty final." She quickly ate, knowing that her time with Whalen would run out pretty fast.

"Are you done after this?" Whalen asked her.

She nodded. "I want to grab a couple hours before I return to the kitchen later today, to see if I can get a little bit more sleep. I can't say I had a whole lot myself overnight."

"No," he noted, "I think a lot of people are in that same boat. Even worse, we've got a blizzard moving in again."

She stared at him and shook her head. "When you think about coming up here and doing this special training, you don't really think that *every* day will be a bad weather day, but since I've arrived? It sure seems as if every day has been a bad weather day."

He smiled and shrugged. "I think that's probably pretty common up here. We just aren't used to it because it's not our normal habitat," he replied.

"Maybe." She shook her head. "I'm not sure anybody could make it their normal habitat either. Think about it. These are quite the weather events and they happen on a regular basis. I don't know how even the villagers survive."

"They're hardy. They're used to it, and they want to be here," Whalen pointed out, "and all of that makes a big difference."

She smiled. "I guess. And, for me, it's not necessarily where I want to be, so I keep looking at ways to get through it and hopefully get home in one piece," she muttered.

"You and everybody else, from what I'm hearing," Whalen replied.

She nodded. "And that's even more disconcerting too. … When you think about it, you think *not* surviving this is dying on the job because, if you die, you'll die out there in the midst of a mission or a training exercise." She pointed to the vast wilderness outside them. "You're not thinking that you'll die in here, inside the base, and certainly not from suicide, like Jaden chose to do. That makes his choice all the more interesting because it's almost as if, in his mind, he had no choice."

"Exactly," Whalen agreed, "which is why we're trying to figure out just what went wrong here, so that we can stop it from happening again."

"Clearly something is going on here that none of us know about." He frowned at her, and she shrugged. "You think I don't see and hear things?" She shrugged again.

"And, of course, we talk about it in the kitchen too." She glanced back where Chef Elijah was even now cleaning up after serving the meal. "And most of us don't really understand what happened or how it happened."

"I don't think anybody does, and the fact that I can't say anything in terms of details just makes everybody even more standoffish."

She smirked. "Yeah, that's true too. If you don't tell people what's going on, they tend to look at you as if you're the enemy." He shook his head at that. "But I know you're not the enemy," she added, with an eye roll. "You have that *need to serve and to defend the group* thing going on."

"And you don't?" he asked, a note of challenge in his tone.

She considered his words and slowly shook her head. "I know it'll make me sound as if I'm a whole lot less, and I don't mean it to be, but this can't ever be my life or my first love," she stated, with a nod, "but I do recognize and respect that it's yours. I don't know if you've acknowledged that you'll be alone all your life and whether that's totally okay for you," she added, "but that's not what I want."

"You don't have to be alone the whole time," he corrected, looking at her. "Lots of people have relationships."

She cast him a glance. "I wonder if they work out long-term, though."

"I would like to think so, but I can see that your perspective is tainted by our history."

She laughed. "I'm not sure that *tainted* is the right word, but it's certainly something that makes life a little bit more interesting, when you consider just how much I've changed."

"I have changed too," he stated. "I think this life does that to you."

She nodded, smiling. "I guess. I hadn't really thought about it. But, for me, it was a case of just growing up and realizing that I had to make the changes I wanted and that nobody else could make them for me."

"Which is a huge step in everybody's book," Whalen murmured, studying her intently.

She waved her hand. "You don't need to look at me like that. I'm not going crazy. I'm not doing anything weird or abnormal. I just think this has been a really good opportunity to sort myself out, and I'm grateful that I've had that chance. And honestly," she added, "I'm grateful that you're here too. It's given me a chance to work my way through what I had thought was resolved, but apparently isn't."

At that, he winced and she laughed. "Don't worry about it," she said, "I'm getting over it all. I'm actually over it all, which is even more empowering."

He didn't know what to say to that and looked as if he was attempting to say something, as his mouth opened and closed several times, and then he just gave it up.

She smirked. "That's probably a wise thing."

He shook his head. "I'm not so sure it is," he disagreed. "You're a very special person, and believe me, an awful lot of times I knew inside my heart that I'd made a mistake by walking," he shared, "but some things, … you just don't know how to go back."

"I don't think you wanted to go back anyway," she stated. "I guess I just needed to see that whatever we had wasn't me or it wasn't connected to what was wrong with me." She smiled at him sadly. "And that helped me in a way too."

"It never was about you."

She laughed. "And you say that as if it's a good thing. But honestly, it *should* have been about me, and, if you had cared, it would have been. But, because you didn't, you did the right thing, and you moved on. I didn't move on in a good way. I was holding grudges, and, for the longest time, I was angry. So this has been my way to move on, and I'm grateful for that opportunity."

Even at that, he seemed a little nonplussed at her wording.

She just smiled, shook her head, and said, "Honestly, it's all good."

"Yeah, you say that, but having just spoken to somebody who shot himself right in front of me, it doesn't sound good at all."

She frowned at him. "I am not in any way suicidal."

"No, I'm not implying that," he corrected. "I just want to ensure that wherever you're at right now, … that it's a good place."

"It's a good place," she confirmed, then got up. "Thanks for the talk." And quickly she went back to where Elijah was working.

As she passed him in the back room, Chef looked at her too closely. "You okay?"

She smiled, nodded. "Yes, just trying to find a way to bring closure."

He snorted. "Why the hell are you trying to bring closure when what you really want to do is bring him back into your life?"

Startled, she looked at Chef and shook her head. "I don't know where you got that idea from, but I won't be second best in any relationship."

Chef eyed her in surprise. "It's not being second best," he argued, understanding her struggle. "It's a matter of being there for him because we need more people like him. It's being that special part of his life that makes it worthwhile for him to go out on a mission and to come home at the end of the day. Without that, most guys don't last very long," Chef noted. "They get careless and reckless, and then something happens, and they take on jobs that are a little riskier than they should because they don't care anymore. Is that what you want for Whalen?"

She gaped at Chef, her heart sinking. "No, of course not, but he doesn't want me. We've cleared the air a bit, which is good, but the fundamental issue remains."

"And that's why he watches you whenever you walk into a room? That's why he watched you walk away just now, his jaw working, as if he wanted to stop you but didn't know how?"

She turned and looked back in the direction where Whalen had been sitting, but she saw no sign of him now. She turned back to Elijah, and he nodded.

"You're not seeing what's right in front of you," he said. "You already missed it once. Do you really want to miss it again?"

She winced at that. "You make it sound so easy."

"Nothing's easy," Chef declared, with the wave of his hands. "Nothing is intended to be easy. Life is all about work. It's all about finding somebody out there who's special."

She glared at him. "That doesn't mean it'll be him."

"No, it doesn't have to be him, but you know you want it to be. You know that something is unfinished between the two of you. You know it, and I certainly don't have to tell you that. What's interesting to me is the fact that you're not willing to go in that direction, just in case you get rejected."

"I was rejected once before," she snapped, "and it sucks."

"It does, but being alone sucks too," Chef pointed out. "Ask me about it."

She frowned at that. "I was going to ask you, so why is that?"

"Because, after my son died and my wife died," Chef explained, "I didn't care anymore. I was all about making sure that the guys here had what they needed. I've been good friends with the CO for a very long time," he added, "so I've followed him around, making sure that his world happened."

"What about now, when his world goes to pieces?"

Chef sighed, even while nodding. "It's hard. It's hard for me to see it. It's hard for me to watch everything come to a head like this—but that's what friends are for. You think I'll just bail on him because he's in a tough spot? If he gets fired, kicked out, or whatever, I'm at retirement age anyway," he shared. "We always planned to go fishing. Just take off and get a cabin somewhere and just fish."

She smiled. "Are you sure there isn't something closer than that between you?"

He rolled his eyes. "No, and that's the thing. You can be good friends without it being a relationship," he said, staring at her. "But, in your case, you want a relationship with Whalen, so why the hell are you not prepared to go after it?"

"I'm not prepared to go after it because he made it very clear that he didn't want me. If he should change his position on that and lets me know in some way that he wants to try again, that would be an entirely different story."

"But you're putting the onus on him."

She nodded. "And why not?" she cried out. "Haven't I already had enough of this pain?"

"I don't know," Chef admitted, with a casual smile. "A little bit of pain now for a huge gain later seems to be a fair trade-off to me."

"Not if it means walking home with my tail between my legs."

"What if it means that because you're too scared to try it that you'll be alone, and, at least if it's with your tail between your legs, you'll know that you've done absolutely everything you could to try to have more. So, if it didn't work, it didn't work, but at least then you would know that you had tried. But instead you put in five years of your life in the military, which you say was to understand what he did. And then you came up here, but how much of it was in the hopes that he'd see you here, admire what you did, and see you in a different light, one worthy of his time and attention?"

She flushed beet red at that and shook her head. "Dear God, I hope not," she muttered, her voice faint, "because that would be seriously stupid. If he wanted me, he could tell me."

"Yet, in many ways, he's already started to. He's confused and doesn't really understand what he's doing, but you have to give him a chance to work his way through it. You knew that you were coming here and that you were in the military. Whalen didn't. He's dealing with a lot of shocks right now, so give the guy a break and let him have a chance to adapt, before you cross him off the list."

WHALEN WORKED WITH Egan steadily for the next couple hours, reading all the data Tesla had found on each of the trainees here, finding interesting connections in their past.

Whalen sat back, staring at all the documents in front of them. "Almost all of them had contact with various people here," he noted, with a frustrated tone. "But, in all cases, it's not as if it was major contact. They might have been in the same Forward Operating Base, which maybe gave them an opportunity to meet each other," he suggested, then pointed to the overlapping timelines he had written down, "but no complaints are on record about any of them. There's no … If there were disagreements, none of them have been written up, so nothing says that a past issue existed between anybody here."

"And sometimes it's not that clear-cut and simple," Egan pointed out. "Sometimes complaints don't make it to the file and aren't taken to the brass because nobody got threatened."

"Or because people were too scared to speak up, like Ralph and Jaden. If that's the case, how are we supposed to figure out who and what might be behind any of this?" Whalen asked, with a shrug. "If anybody's behind any of it at all."

"That's the problem," Egan admitted, with a nod. "We can do all this and compare, but the fact is, because some of these people have been in service for a very long time, we still have to double-check to confirm that they were at a particular base, that they were actually there at the same time. We've got correlations between four of our trainees, but over thirty of them are here," he stated, checking out the files. "Then if we take out all the foreign ones …"

"Which we can't," Whalen said immediately, "because some of them attended other joint sessions." Egan nodded, as Whalen continued. "But, if we can't connect everybody, how can we assume that we can connect anybody?" He frowned, pondering the information in front of him. "Unless of course—"

"What?" Egan asked, looking up at him. "You can't just stop after starting something."

"No, it's stupid," Whalen replied. "Seems to be a really dumb idea."

"Doesn't matter if it's a dumb idea or not. Throw it out there. It might spur us on to something else, to some angle we hadn't considered yet."

"I don't know. Is somebody trying to get out of the military? Is somebody trying to pay back someone for shitty decisions or the loss of a friend? Are they leaving soon and planning on leaving in a big way and never doing this again?"

"Motivation?" Egan asked, staring at him.

"That's the thing. Motivation doesn't seem to exist here, even with all these circumstances, or at least nothing that really makes any sense to me."

"And yet there's always motivation for things such as this."

"I hear you on that, and I agree. I'm just not so sure that anything we've seen so far will give us the information we want." He stopped again.

"Spit it out," Egan said, with half a smile. "No matter how stupid."

"It's just … What if, as you hear about with serial killers sometimes—which we do have here, if certain of these deaths were caused by just one person. Of course what has always confused the issue is that some of these deaths really were or just seemed to be well-executed accidents, giving them a free pass. But what if it wasn't such a well-executed accident and instead were trial killings?"

At that, Egan sat back and stared.

Whalen shrugged. "Obviously I'm just saying this off the

top of my head, but what if somebody was after one specific person, but, in order to throw off any investigation, he figured he had to kill several people, so he could obscure his prime target. Or maybe he didn't quite know how to make the killing happen, so he did a couple trial attempts."

"And all of them worked?"

"Or maybe they weren't attempted killings, but it turned out that it worked really well … at least for those deaths. Think about it. When it comes to killing machines, some of the most lethal people are at this base. You and I both know what training we've had, so successfully killing somebody isn't necessarily an issue."

"But hiding it on this base," Egan pointed out, "that's a whole different story. It's one thing to go into war and to take out the designated enemy, but in wartime we're not trying to hide our tracks or to hide who did it or even to hide who we killed. Except sometimes, in special cases, maybe," he muttered. "Still, that's really not part of what we're looking at right now."

"No, of course not," Whalen agreed, "so this all just ends up being more confusing. And maybe on purpose."

"And to add another element to your serial killer theory, what if he's done it before? Maybe at other bases?"

"Oh my God," Whalen replied. "Other missing persons, other suspicious deaths?" He shook his head. "That would make this more confusing than ever," he muttered.

"Yet the answer's here," Egan declared, as he stared down at the paperwork in front of him. "I'm convinced of that."

"I'm glad you're convinced, because at least that gives others the motivation to follow along in your tracks," Whalen admitted, with a snort, "because I'm not sure anybody else is convinced."

"No, and that's not helping either."

Whalen groaned. "Let me, … let me ask this question. Is anybody here *not* on the suspect list?"

Egan nodded. "Sure. Mountain, you, me, Magnus, Rogan, Barret. I have to admit I've checked the women paired up with us, all of us, … pretty intently, and I'm fairly certain we can knock them all off our suspect list."

"Pretty certain, but not 100 percent?"

"I would absolutely love to say 100 percent, but, if that is the standard, I can't even knock us off the list. I can knock me off," he added, with a laugh. "But you know, 100 percent is a pretty finite figure. Do I suspect any of them? No. Would I feel comfortable saying not one of them is involved? Yes. But does it make a damn bit of difference? No, because, if we go by the thirty original names, not really counting those added in later, we still have roughly twenty-four remaining, including our CO and Chef."

"What about knocking them off?"

"I can't knock them off. Yet I can't keep them on for any particular reason. I don't have *any* reason," he said, shaking his head. 'Either way, our CO and Chef are good friends and have worked together like brothers for a very long time. They're also retiring, and that's one of the things that I wondered about."

"What? That they would kill a lot of people on their way out?"

Egan shook his head at that. "No, I'm not saying that at all. It's just, well, I'm wondering if *somebody else* is holding a grudge against the colonel, and maybe this person is doing all this to ensure that the colonel goes out in tatters, his reputation a mess."

"That would be pretty unpleasant," Whalen noted, "and it would take a lot of hate to do that."

"Revenge is a powerful motivator, but, at this extreme, it would mean something personal, such as the loss of a team, the loss of a family member, the loss of somebody very close to them in some way."

"And yet we aren't trying to justify an excuse, we're just trying to … I hate to say that we don't have enough information, but clearly we don't have enough information. There's also the possibility that maybe whoever was responsible for this has managed to escape."

"Except that nobody has escaped." And then Egan stopped, winced, and corrected himself. "Of course we also have the case of the missing Dr. Amelia Morrison."

"Yeah, but I don't think she'd be responsible for killing a lot of people in our base or in her camp," Whalen stated. "Anna admitted she tried to kill the scientists with that carbon monoxide maneuver, plus she killed two scientists in a more direct and one-and-one manner."

"I know," Egan replied, "but it doesn't mean that Amelia isn't harboring somebody who might be our killer."

At that, Whalen's eyebrows shot up. Then he nodded and made a mental note. "I think it's far-fetched, but valuable to consider," he muttered. "Remember. We still have a missing Russian named Eric."

"And then, I hate to say it, but we also are still missing Teegan Rode."

"I know," Whalen said. "Just don't say that out loud."

"I know, right? Mountain would have my head. And yet, if it came to solving this problem and finding his brother, regardless of where his brother is at and what he may or may not have done, you know that Mountain would be happy for a resolution as to whether his baby brother is alive or dead at this point."

"But Teegan had a thumb drive, so he was investigating the trouble up here. That is one of the few things we know. But there wasn't much on that drive, *huh*?"

"Not enough," Egan said, "but Teegan did point out how every one of the accidents early on could have been manmade, and I agree with that in every instance. Yet I haven't been able to track who could have been around at that time," he admitted, his tone turning hard. "Almost everybody was off doing something on these training sessions. However, when I checked with people, there were a lot of instances where they have come in and come out of those training sessions freely, which makes for a lot of opportunity for a lot of people to stir up some mischief."

"Which is why it worked so well to cause these *accidents*," Whalen muttered.

"That was my take on it too," Egan agreed. "Then, because we tightened things up, there's a good chance that we've put a stop to that. However, now we still have whatever else is going on, and we know it's not good, and it's nothing we have any good information on."

"If only Jaden had talked to us before he decided to take his own life," Whalen muttered.

Egan grimaced. "But still he said *them* and that he got a message. What I can't figure out is what that message was, and how he got it."

"Having seen him at the time, he didn't seem to be himself at all," Whalen noted. "I don't know whether he was high on drugs or just petrified, but he was a mess."

"Saying *them* implies that he was being pressured by more than one somebody and, in this instance, to not say anything."

"And to not say anything would imply that other people are involved. This is bigger than just a case of two guys being friendly and having a same-sex relationship and all."

"But the question is, involved in what? What would any of that have to do with Ralph's death? Jaden's the one who sent Ralph outside, headed to the village for his escape. Jaden made it happen on the surface, so why?"

"And yet maybe he sent Ralph out more so because Ralph knew what was going on and was cracking under the pressure. So maybe Jaden was petrified that, if Ralph talked, Jaden would get caught too."

"That's another possibility." Egan nodded with a wince. "We're discussing possibilities and all, so it'll come up all the damn time. What we're not getting is any evidence or any leads. All we have is yet another dead body."

At that a shadow crossed them, and they looked up to see Mountain bearing down on them. He sat down with a hard *thump* and glared at them. "Well?" he barked.

"Nothing," Egan replied. "We have suppositions but nothing concrete. We've tracked Jaden's last few days, but absolutely nothing is there. He spent all his time with Ralph, up until the point in time that Ralph went out that door, which is already a disturbing thought."

Mountain nodded. "You guys checked Jaden's room?"

"We did, before he was taken prisoner," Egan confirmed.

"Did he ever share a room with anybody?" Whalen asked suddenly. "What about Bruce, the relief guard?"

"I spoke to Bruce. He said he doesn't know anything. Everything was normal. Had no idea what Jaden was up to, supposedly." Egan thought on it for a minute longer. "And, yeah, seems Jaden was roommates with one of the missing guys." Egan reached for his papers. As he looked through them, he suddenly frowned, then spoke in a hard voice, as if two stones were grating together. "Actually he shared a room with one Teegan Rode." Egan turned to face Mountain.

Mountain's eyebrows shot up. "Jaden shared a room with my brother?"

Egan frowned at that and said, "There wasn't space to have their own room at that point, so he had to share it with somebody."

"And, when my brother didn't return, obviously that bed was reassigned to Thomas—who has since been arrested and relocated, after trying to roofie Avalon, in the name of standing up for Ralph."

The other two just nodded, waiting as Mountain thought about it for a moment. "I want to search Teegan's room again." He bolted so fast that he knocked over the chair in the process. He picked it up and put it back into place.

Whalen hopped up and said, "I'll go with you." Mountain just shrugged. "I saw the Jaden guy die," Whalen added, with a distasteful shake of his body. "I just know we're missing something."

"Come on then. Let's go take a look."

"What about that stupid journal from the science center?" Egan asked. When they both stopped to look at him, he added, "I don't know, but could that have anything to do with this?"

"Did Jaden have anything to do with the scientists, whether alive or in death, including that missing female scientist, Amelia?" Mountain asked suddenly.

Egan looked at his notes and stated, "Jaden and Amelia

appeared to be somewhat friendly, but they were only here for a few days, before Amelia went missing. Besides, everyone was friendly to everyone back then. And there's not much that we know when it comes to both of them."

"But I understood that Jaden also had spent time over at the scientists' camp too," Whalen noted. "Maybe the scientists are that 'them' who Jaden was talking about."

"And yet that 'them' is pretty well all wiped out, gone back home, either dead or alive. Except for the ever-missing Amelia."

"Maybe not though. Maybe the ones airlifted out of here are who Jaden and Ralph were afraid of because, as soon as Ralph left this base, he becomes more vulnerable to that threat from the scientists, if any."

"Not really," Mountain disagreed, looking at him. "Jaden would be heading back home. Ralph too. Where are the relocated scientists right now?"

At that, Egan snatched up a notepad and started writing. "I don't know, but I'll find out."

With that, Whalen and Mountain headed toward Jaden's room.

As they stepped inside the bedroom, Mountain tapped the wall. "Those … Those are my brother's initials."

"Yeah, I knew the guys were doing that, carving their initials into the wall, leaving their mark," Whalen noted.

Mountain nodded. "Goes along with that age." He snorted and then shook his head. "I would have done the same thing ten years ago myself."

"Is that how many years are between you?"

He nodded. "Yeah, pretty close." He turned and looked around, and it was obvious that various emotions twisted his expressions, as he stared at what had been his brother's room.

Whalen looked at him and asked, "Any chance your brother would have hidden anything here?"

"He did, and that's what he gave to me," Mountain shared, his voice harsh.

"And what if he had something else as a backup, you know, just in case you didn't get it?"

Mountain turned and looked around the room, his gaze narrowing. "You do realize that now we'll have to destroy this room, right?"

DAY 5 AFTERNOON

CHRISSY COULD TELL that something was up via the grapevine, as she walked through the dining area back to the kitchen, where Chef stood, and asked, "What's going on?"

He shrugged. "I'm not sure. Something to do with Jaden's room."

"Okay, that sounds ominous," she replied.

"I haven't heard anything specific," Chef clarified, "so I can't tell you if it is true or not." She nodded but didn't say anything. "You'll probably know before me anyway," Chef noted, with a grin.

She shook her head. "Nope, not privy to any of that." When he frowned at her, she shrugged. "As much as anything, they're probably trying to keep me out of it."

"Yeah, and maybe to keep you safe," he pointed out to her.

She winced at that and nodded. "That could be. Maybe I don't want to know either."

"No, and that's another good point," Chef admitted. "All of this can get pretty rough."

She nodded and didn't say a whole lot. She looked around and asked, "Where's Avalon?"

"She's not doing too great," Chef shared. "I was hoping maybe you could help me with dinner service."

"Absolutely, particularly if you don't need any baking done."

"If you want, you can get something for dessert in the oven, but we need a little more prep work done first."

"Got it. Just tell me what you need."

And, with that, they buckled in and got food prepped for dinner. By the time they were done with the dinner service, she looked back at him and noted, "That was a fair bit of work today."

He nodded. "Every once in a while, it can pile up, and I could have done without some of it, which would have made it a little easier in some ways, but, with your help, we got through it just fine."

She smiled. "I'm glad we managed it. I hope Avalon feels better."

He nodded. "Are you okay to come in the morning?"

"Sure. I'll take over the slack, until she's back on her feet."

"Good." Chef nodded. "Now this was why I requested you."

She raised her eyebrows. "Did you request me?"

He nodded. "I sure did."

"Wow, I think I'm honored."

He snorted at that. "Don't be." He shook his head. "I just wanted to put you to work."

She burst out laughing and nodded. "Message received."

"Good, see you in the morning."

And with that dismissal and dinner over, she blurted out, "Dang, I didn't even eat."

"Ah, and we already cleared it all away. What the hell were you thinking?"

"I wasn't thinking. I was working."

"Right, well, in that case, you should pull out something for yourself."

She shook her head. "I'm fine. I'm not all that hungry anyway."

He stood there and glared at her.

She raised her hands and gave in. "Fine, you've still got ribs cooling here, don't you?"

"Yeah, you want a couple?'

And, with that, she quickly grabbed a plate and took it out to the dining room. Nobody still ate, but people remained, sitting around and talking—although the conversation immediately stopped as soon as she arrived. She sat down in a corner all on her own and ate, happy to have a break, happy to have a few minutes to just sit down, relax, and eat in peace.

She sat here quietly, and eventually the others ignored the fact that she was here and began to visit among themselves again, speaking a little more freely. She didn't try to listen in, but it was hard not to when she was sitting right here, all alone, with nothing else to distract her. It was late at that, and she was tired, after stepping up to help out more than she normally would, having already done her shift earlier that morning. As she sat here, she heard Whalen's name mentioned in a hushed whisper, which immediately got her attention.

Her ears cranked up, and she listened as one of them said that he wouldn't doubt if Whalen hadn't planted something in Jaden's room, since, after all, it was an easy way to make a dead man look guilty. She kept her expression calm as she listened in, and several other people agreed. One person disagreed, saying that maybe Jaden was guilty right from the beginning, and nobody would know. Then they all joined in, talking about Jaden and even Ralph. She didn't know what anybody needed to discuss, but, of course, human nature meant people would gossip and gossip hard. When the voices stilled suddenly, she realized somebody had walked in.

As Whalen sat down beside her, she looked up and smiled. "Hey, you look pretty tired."

He nodded, but it wasn't the fatigue in his expression as much as the grim look he wore.

"You look pretty upset," she muttered. Glancing around, she suggested, "You want to go for a walk?"

He laughed. "Where do you want to go?"

"I guess it's too cold outside. Isn't it time to go and, I don't know, check on the generator or the dogs or something?"

He looked at her and then slowly nodded. "Actually it probably is. Besides, I'm happy to go visit Patches any day."

She chuckled. "Oh my, isn't she gorgeous?"

"She is. If Joe is interested in selling her, I would take her home in a heartbeat," he confessed. He looked down at her food and asked, "Aren't you eating awfully late?"

"I am. Avalon wasn't feeling well, so I took over her shift. Just give me a second to finish this and to put it all up." She finished her meal, then went into the kitchen, quickly washed her plate and silverware, tucked it away into the rest of the dishes, then came back out. Whalen already stood at the doorway, waiting. As she walked out, he looped an arm around her shoulders.

She looked up, laughed, and asked, "What's that for?"

"I don't know. It seemed instinctive as much as anything. ... Maybe to let everybody know that you're taken."

"Am I taken?" she asked, looking at him.

He shrugged. "It seems safer for them to all believe that."

"I don't think anybody in there would hurt me."

He raised one eyebrow. "Yeah, and I don't think any of the dead men thought that either."

At that she stiffened, then slowly relaxed. "That's one of the reasons I wanted to talk to you."

He nodded, and they quickly bundled up, and he ushered her outside. She stood for a moment, gasping at the shocking cold, and he laughed. "Come on. You wanted to go check on the generators."

She rolled her eyes at him but followed obediently. In the generator shed, she looked around, the noise of the generator loud but not so obnoxious that they couldn't hear each other over it. "I wanted to tell you that some of the guys were talking about you at dinner. One even suggested that you may have planted evidence in Jaden's room, saying something about it being easy to make a dead man look guilty." She tried to give an exact quote but ended up paraphrasing. When he stared at her, she nodded. "Another one defended you, but several others agreed."

"That's getting pretty ugly then, isn't it?" he said, the frustration evident in his expression.

"That's what I thought. I didn't hear much else. They just started gossiping about both Jaden and Ralph. I'm pretty much classed as part of the enemy most of the time, and you're not helping that, by the way."

He tilted his head and then shrugged. "I was trying to keep you safe, and having you pinned with us does make it seem as if you are part of the enemy," he acknowledged, "but we're also doing our best to uncover what the hell's going on, and nobody likes it when we interrogate."

"Of course not," she agreed. "Nobody likes to be interrogated. Is Avalon really sick?"

"I didn't even know she wasn't feeling well," he said. "I'll check it out after we get back."

"That would be good," Chrissy agreed. "I guess I could too, but I don't know if Barret is out and about."

"He's gone to the village. He's been doing a lot of village trips, just scouting," Whalen shared.

"*Scouting.*" She shook her head. "That doesn't even sound innocent anymore."

"Nope, probably because it isn't," Whalen added, with a smirk.

"No way anybody outside of the base could be doing this," she said, then frowned at him. "Is there?"

"Not likely. We're pretty sure that Amelia from the scientists' camp broke into our storeroom and took groceries one day a while back, but I'm not sure since then."

"I don't think there's been any more break-ins at the kitchen. I only heard about that from Elijah, and he wouldn't really talk about it."

"I'm not surprised. He doesn't talk about much anyway." Whalen gave the generator a good once-over, checked on the fuel, then nodded. "Okay, we're good here."

"If you say so. I just wanted to let you know that people are suggesting that you might plant evidence."

"And that sucks," he stated. "I'd rather think that people here were a little more open-minded about finding the truth."

"Maybe, but one of them was from the Russian team, if that makes a difference."

"No love lost there," he said. "Not after Yegorahn's death, which I'm pretty sure they're more or less blaming us for, even after Raffi admitted to it because he wanted Cherry to himself."

"And how was that even connected to you?"

"I don't think logic matters at this point. There's always been enough rivalry between the countries already, so things such as this just make it even uglier, very quickly."

"Maybe, but, if you didn't have anything to do with it, they shouldn't be attacking you." She felt her own ire rise at the thought of the injustice.

He shot her a look. "It's part of the job." She glared at him, but he shrugged. "I don't like it," he admitted, "but it is what it is. Nobody in my position can be the *happy-go-lucky, always right, always smiling* guy and every man's best friend. I come into these places and do investigations, so it's never a good time for anybody when they see me," he muttered. "And believe me. I already know that very well."

"I'm sorry. I hadn't realized."

"No, of course not, and we don't advertise it, but word gets around pretty fast."

"It would," she agreed. "Yet that does explain some of their attitude and disgruntlement."

"Sort of, but not really," he said, looking at her. "If they haven't done anything wrong, they've got absolutely no reason to be pissy about it."

"But most people are pissy to some degree just because of the circumstances, and I don't think they've done any-thing wrong," she argued. "I think they're just worried and looking for an outlet."

"They're looking to gossip," he corrected. "Now, if any-body would speak up about things they know, that would be a different story."

"But, if it isn't things they know, then they'll just gossip."

"Exactly, and that's what gossip is. Now Jaden was about to tell us something important about this mess, and then he killed himself, saying that he couldn't live with it."

"And yet that makes no sense." Chrissy stared at Whalen. "He should have told you and *then* killed himself, in theory, but to keep his silence means that he's protecting somebody. Otherwise there's no reason to not speak up."

Whalen nodded. "But we haven't found any family connected to him."

"Doesn't have to be family," she noted. "Could be a loved one you don't know about. Could be anything, such as his reputation. For that matter, maybe they threatened to ruin somebody, a buddy in the service maybe?"

He considered that and then nodded. "We've been trying to hash out any and all kinds of ideas."

"That's good," she noted. "I think the fact that Jaden killed himself has everybody spun up. They feel as if he was backed into a corner and didn't have any choice."

"And that may be true, but it wasn't us who backed him into the corner," he told her. "We went down to talk to him at his request." She looked at him, startled, and he nodded. "That's the thing. Jaden was ready to talk."

"So, what stopped him from talking then?"

"He said he got a message, a message that would make his life miserable if he did talk, so he chose the easy way out. Knowing that he would be in trouble with us, and above us," he added, "Jaden couldn't see any future for himself, and, therefore, he wanted to get out of the situation."

"Yeah, but still he could have just made no comment, served a few years for the deal with Ralph, if he even got that, then just quit the service," she said in an exasperated tone. "It's not as if he did very much that you could really nail his ass to the wall over. So, I would say that whatever the threat was wasn't so much about watching his back as much as somebody not only would take him out permanently but, if he didn't do something along this line, they would take somebody else out permanently."

Whalen studied her, with a narrowed gaze.

She shrugged. "Just seems more along the line of human nature."

"He didn't have to kill himself, not unless it was part of the instructions and potentially, as he saw it, the best way forward."

"And, as sad as that may seem, it does seem to be an easy out. He's not here to be questioned. Nobody else is out here bugging him, talking about him, and nobody else can get hurt because of him," she pointed out.

"No, you're right there," Whalen agreed. "I will have to think about that."

"You do that." She shot him a glance. "I know that, in your mind, I probably don't know very much about life, but I do understand humanity. You forget what it was like with my sister. People were not kind to her. Everybody looked at her as if she was mentally deficient in some way, just because she couldn't hear. It was frustrating for her."

"No, I understand." He smiled as he thought back. "She was a sweetheart."

"She was, and that's another reason I want to get that bakery set up. I want to honor her memory. It was our dream, so I want to see it through."

"I totally get that," he said. "That's another reason I was surprised you joined up."

"I think she would have been very supportive of that

decision."

"Maybe because she wanted some independence too," he agreed, with a laugh.

She widened her gaze, as she looked at him. "Yes, I know, that was another issue you had, wasn't it?" she asked, with a headshake. "You thought I was too protective."

"I didn't know what I was talking about. I'm sorry about that too."

"No, you were right on that one," she stated. "I was too protective. I needed to let her fly a little bit. I was just so afraid that, if she did try to fly, she'd fall instead and get hurt."

"Getting hurt is part of life, you know?" he pointed out.

"Yeah, I know," she declared, with a wry look in his direction. "You see? You're also very much in tune with humanity. I'm only a late bloomer to the cause, but I've seen a lot of what humanity can do to each other, and it's not nice."

"No, often it's not very nice at all," he confirmed, with half a smile, "but there's still hope for the species as a whole."

She grinned at that. "I sure hope so because I've got a whole lot of doughnuts I want to make for the world."

"Oh my, doughnuts," he said, with a groan. "That would be hard to pass up."

"It would be. I've been working on my own recipes. I've even got a couple cookbooks ready to launch." He stared at her in shock. She laughed. "Yeah, I know, and you thought I would sit around and mope because you were gone." He flushed and she nodded. "And you're right. I did, but then I got angry. I just made a decision that wasn't necessarily to my benefit."

"You mean, joining up?"

"Yep, joining up." She smiled. "But that's okay. I still think it was the best thing I could have done."

"I'm glad you aren't angry about that decision," he replied, "because, really, an awful lot can be said for enlisting."

"There is," she agreed, "and I really hadn't expected to enjoy it as much as I have. I also hadn't expected that, when the time came, I would understand it was time for me to leave." She nodded to stress her point. "But knowing that it's the right time just makes a huge difference."

As they went to exit the generator room, the door was jerked wide open right in front of them. Someone wearing a full-on parka with balaclava stood before them, and it was hard in that light to even see their eyes.

She looked at him and said, "Hey, we just checked the generator. So, if that's what you came here for, it's all good."

He nodded and looked over at Whalen, who walked toward her, and the stranger added, "It's mostly good." And without warning, he hit her hard on the side of the head.

As she fell, she saw the gun flash and heard a shot fired. When she collapsed onto the floor, her last thought was that they'd been ambushed.

WHALEN LAY IN the generator room, slowly shifting, the pain rippling through his body like nothing before, and yet he had been shot before. Whoever the stranger was had long since departed, yet, at the same time, Whalen had a distinct impression that their attacker would come back as soon as he could. Either he was putting plans in place or something else was going on, but they didn't dare still be here. And, if their attacker lit this place on fire, everybody would suffer, first and foremost, him and Chrissy.

He fished his phone from his pocket, as he slowly made his way to his feet, holding his shoulder. The shot had gone high and had also traversed multiple layers of padding. With his phone in his hand, he dialed. When Magnus answered, he whispered, "Generator room, shot. Shooter at large."

And, with that, the response was crisp. "On the way."

Whalen sank down slowly to the ground beside Chrissy. He reached out a hand, knowing that he was dripping blood all over her, but he needed to see if she was alive. Sometimes head blows could cause the most incredible damage and all without anybody suspecting anything. She didn't appear to have any other injuries, but her breathing was labored.

The door burst open behind him, and he wasn't surprised when he heard Magnus calling out, "Whalen?"

He shifted so he was sitting up, then looked over at his buddy, grim-faced and nodded. And saw Sydney barreling in right behind him. "Check her, please."

She looked at him with a sharp eye, saw where the bleeding was coming from, and shook her head, her gaze moving to Chrissy. Immediately she dropped to her side.

"Head injury," Whalen began. "He hit her hard on the side of the temple, and she went down hard. Then shot me in what seemed to be the same movement. I didn't even see the gun, didn't see it coming," he whispered.

Magnus helped Whalen to his feet. "Don't stress over it. Let's get you back inside."

"No, she has to come too."

Egan and Barret were both right here. They each gave Whalen an arm and helped him back to the main building. Whalen looked back at Magnus, who had picked up Chrissy and was carrying her, Sydney hovering at her side. Once they were all inside the medical clinic, thankfully not having encountered anybody on the way, Whalen sank down on one of the two hospital beds and groaned.

Magnus laid Chrissy on the other bed, with Sydney going to work on her. Then Magnus came to Whalen's bed. "Let's get a look at this." They quickly and carefully peeled away the layers and undressed Whalen so that the wound was exposed. The bullet had gone through the top of his shoulder. However, a second shot had also been fired and had burned along his ribs.

Whalen shook his head. "This isn't how I thought the day would end. Although, if I had listened to Chrissy, maybe I would have been more prepared."

At that, the men looked at him sharply, and he explained what she had heard about people in the dining area not being happy and thinking that maybe Whalen would fabricate evidence against Jaden.

"Jesus Christ," Egan muttered in a harsh whisper. "First, they say we killed Ralph, and now this. Is that what people really think of us?"

"That's what she overheard anyway." Whalen looked over at Sydney. "How is she?"

"She'll be fine," the doc replied, as she walked over and took another look at his injury. "She's better off than you are."

He shook his head at that. "That doesn't sound very good."

"No, and you'll notice more pain as I check you out. Sorry." She shook her head, as she poked and prodded. "The good news is the one in your shoulder's gone through and through. You'll have to go back into the generator room and find it." She turned, looking at Magnus.

He nodded and faced Whalen.

At that, Whalen added, "I was standing near the generator. We were headed to the door, when the shooter ripped open the door, slugged Chrissy. Then I took the bullet, well, the first bullet," he corrected, not quite as coherent as he should be at this point. "When I came to, I made my way to where she was, where you found me," he said, "so that's not where I was shot."

With that, Egan and Magnus disappeared from the room, but Barret stayed at Whalen's side. "Did you get a description?"

"No, he was bundled up head to toe, as we all are," he replied. "Full balaclava, so I couldn't see his face. I couldn't see anything. … It felt very much like an ambush."

"And yet you were inside?"

"We were inside. Chrissy wanted to tell me what she had overheard in the dining area and didn't want anybody listening in, so she suggested we go for a walk. We decided to go check on the generator. Maybe he was messing around with it."

Barret winced at that. "And that would be fatal for all of us."

"I don't know about fatal, but it sure as hell would be uncomfortable for a while, and none of us need that right now. It seems as if we've been to hell and back already," he whispered.

"Isn't that the truth?"

"Go see if you can track this asshole."

"I was told to stay with you."

Whalen gave him a lopsided grin. "Get my handgun from my room. I'll keep it here as protection for the two of us."

Barret hesitated, then nodded and quickly disappeared. When he returned a few minutes later, he had the holster. He put it under the pillow on Whalen's bed and said, "And don't you move." He looked at Sydney and asked, "You're under full watch, right?"

"Already on it," she stated with a rush. "Send Simon the guard over."

"Oh, I can do that," Barret replied, relieved to have an answer.

And with that order being sent out, Simon showed up a few minutes later, and Barret took off. Sydney looked over at Whalen. "They really should put the whole base on lockdown."

Mountain spoke from the doorway. "In progress," he declared, his gaze going from one patient to the other. "How bad is it?"

"They'll both live," Sydney replied, "but honest to God only because of Whalen's coats. It probably made for a bigger target so the shooter's aim was shit. Shot him twice and didn't manage to kill him."

"So, somebody without wilderness experience," Mountain noted.

At that, Sydney slowly nodded. "Yeah, you and I would have shot him dead center in the chest."

He laughed and nodded. "Exactly, though I would have gone for a headshot to ensure that sucker didn't get back up again."

"I'm grateful," Whalen noted in exasperation, "that he didn't think that far ahead. I think we surprised him by being so close to the generator door. He was in a rush too. Either he didn't take time to line up, wasn't a good shot, or isn't as well trained as the rest of us." Whalen gave a headshake.

Mountain looked over at Chrissy, who was still unconscious. "Another head wound?"

"Yeah, he hit her but didn't shoot her," Whalen stated.

"Why is that, do you think?" Mountain asked, his gaze zinging right in Whalen's direction.

"Honestly, I'm not sure why, but, when I woke up, my first thought was that he would come back and light the place on fire."

Mountain's eyebrows rose. "Which would effectively put all of us in grave danger."

"Once that generator goes out, you and I both know how much trouble it is to stay warm."

"Obviously we would have more experience in that element of survival, but most of us would live through it."

"Maybe he didn't think he would," Sydney suggested quietly from the other bedside. "Maybe he's here for training but doesn't have the history and the experience that you guys do. Maybe he thought that would take him out. And he's not quite desperate enough yet."

"It's possible, and yet he still tried to take out Whalen," Mountain stated, as his gaze went from one to the other. "So, was he after you or her? Or was it the fact that you were in the generator room? Who was there last?" he muttered out loud.

"I don't know. I generally check it a couple times a day," Whalen shared.

Mountain frowned at him. "Why?"

"Because I don't like the shit going on here." Whalen snorted. "That generator's a lifeline for all of us and way too easy for anybody to take out."

"Agreed. I just hadn't realized that you felt that strongly

about it.”

“I do, and obviously for good reason.”

“I don’t know. At the moment it feels as if somebody’s got a plan, and they sure as hell aren’t sharing anything with us.”

Whalen shook his head. “Magnus and Egan went to the generator shed to look for the bullet and anything else they can find, and Barret has gone out hunting, looking for tracks,” Whalen shared. “I’m pretty sure the guy came from the scientists’ camp though.”

“Yeah, but did he go back to their camp?”

Whalen nodded. “That would be my take on it, and he just seemed way too comfortable.” He hesitated, then looked at Sydney and added, “Another point …”

“What’s that?” Mountain asked, a bit too harshly.

“I’m not sure our shooter was a man.”

DAY 5 LATE AFTERNOON

CHRISSY WOKE SLOWLY, hearing voices around her. She moaned as the pain in her head kicked in with her first movement.

"Take it easy." Sydney's gentle voice came from her side. "You got your head clunked. It'll take you a little bit before you want to move very much."

Chrissy opened her eyes and stared at the doc in confusion.

Sydney's gaze was ever sharp, as she studied Chrissy and asked, "How are you feeling?"

"Like I got my head clunked," she murmured. "I just don't remember it happening."

At that, Sydney asked, "What do you remember?"

That question almost seemed to be a test. Chrissy closed her eyelids and sank back into the bed. "I was in the generator room with Whalen," she murmured. "The door suddenly burst open, and somebody else came in, and I spoke to him, but I don't remember more than that."

"Even remembering that is pretty good at this point," Sydney noted, "because that guy came in and clunked you one."

"Why?" Chrissy asked, her eyelids flying open to stare at the doc in confusion.

"I don't know that I have an answer to that," Sydney

replied, "but everybody is on the lookout, hoping that somebody will have an answer, and that's why we're very grateful to see you awake and back to the land of the living."

"Right." Then her eyes widened. "What about Whalen? Where is he? How is he?" And she shifted in bed, trying to get up. "He was with me."

"Hey, hey, hey," Whalen said from the corner beside her. "I'm right here. It's okay."

She looked at him, blinked several times, and then collapsed back down. "God, what a nightmare. Why did he hurt us? What did he want?" she muttered.

Whalen explained, "Either they were not expecting us to go into the generator room, or they were hoping we would, but, either way, somebody took advantage of the fact that we were there and pretty-well isolated. You got smacked in the head and knocked unconscious, and I got shot twice."

"Oh my God." She struggled to get upright again. "Jesus, are you okay?"

He gave her a rueful smile. "Let's just say I've felt better, but both bullets technically didn't do his firing record any good, and I presume whoever it was failed that part of the mission."

She frowned. "What do you mean?"

"Meaning that he didn't do a good-enough job, and I'm still here to talk about it."

"We don't want him doing a better job," she snapped, as she looked at the bandages on his shoulder and his chest. "Looks as if he got you well enough."

"Not really," Whalen noted. "Both bullets missed anything essential. All the major organs are still good. Up here in these conditions, you know that a serious wound would be the end of me."

She stared at him, and her heart sank, as she realized that he was right. In these conditions Sydney would do the best she could, but it would be pretty-damn hard to survive if advanced care or tricky surgery was required. "It's a damn good thing it isn't that bad," she murmured.

"Absolutely, but it's bad enough," he admitted. "I won't go anywhere quickly. The burn on the chest here is just a burn, and the shoulder? Well, it's a through and through. So, yeah, the shoulder feels like shit, but I think it'll probably all be just fine."

She let out a breath that she didn't realize she was holding. "So did you see what he did after he hit me?"

"No, because he hit you and shot me at nearly the same time," Whalen noted. "I just barely registered that you were going down when I already felt the pain."

She winced. "So, in other words, he took out two of us, and we didn't even expect it, didn't even defend ourselves."

"Thanks for the reminder," he said cheerfully. "Believe me. It was great trying to explain to everybody else what happened."

She looked at him. "I can imagine." She let her head fall to the side. "As much as I can see the humor in that, at the same time, I'm also in the service now and should have done something to protect myself." She started to shake her head then stopped gasping from the pain.

"You both were ambushed," Sydney stated in a serene voice. "You can't take on more than you can take on."

"Meaning, we aren't allowed to feel guilty, is that it?" Chrissy shook her head. "It sure seems as if we should feel guilty, since we're both trained for this." At his surprised look, she shrugged. "And I know that you don't really see me as a fighter, but I am, and I've had plenty of defense and military training in terms of warfare," she murmured. "So, it's not a case of you looking after me. It should have been a case of both of us having each other's backs. Apparently we suck at that."

He shook his head. "I'm not so sure about that either," he disagreed. "It's easy to say something like that, but the truth of the matter is, these things are always much more complex. For all we know, this guy or gal, whoever was there, was lying in wait."

"I suppose that's possible too," she agreed. "Hadn't really considered that."

"You should because we can't take on all the blame of the world, and, right now, somebody is getting very desperate to stay hidden."

She stretched out on the bed, looked over at Sydney, and asked, "Do you mind if I just crash here a little bit?"

Sydney nodded. "Go for it."

Chrissy closed her eyelids and drifted in and out. In the distance, she heard whispered voices behind her and realized that the two of them were talking. "If you want to get him coffee or something, feel free. I'm just relaxing my eyes."

"Sure you are," Sydney said. "If I give you enough time, you'll crash, and that's a good thing. Your body needs to heal right now."

"Yet I'm too wired, too hyped, and too wide awake," she muttered.

"Fine." She looked over at Whalen. "Do you want a coffee?"

"I'd love a coffee," he said, "and maybe get her something too."

"Yeah, except I want her to sleep and to not get revved up on caffeine," the doc said, with a half laugh.

Sydney left soon afterward, and, when there was just nothing but a warm, gentle silence around her, Chrissy closed her eyelids and drifted off to sleep.

WHALEN CHECKED ON her breathing a couple times, but it seemed as if Chrissy was doing just fine. He was amazed at how fine she was, and she was calm, relaxed almost, as if getting hurt was an everyday occurrence. For him, in a way it was, but that wasn't what he thought of her life. He was really proud of how she'd handled herself here, proud of everything he'd heard about her service as well.

She'd proven herself to be somebody he hadn't expected. He hadn't given her much chance, he knew that, but, at the same time, seeing her shine, almost blossom in a way, had been really good to witness. He'd always cared about her. Hell, he still did care about her. To be honest, he probably cared far too much, considering that she was trying to shake loose of him. That would mean heartbreak for him, something that he wasn't really good at handling.

Then she rolled over, opened her eyelids, and looked at him.

"Hey, how're you doing?" he asked.

"I guess I drifted off, didn't I?" She yawned gently.

"You did, but just for a few minutes."

"Sydney still not back yet?"

"Nope, so that goes to show you how long you didn't sleep. Why don't you try to roll over and sleep again?"

"Nope, I'm fine," she said, with an exasperated tone. She shifted upright onto the bed.

"Whoa, whoa, don't try to get up."

She looked at him funny and said, "It'll be a little hard to get to the bathroom, if I don't."

He smiled and then frowned. "I don't think you should be walking yet."

"That's nice," she quipped, as she used the bed to hold herself up, while she tested a few steps. "I still have to go to the washroom," she repeated tiredly, "so it doesn't really matter if you agree or not. I'll make my way down there and back again without you." She looked over at him and that longing in her tone he understood all too well. "So, take that."

But a smile was on her face and a spirit in her tone that once again reminded him just how much she'd changed. "I think these last five years have been good for you," he noted.

"They have been good. I just didn't realize how much I needed them."

"You've had them now," he said cheerfully, "so you can go home after all this, with a smile on your face and your back straight, knowing that you've done a wonderful job."

She frowned at him, while slowly walking toward the door. "That's a hell of a conversation to have at this point. I really do need to go to the bathroom though, so hold that thought." And, with that, she walked down the hall.

He hated to see her walk away. She was using the wall, but he wasn't sure if it was more for guidance or stability. But he got up too and took a few tentative steps himself over to the doorway, where he could keep an eye on her, as she headed into the bathroom.

Even with Simon still on guard, as soon as Chrissy turned into the bathroom, Whalen relaxed. However, when it seemed she was taking too long, he slowly made his way down the hall too, but she came out just before he reached the door.

She looked at him in surprise and shrugged. "That was a little longer than I planned. I was checking out my head, but it's not bad at all. I will survive."

He nodded. "I don't know that it even broke the skin, did it?"

"Just a little bit, but not enough to worry about," she said, with a smile. "Now come on. Let's get you back to the clinic."

She put an arm around his waist, and he chuckled. "I came down here to confirm you were okay, remember?"

"Yeah, but you forgot to check that you were okay yourself," she said, with a headshake. "Always have to be the tough guy."

"No, I can't say I *always* have to be," he clarified. "It's just the role I'm used to being in."

"Sure, but everybody needs a break sometimes. And, right now, you need looking after, not the other way around."

"I just wish we'd gotten him. Or her or whomever."

"Yeah, you and me both. I didn't see anything, did you?"

"Not enough to identify him," Whalen stated. "I'm not even terribly sure that we can count on the fact that it was a man."

Chrissy thought about it and added, "I'm not sure either, and, with all the clothing and the bulked-up layers, it's really hard to identify anybody here."

"Which is what he, she, they, were counting on," he noted.

Back at the clinic, he sat down again and motioned at her bed. "You lie down too."

She rolled her eyes at him. "Sydney's probably not bringing me coffee."

"I did suggest it, but she didn't want you to get hyped up on caffeine."

"I think *hyped up on caffeine* sounds pretty-damn good right about now."

"What will you do when you head back?" he asked, a smirk on his face. "Will you miss this?"

"You know what I'll do. I already told you. And will I miss the service?" She pondered that. "I'll miss some things about it. It took a while to adjust. It took a while to really sort myself out." She wore an expression like she was thinking too hard, her eyes squinted and her brows drawn together. "But the fact that I did have the time to sort myself out will be part of what I do miss, but not enough to stay," she said, with a smile.

"What about a family?" he asked, blurting out the question without thinking first.

She stared at him for a long moment. "Not sure where that question's coming from," she noted, "but I've always wanted kids, so hopefully, at some point in time, I'll get there."

He nodded and stared off in the distance.

"What about you?" she asked curiously. "It'd be pretty hard for you to have a family and to leave the wife and kids, while you're off on missions all the time."

"I would set out to do other things at that point in time," he replied, "because I want to very much be a hands-on dad, if and when I get to that point."

"You'll get there," she confirmed, with a smile. "I'm sure of it."

"I'm not," he admitted. "I feel as if I walked away from that option a few years ago. A part of me says I don't deserve more than that. And I know everybody would say that, sure I deserve it, everybody deserves it. But," he took a deep breath to add, "when you've made a choice like I did, it kind of … it almost seems to be a fatalistic choice where there's no going back."

"You don't have to go back," she pointed out. "You just have to go forward and change it."

He nodded, considered her for a long moment, and then asked, "I was wondering if you were interested in maybe picking up the reins of our relationship."

DAY 5 EARLY EVENING

CHRISSY STARED AT him for a moment, mute. "I didn't expect to hear that from you," she replied.

"I didn't really expect to say it either, to tell you the truth," he admitted. "But maybe the fact that we just saw our lives pass before our eyes might have had something to do with it."

Her eyes widened at that. She nodded slowly. "It does make you reassess your future, doesn't it?"

"In your case you've already done lots of reassessing," he noted, with a smile. "I don't know if I've told you, but I'm really happy for you."

"So I've been told time and time again," she replied. "You're surprising me a lot these days."

"That's okay. You're surprising me too," he added, with a smile.

"I don't know what I could possibly do that would surprise you," she replied, staring at him.

"I think I'm really proud of who you've become, for one," he stated, "and proud of what you've accomplished. Following your heart is huge, even if you got here by following me into this madness."

"I didn't follow you into this. I followed the path that you forged," she pointed out.

He tilted his head to the side and nodded. "I really like

that," he said. "I can't say that I was ever planning on being a person who forged pathways, but I do like the implication that I was leading in some way that other people found valuable." He took a moment to collect his rampant thoughts. "Of course I'm certainly not leading anything here. The leading is all happening individually, as people find their own way through this, through their lives, and what it is they need to do for themselves."

"And are you still gung-ho on doing what you're doing?"

"I am, but I can say at some point in time I'll shift directions," he shared. "I don't … When I have a family or get ready to settle down and have that family, I want to be home more."

She stared at him intently. He really was surprising her.

Whaled noted, "You're being quiet when it comes to my question."

"It's not that I'm being quiet," she said carefully. "It's more a case of trying to understand just where that's coming from."

He looked over at her and smiled. "Seeing you again, for one. Realizing that I never really got over you, for another. And admitting I still have feelings for you. That's three," he declared, with a half smile. "How many more do you need?"

"All of them," she said. "I need all of them."

He looked at her and slowly nodded. "Let's see. I'm sorry for what happened and for the way it happened. I'm sorry that I wasn't grown-up enough to handle the conversation that needed to occur, but, when I walked, it wasn't because I didn't care. It was quite the opposite." He dropped his head further. "I'm finding out that I never got over you, and I'm here staring at you and wondering whether our past has got any place in the future or we're *done*-done. I feel as if I have to leave that decision up to you because of the way I walked out." He paused for a moment. "It would have to be your choice to open up a door that you probably slammed shut many, many times over."

She winced and admitted, "I did, at least a time or two."

"Right," he said, "and that's why I would leave it up to you to decide."

She stared at him, mute for a long moment, then said, "I didn't really expect this."

"I know," he acknowledged, "but I'm not sure that you didn't intuitively know it was there somehow. I feel as if we had an instant connection from the time you got here, whether it's one you want to acknowledge or not."

"In that you are probably correct," she stated, "but it's not necessarily something I want to admit."

He smiled. "Sometimes life throws us a curveball, and, right about now, that's what this feels like. I didn't expect to see you, but now that I have, it's as if I've been waiting for this moment for years." Looking at her sideways, he continued. "I didn't know you were in the military, had no idea that you were here, and yet I couldn't be happier for this opportunity to talk to you, to reconnect, and to sort it out."

She smiled. "And yet now you're talking about opening up a pathway we both closed."

"Only if you want to," he said. When she hesitated, he added, "And, for the record, yes, absolutely I want to."

She blinked. "I'm really not used to you talking about all this."

"No, but somewhere along the way over the last five years, I also learned to communicate better," he said, with a chuckle. "It was something that I struggled with back then because I didn't want to hurt you. But I ended up hurting you anyway, probably even worse. Yet, at this point in time, it's not you who'll get hurt. It's me, and, if that's what you choose, then that's your decision, and I'll accept it." He stared at her, as if she were something ethereal. "But I didn't want both of us to walk out that door without saying anything, just in case it is a door we need to reevaluate together, so we both want to walk through it again."

Just then Sydney returned to the medical clinic. She stopped when she saw the serious expressions on their faces. "Am I interrupting?"

At that, Chrissy snorted. "No, and, well, … yes."

Sydney burst out laughing. "Here are two coffees. Enjoy, and I will disappear and go get myself another one, I guess. You guys can continue talking, since clearly you have a lot to talk about."

"Is it that obvious?" Chrissy asked.

"Absolutely," Sydney declared, "and you know it. Whether you're willing to look at it or not, it's crystal-clear to the rest of us, and has been this whole time." And, with that, she was gone again.

Chrissy stared at the door and nodded. "Everybody kept saying things to me about it, about seeing you again, about being with you, as if we were together," she explained, "and I kept shaking my head, going, *Nope, no way, we're not going there*." She laughed. "Apparently nothing deceives us quite like ourselves." She smiled, then hopped up a little bit more exuberantly than she realized and grimaced.

He immediately reached out a hand, then winced at the pain in his side. "Hey, take it easy."

She reached back, and their hands linked. She stared down at their fingers and said, "I didn't enlist in the military for this. You know that, right?"

"I expect that you probably came in vowing that, if you had the opportunity, you would kick my ass into next week," he said, with a big grin.

"Yeah, that's not far from the truth," she muttered. "However, at the same time, I didn't really expect to ever see you. The military is a massive machine, and I was pretty far away from you for a long time."

"I know, but, if you still want to kick my butt for all that I put you through, I would certainly understand."

She gave him a lopsided grin. "Yeah, you might understand, but that doesn't mean I could allow myself to do it. But I can't promise there won't be times when I throw it in your face."

"And that would probably be normal too," he noted, with a growing smile, as he tugged her slowly and inexorably closer toward him. "Does that mean it's a yes?" He pulled her into his arms, so she was half sitting on the bed and half leaning against his chest.

"Are we sure we're ready to do this?" she murmured, as she looked up at him.

"I am, but I would certainly accept and understand that you might need some time."

"I don't need time," she replied. "I just need to know that you won't do that to me again."

"That I can promise," he stated, as he leaned down and kissed her on the cheek.

She popped back ever-so-slightly, as sparks literally flashed between them.

"There's not even any carpet here for static to have built up on," he noted, with a chuckle.

"But then it was always like that with us."

"It was," he murmured, as he tugged her back into his

arms, pulling her up so that she was sitting in his lap.

She looked at him and said, "You're injured, remember?"

"I am healing quickly. Something about this beautiful woman in my arms is good for what ails me."

She snorted at that. "I don't think Sydney would consider it *healing*—like maybe antibiotics, pain meds, and some rest."

"No, but you might be surprised. I think she'll be right behind us on this one."

"Maybe so," Chrissy muttered, "but I'm still not quite sure how this will work."

"I suggest we spend the next couple weeks healing, sorting ourselves out, figuring out how to make it work, and deciding what we want to do," he suggested, with a smirk. "I do have a house in California."

She frowned at him and asked, "Seriously?"

He nodded. "Yeah, I bought it a few years back. So, that gives us a start, a roof over our heads."

"I won't have much money for a while," she shared, "since everything will go into the business."

"Of course," he agreed, "and, since it's the dream business you've spent a lifetime working toward, you need to keep doing exactly that."

"Meaning, if I get to do my dream, you get to do yours?"

"Will you be okay with that?"

She nodded. "I am now, because I've seen what it is. I've seen how it is, and I understand it a whole lot more than I ever used to know about. It makes me feel very small to think I was jealous of something so important to those you are helping."

"I don't think it's a case of being jealous, but I would

need to know that you would be okay and confident in the knowledge that it will always be you I'm working to come home to."

She smiled at that. "That sounds perfect." He leaned over and gave her a very soft kiss. She gently looped her arms around his neck and kissed him back. She whispered, "You know that we won't do anything too exciting until you're feeling better."

He chuckled. "That'll just make me heal all that much faster."

JUST WHEN THEY were too engrossed, too occupied to notice, a woman from the doorway spoke. "Even still, you won't be cleared for any shenanigans for at least a couple days," Sydney pointed out.

Whalen looked over at her and smiled. "You are a spoilsport, aren't you?"

"And you are injured."

"Not that bad," he added.

"You let your coffee go cold," Sydney noted.

"We had a few things to discuss," he stated.

"And I'm glad you seem to have sorted it out. I'm not sure that you need to stay here overnight, either of you," she added, looking at both of them. "So maybe the two of you should head off to wherever it is you'll head off to."

They looked at her in surprise. "Are we really cleared?"

Sydney shrugged. "Conditionally, as long as ..." She hesitated for a moment, then added, "It would mean, ... I don't want either of you alone."

"No, no, we won't be alone," Whalen stated, with an eye

roll. He looked over at Chrissy, then grinned and whispered, "I think she means we need to spend the night together."

Chrissy rolled her eyes at him. "Yeah, well, if Sydney means that, she would have said that."

"Actually I do mean that," Sydney confirmed. "You're either staying here in the medical bay with a guard, or you're heading back to your quarters and spending the night together with a guard. Neither one of you is to be alone, so you can monitor each other, and you both need a guard."

"That makes total sense, except the guard," Whalen noted, all the joking gone. "I'll look after her."

And Sydney smiled and asked, "Who'll look after you?"

"I will," Chrissy replied immediately. "Hell, it seems as if we've always been heading for this anyway."

"You have," Sydney agreed. "You just needed to both finally get your shit together." Rolling her eyes, she ordered, "Now scat. However, the guard remains on duty with you two." She shooed both of them to get up. "I'm hoping to grab some sleep tonight myself."

"How late is it?"

"It's well past eleven," She yawned.

"Right," Whalen murmured, as he slowly got off the bed and said, "Come on, Chrissy. Let's go."

"Yeah, and where are we going?" she asked, looking at him. "Your place or mine?" Then she chuckled. "That's not a question I'd ever thought to ask you again."

He smiled as he removed his gun from under the pillow, tucking it into his pocket. "Just goes to show you that sometimes life happens while you're busy making other plans."

"Yeah, I would say so."

Slowly they moved toward his room, trying not to pay

attention to the guard in their wake. "You okay at my place, or do you want to go to yours?"

"Yours is fine," she said, yawning. "On the other hand, I do need to hit my room and get some clothes and maybe some of my stuff."

"Okay, so we'll go there first and then back to mine."

"And you mean it because you won't leave me alone, will you?"

"Absolutely not," he declared. "Sydney wasn't kidding."

Chrissy nodded. "I guess we don't want to face her in the morning to tell her that we didn't follow through, *huh*?"

"Not with a guard as a witness, no. I'm afraid we'd see the very serious Dr. Sydney come out, and she wouldn't take our failure to comply very kindly," he noted, with a grimace. "I also wouldn't be at all surprised if she didn't come and check on us in the middle of the night, just to be sure."

"Hell, she might do that anyway," Chrissy muttered. "Honestly, I might too, if I were a doctor and if I had patients with these injuries and all this other shit going on."

He nodded. "Let's go."

By the time they had collected her stuff, made it back to his room, and everybody had their teeth brushed and ready for bed, he sat down on the bed, exhausted, which worried her. "Look. Maybe I should go back to my room, you know, so you'll sleep better."

He stared at her. "Remember Sydney?"

Chrissy flushed. "Maybe I'll go back to the medical clinic."

"Then she has to stay in there with you," he replied, "or at least she would."

"So, what's the option then?"

"The best option is for both of us to get a good night's

sleep, right here, and check on each other periodically."

"And yet I don't think you'll get any sleep with me here beside you."

"I don't know," he argued. "I'm about to take some painkillers and knock off for the night. I sure won't move a whole lot, since these things knock me out."

She got into bed and propped herself against the wall. "Am I supposed to make it to my shift in the morning?"

"Not now you aren't," he said. "That's somebody else's job. Pretty sure that's already been handled, given the state you're in."

"Yeah, but I don't know that it has been, and I would hate to leave Chef in the lurch, what with Avalon sick and me down too."

"Elijah will have heard by now, and hopefully Avalon is on her feet, so she can relieve you and get her shifts back."

"We'll see," Chrissy muttered, as she yawned. "God, I'm tired, and, as much as I hate to admit it, my head is pounding."

"Yeah, and that's what injuries do to us. Take your painkiller and get to sleep. That's the best thing for both of us."

And, indeed, as soon as she closed her eyes, she was out cold, and he was right behind her.

DAY 6 MORNING

CHRISSY WOKE BRIGHT and early to a dead weight around her. She rolled over, shifting gently to find Whalen looking at her, his blue eyes twinkling.

"Look at that," he teased, as he awkwardly tucked her up close with his good arm. "We spent the night together … again."

She smiled. "Not exactly what I thought would be happening … ever."

"Nope, but I'm feeling really good about it."

She leaned up and kissed him on the cheek. "Guess I missed my shift, *huh*?"

"Looks like it, and that's all right too."

When a knock came at the door, he groaned and asked, "Who is it?"

"It's Sydney," she replied, popping open the door ever-so-slightly. "How are you guys doing?"

They both shifted in bed, so that Sydney could come in and check them out.

"You both look pretty decent, considering," she stated, with a smile. "Nothing like a little bit of love and healing of the heart to do the job on the other layers."

"Hey, if I'd realized that's all it would take, I would have given it a shot earlier," Whalen replied.

At that, Chrissy snorted. "Like hell," she muttered. "Am

I good to go back to work?"

"I would like to see you take the day off today," Sydney replied, "and Avalon is back in the kitchen, if that makes you feel any better about it. Elijah was asking about you. I told him that I hadn't checked on you yet this morning, but that I would report back."

Chrissy chuckled. "Everybody reports back to Elijah, and that in itself is mind-boggling," she noted, with a smile. "I guess a good chef is worth his weight in gold."

"I also heard that a good baker might be too." Whalen laughed, as he chipped in with his two cents.

"But not today," Sydney stated firmly. As they relaxed, she added, "One of you can get coffee, but you're both on bed rest for the remainder of the day."

Whalen turned to Chrissy and winked.

She rolled her eyes. "You're still hurt."

"Not that hurt," he muttered. "I'll go get coffee to prove it." Then he got up and got dressed awkwardly, but he still managed to do it.

Sydney frowned, as she watched him. "Your shoulder really isn't bothering you that much, is it?"

"Oh, I've got good painkillers for one thing," he explained, "and I did take one already this morning, but I'm in much better shape than I thought I would be. I'm sure it'll be a slow recovery because these things always are."

With a nod, Sydney left them alone.

Frowning, he added, "I guess it's possible that they'll ship me out," he told Chrissy. "I hadn't really thought about that."

"So don't think about it now either," she said, with a chuckle. "And maybe we'll both get to stay."

"You want to stay?" he asked, looking at her closely.

"I do, especially if you're here."

"That's why Sydney is here too, I'll bet."

"I don't know if that's why Sydney is here or not, though maybe that's why all of them are here. It's easy to keep an eye out if you're on the spot."

He nodded. "Absolutely, and I, for one, want to make sure that you don't get hurt anymore."

"Yeah, I don't want to get hurt again myself," she agreed, with a gentle smile. "Now, you go get the coffee, and I'll get up and make my way to the bathroom, so I'll be ready when you get back."

"Ready for what?" he asked.

She opened her eyes wide and said, "You heard the doc. We're both officially on bed rest for the day, together. Surely we can find something interesting to do," she teased, raising an eyebrow as she looked at him.

He blinked and said, "I'll be right back with the coffee."

She laughed, got up, and went to the bathroom down the hall, the guard eyeing her the whole way there and back. By the time Whalen returned, she was curled up in the bed again.

"How're you feeling?" he asked.

"I'm feeling decent," she murmured. "And that coffee will help a lot."

"I told Chef that you were doing okay, but Sydney had put us on bed rest for the day. He gave me a wink and a nudge and told me to enjoy myself."

She burst out laughing. "So, I guess that's what everybody thinks we're doing today, *huh*?"

"Works for me," Whalen declared, "and I really don't give a shit if they talk about us or not. We have some healing to do on a lot of different levels."

She smiled and pulled back the covers for him to join her. "Yes, but you're wearing way-too-many clothes for what I've got in mind."

He looked at her hopefully. "And it won't hurt either one of us? You can just imagine what Sydney will say."

Chrissy chuckled. "And here I thought you were the kind of guy who could improvise."

"I can absolutely improvise," he said, "but I just want to confirm we're on the same wavelength."

"Not sure about the same wavelength," she quipped, "but we're definitely in the same ballpark."

And, with that, and a little help from her, he quickly undressed and curled up in the bed, shuddering at the cold. "I think an injury makes the cold so much worse."

"It definitely does," she agreed, "and doctor's orders are to stay in bed and to rest all day." She wiggled up against him and whispered, "Who would have thought that we'd get a day like this together?"

"Yeah, and I had to go and get shot," he pointed out, with a groan.

She thought about that for a moment. "It's really silly, isn't it, that it took us this long."

"Maybe, but we're here now." He wrapped his arm around her and shuffled her up a little closer to him. Suddenly he stopped. "Did you take off your clothes?"

"I took off my pajamas, yes, and you didn't even notice."

"God, what's wrong with me?"

"You're injured, and maybe that was a test to see how injured." She chuckled.

"Not that injured," he argued. "However, last night I was trying to avoid thinking about such things, but, dammit, now that I know …" She burst into joyous laughter. "I'm glad you're having fun," he muttered.

She smirked as she realized his body was already reacting. When she wrapped her hand around him gently, he sucked in his breath and groaned, as he closed his eyes.

WHALEN TOOK OVER almost immediately, knowing that his shoulder and his ribs would determine how this would work out. But he wanted to make it work, and he wanted to make it last, and he wanted this moment to never end. Yet he also knew that it would pass very, very quickly. He nestled up against her neck.

As soon as he tried to control the action, she gently shifted him and warned him off. "Lie down."

He hesitated, but then relaxed back as she stretched out on top of him. She murmured, "I think it might be better if you just laid there and didn't do much."

He chuckled. "That sounds like torture."

"I don't want you hurt," she explained, with a flushed face.

"And I don't want you hurt either. Remember your head."

"My head is … just … fine."

He chuckled, and then groaned as her hand found him again and gently stroked him up and down. "You know what will happen if you keep doing that, right?"

She nodded. "I absolutely know what will happen," she murmured, a smile in her voice.

"But that's not allowed to happen alone," he muttered in alarm. "That's not how I roll."

"That's fine," she said. "I was planning on going with

you." She wiggled up higher on his body, and his immediate reaction was hard to miss. She chuckled. "I always remember that. You were always ready."

"Hey, it's hard not to be when this beautiful woman is in bed with me," he murmured, gently shifting his hips and changing her position just enough that he could reach up and grasp her with his good arm. He tucked her up higher so that she was closer and kissed her gently.

She murmured against his lips, "I really have missed this."

"I'm sure you've had lots of relationships since."

She paused for a moment, then looked up at him and shook her head. "No, I haven't. I didn't want to go in that direction anymore." He winced, and she shook her head. "I understand and no need to apologize," she said. "I just needed to get my head together for a bit."

"Still, I'm sorry."

"I'm not," she declared cheerfully. "It'll make this all the sweeter." And, with that, she leaned up and kissed him, their tongues gently warring.

Soon it was hard for Whalen to even breathe, as his blood pressure rose in response to her hand motions working him over. Finally he broke free, gasping, tossing and turning his body. "You need to stop that."

"No, not stop, but definitely shift a bit," she noted, as she sat up and, in so doing, placed herself directly above his erection. When she slowly lowered herself on it, his hips surged upward, settling deep inside her. This was where he wanted her, and he groaned as everything inside him shuddered with the need to control it.

"You don't have to control everything, you know?" Chrissy told him.

"If I don't control this, it'll all be over, and you won't get anything out of it."

"If that's the case," she said, "I'm okay with that too. It's not as if we're going anywhere, and we do have all day."

His laugh broke free, and Whalen added, "Still, I'd much rather have the two of us go together."

"Ah, well, I won't argue with that."

She leaned forward, and using her arms to hold her balance and to ease up any pressure on his shoulder and ribs, she started to move, gently at first, as if testing the water, then faster and faster. He held himself back as long as he could, fighting it, his head tossing and turning, the pain inside almost exquisite, until he finally couldn't hold back anymore, and his orgasm ripped through him, forcing him to shudder in place, as she rode him through it.

And, just when he was done, his body awash in sweat and satisfaction, she came apart in his arms and collapsed on top of him, even then gently avoiding his injuries.

Gasping, the two of them curled up together, and she whispered, "You know something? That was worth waiting for."

He would have laughed if he could, but it was past him. He whispered, "That was delicious."

"Good, so we'll do it again in another little bit, *huh*?" She lay beside him, facing him. "Right now, I think I need to sleep." And with their coffees going cold beside them, they both fell into a deeply healing restful sleep.

DAY 7 WEE HOURS OF THE MORNING

CHRISSY WOKE IN the stillness of the night, a disquiet rippling through her. What was it? She lifted her head and looked around. She was in Whalen's room still, the two of them having made love several more times, just curled up in each other's arms and enjoying the day, enjoying having time with each other. But even now as he slept beside her, she sensed something was out there.

She stiffened in his arms, and he tightened his grip, whispering against her ear, "I hear it too."

She relaxed back, as they both waited to see who was seemingly sneaking around outside his room. Whalen pushed himself up with his good arm and tilted his head to the side, listening, and she did the same but from where she was. He looked down at her and frowned. She shook her head. "I don't know what it is," she murmured.

He placed a finger against her lips, and she remembered just how thin the walls were, particularly at nighttime when everything else was silent. As they listened, it seemed somebody was sliding along the wall. Whalen slipped on his boxers and, moving carefully, walked to the door. Meanwhile, Chrissy slipped on Whalen's T-shirt.

As Whalen got closer, somebody picked the lock, grabbed the handle on the other side, and slowly turned it in front of their eyes. Whalen looked over at her, held up his finger, then immediately grabbed the door and pulled it open. The intruder tumbled forward with the momentum, and Whalen immediately kicked him in the back and dropped him to the ground. A hard *oof* came, and somebody came up fighting mad.

Chrissy jumped him from the bed, her arms wrapped around his neck, as she kicked at the back of his legs, forcing his knees to bend, dropping him to the ground.

With a smile on his face, Whalen said, "Now that's a smart move." He grabbed the intruder, snapping his head to the side and pushing him to the floor, where he held him.

She immediately hopped up, turned on the light, and stared down at the figure in front of them. "Dear God, I was so afraid it was Sydney."

"Sydney would have identified herself," Whalen stated, "and this asshole did not."

Chrissy immediately bent and pulled the balaclava off their intruder.

She looked at the stranger, then to Whalen, and back again. "Who the hell is this?" A note of confusion filled her voice.

Whalen tilted the intruder's head, so he could look at the glaring male on the floor in front of them. "I don't know. I don't recognize him." At that, he motioned at her. "Grab the phone."

She picked it up off the nightstand and handed it to him. Just as he went to make a call, the intruder bucked up backward, dumping Whalen off and spinning around. With a weapon that seemed to appear out of nowhere, he shot toward Chrissy, but she was already on the move, having ducked and rolled. Coming up on the side with her own handgun, she immediately shot him. He took one hit to the chest, looked at her, blood bubbling from his mouth.

"Oh my God," she cried out.

Whalen secured the shooter's gun and then grabbed her and held her close. "It's all right. It's all right. Just hold steady."

As they watched, the stranger died in front of them.

BOTH DRESSED QUICKLY, and, by the time they had pulled on their pants, Sydney was already here, with Magnus, while Egan and Barret poured in right behind her. The only one missing from the party seemed to be Mountain. And their guard.

"What happened to our guard?" Whalen asked.

Sydney pointed toward the door. "Knocked out in the hallway. He's breathing, and I saw no blood, so I will check him out further in a bit."

They all looked down at the man in front of them, frustrated that nobody recognized him.

"What the hell?" Magnus asked. "We seriously have somebody who nobody even knows, yet is inside the walls of this base and nobody is aware of it?"

"Or he's been here all along and somebody thought that he'd left," Egan suggested. "I don't recognize him, but that doesn't mean nobody will."

At that, Sydney surveyed the dead body. She looked over at everybody, then dropped to her knees. "Could you guys stop bringing me business?" she muttered. "I really don't need it, not after Lisa, my latest nurse, was shipped out to help another base." She quickly checked him out and shook her head. "One shot to the heart, so whoever did this was definitely paying attention in class." She looked around and asked Whalen, "Who shot him?"

In a wavering voice, Chrissy said, "I did."

Sydney looked at her and nodded. "Good shot. How are you doing? Did you hurt yourself?"

"No, I'm fine," she replied, "although I'm not so sure about Whalen."

Sydney noted Whalen sitting down, pale and obviously in pain, and she nodded. "A little more activity than you expected, *huh*?"

Chrissy flushed at that comment and then nodded. "We were asleep, then suddenly we both woke up after hearing what sounded like someone moving down the hallway against the wall. It just didn't sound right," she explained. "As Whalen went to the door, the shooter had already picked the lock, so Whalen jerked open the door. We were able to subdue him for a minute, but then he got loose and came up shooting."

"Interesting," Sydney murmured. Then she looked down at the dead guy's face and gasped. "Oh God."

"What?" Whalen asked, leaning forward. "We didn't recognize him. Do you?"

"I'm not surprised because you haven't been here that long. Magnus, you better take a closer look," she said, turning the dead guy's head, so they could get a full view.

Frowning, Magnus crowded in and shone a light on the man's face. "What the hell?"

"This is one of the men who disappeared early on, is it not?" Sydney asked, while Magnus flipped through his phone, looking for photos of the missing men.

At the newly arrived and now-scowling Mountain, they all turned and looked up. Mountain had blocked the light with his very presence as he entered the room.

"Mountain, look," Magnus called out. "Look at him. Sydney's right. This is one of the missing guys, ... so what in the hell is he doing shooting people and causing all this ruckus?"

Mountain shook his head. "I can't tell you that, but I'll be on it. Believe me. I'll get to the bottom of this and damn fast." And, with that, he took off.

Sydney looked over at the others and said, "Look. These two need to get some rest. They had a busy day before all of this," she noted in a droll tone.

Everybody else looked over at them, smirking, and Magnus added, "Glad you enjoyed your day off."

"Yeah, a recuperation day," Chrissy whispered. "But now? ... How do you deal with the fact that you, ... that I just killed a man?"

Immediately they all looked at her. "You learn to deal with it because it was necessary," Whalen told her. "Him or us, Chrissy."

"Don't worry," Egan added. "We can talk to you, and, if you need some counseling afterward, you'll get it," Egan nodded. "Your first kill is never easy."

She nodded. "I could have cheerfully gone through my whole life without that experience. You know that, right?"

"I do know that, and most of us would have," Egan explained in a sympathetic tone. "However, a lot of us have been in situations just like this one, where there was simply no choice, and you hold that thought close. There was no choice. It was him or you guys, so you did the only thing you could. You made the right choice," Egan repeated. "And what we need now is to sort out how and where this guy has been and how the hell he's been lying low so close by without anybody knowing all this time? And, if he's been doing that, who else is?" Egan asked, with a hard voice. "We need a full accounting and to backtrack where he's been. This is BS."

"And, on the other hand," Whalen stated in a more cheerful voice, "this is a huge break. Not only do we have a missing person accounted for, but we also now have a very significant avenue to pursue."

"I agree," Magnus replied, all praise.

A bit too hyped for her own good, Chrissy added, "I get that it's not my fault the guy's dead. It's nobody's fault but his own, but surely now we could break this wide open."

"I hope so," Whalen said from the bed, "but let's do it tomorrow. Definitely tomorrow. Well, later after daylight today."

And, with that, the men carted the dead man from the room.

As soon as the door closed, she looked around, shaking her head. "As much as I appreciate the time we spent here, would you have any objection to moving to my room, like right now?"

He smiled. "Considering the circumstances, I think that would be a hell of a good idea." He motioned to where the body had been and the blood that still stained the area.

Holding each other close, they quickly shifted rooms. And, once there, he pulled her closer and whispered, "Thank you for saving my life tonight."

"I think this was more a case of having each other's back," she clarified, shaking her head, then wincing at the reminder of her head injury.

"That's how it's supposed to be, right?" he murmured. "Glad we learned that lesson."

"Yeah." And, with a big sigh, she muttered, "Can we talk later? I'm exhausted."

"As long as you sleep," he noted.

"I think I will," she said in a dreamy voice. "That doesn't mean I won't wake up with nightmares though."

"That's okay," he whispered. "If you do, I'm right here to help you through them." And he held her close, as she fell into a deep and peaceful sleep.

As he looked around the darkened room, he thought about how different his life would be from this moment on. It's not what he'd come for, or what he'd expected, but, damn, he sure was glad Chrissy had shown up here, and now they could look forward to a lifetime together, and his future had never looked brighter.

EPILOGUE

NIKOLAI STARED DOWN at the man he'd called a friend for many a year, a man he had already grieved as lost out in the winter wonderland, but one who he'd hoped against hope had survived somehow. And to see his body now laid out in front of him in this state—having been shot by the woman his friend had attacked in the middle of the night in the very military training center the shooter had forsaken for whatever dumb-ass reason—was completely beyond Nikolai's understanding.

He didn't even know what to say, yet he knew that this dead man was immediately under suspicion by everybody else. But Nikolai didn't know anything and certainly had no explanation for the actions of his friend. He couldn't even begin to believe that his "friend" had done this.

He looked over at the others and declared, "It's him, no doubt about that, but, before you ask me a million questions …" He paused, shaking his head. "I don't know why he's done whatever he's done. I don't know where he's been or how's he's been getting by since he disappeared. I don't even know why he would have left in the first place," he explained. "I don't really know how he could possibly have been fine out there all this time." Then he stopped and added, "Well, that part I probably could answer, at least to some degree. His family, his uncle, was from Siberia. If anybody would have winter survival skills, it would be him."

"So why was he here then?" Magnus asked. "Why come for this training?"

"I think he wanted to see if you all had any other skills he didn't know about. He used to laugh about it," Nikolai shared reluctantly.

"And yet, you are part of the Russian team, so you ought to have the same skill set."

"No, that's incorrect," Nikolai stated flatly. "I'm not part of the Russian team. I'm part of the Swiss team. Just like you have people from other countries here on your US team, I am from the Swiss team," he repeated. "My family moved to Switzerland when I was very young," he shared, as he looked back to the body of his supposed friend. "This guy," he pointed to the cold dead corpse, "wasn't even part of the Russian team. I don't … He came over on a special assignment for Russia, but he was talking about leaving, about finding a way to switch his team somehow. He wanted to be somewhere else, but I don't know that he ever did anything about it. The thing about him was that he was all talk. He had lots of plans, big plans. I, … I've done actual missions with him. I've been on bases worldwide with him too. But never have I seen him do anything even remotely like he's done this time."

"And yet you would have considered him a friend?" Magnus asked.

"Yeah, well, apparently I don't know what that means anymore," Nikolai stated bitterly. He looked over to see Emily, one of the few women in the base, standing and staring at him. He looked at her and frowned. "Honestly, I don't know anything about this," he said to the men, not wanting this discussion to be out in the open.

Yet Emily wasn't moving. He turned to her and asked, "Don't you have someplace to be?"

"No, I don't," she snapped. "I think, at this point in time, anything that is happening in the training base needs to be something the rest of us get to hear about. Instead of us finding out through the grapevine afterward," she said, shooting Magnus a look, which spoke volumes about the confidence she had in all of them telling the truth.

Magnus stared at her for a moment and didn't say anything, then he turned back to Nikolai. "So, Nikolai, what can you tell me about him? Anything more?"

"Not really, outside of the fact that he came over on the Russian team and wanted to shift to another country. And, yeah, I'd thought we were friends, but I obviously can't tell you much more than that."

"Is he married? Does he have family? Would he have been coerced into doing something like this?"

"No, he would have thought it was a lark," Nikolai declared flatly. "He always thought he was better than everybody else around him. He always knew that he was very, very good at winter survival skills, and he knew that he could live out here much more easily than anybody else. Honestly, he spent complete winters outside with his grandfather. This Arctic tundra is not a hardship for him because he knew how to survive out there."

"And you didn't think to tell anybody that?" Magnus asked.

"Tell them what? He disappeared. Besides, all that he could do and all that he was must be was in his file. I didn't know what had happened to him. After being missing all this time, I assumed he probably died out there. We just didn't know how or why," he noted. "And, for that, I'm sorry because, if he needed my help, I presumed he would have asked for it, and, since he didn't, I have to presume he had plans all on his own."

"And yet, if he wanted to move to another country, such as to the US or somewhere else, this is hardly the place to do it."

"I know. I know, and he talked a lot about that, but I don't know if he ever would have gone." He looked over to Emily again, still staring at him, a hard look on her face. He frowned. "You don't need to be here. This is my private business."

"A man is dead," she stated. "It is no longer your private business."

He flushed, realizing that she wouldn't back down and that none of the men here seemed to want to help him in that regard. "I don't have anything else to tell you. I don't know what happened. It doesn't look good for him, and I guess in your minds, it doesn't look good for me," he stated, as he shook his head. "But I didn't have anything to do with this, and I don't see how you can possibly blame me for something that he's done."

"We aren't blaming you," Emily said immediately. "So take the chip off your shoulder already."

He glared at her. "A little hard to do when everybody's staring at me, as if this is something I'm involved in. I don't know what he was up to. He was my friend, but he was also an arrogant know-it-all, and, if he thought this would be something he could do to mess up everything here, he would do it," Nikolai stated, then raised both hands. "And, right about now, I want to kill him myself, but somebody else apparently already got the job done."

"It was a fair and justified shooting," Magnus replied.

Nikolai nodded, with a shrug. "I know that. I'm sorry, and I didn't mean to imply anything differently. This has been quite a shock for me too." And, with that, he added, "I'll go get a cup of coffee and find a place to sit and think about what this means—and mourn the friend I used to know—because it sure as hell couldn't have been the same guy who did this."

And, with that, he turned and, daring anybody to stop him, walked away.

This concludes Book 5 of Shadow Recon: Whalen.
Read about Nikolai: Shadow Recon, Book 6

Shadow Recon: Nikolai (Book #6)

Deep in the permafrost of the Arctic, a joint task force, comprised of over one dozen countries, comes together to level up their winter skills. A mix of personalities, nationalities, and egos bring out the best—and the worst—as these globally elite men and women work and play together. They rub elbows with hardy locals and a group of scientists gathered close by …

One fatality is almost expected with this training. A second is tough but not a surprise. However, when a third goes missing? It's hard to not be suspicious. When the missing man is connected to one of the elite Maverick team members and is a special friend of Lieutenant Commander Mason Callister? All hell breaks loose …

Nikolai had been at the camp almost since the beginning. His friend had been one of the first to go missing. Although he'd had more specialist arctic training than anyone else in the camp, something had still gone wrong. He can't understand what could have happened and as they slowly find out more bits and pieces, he realizes the hidden connection his friend had withheld from him all these years…

Emily wasn't going to say no to Mason, but his request wasn't along her normal line of duties. Still given the circumstances, she could understand him asking. Although answers were a little thin on the ground particularly when another body shows and shocks them all.

When is enough enough? What does the person behind this mess want? What is his end game? With Nikolai at her side, they need to find out… before someone decides that Nikolai knows more than he's telling…

Find Book 6 here!
To find out more visit Dale Mayer's website.
https://geni.us/DMSSRNikolai

Author's Note

Thank you for reading Whalen: Shadow Recon, Book 5! If you enjoyed the book, please take a moment and leave a short review.

Dear reader,

I love to hear from readers, and you can contact me at my website: www.dalemayer.com or at my Facebook author page. To be informed of new releases and special offers, sign up for my newsletter or follow me on BookBub. And if you are interested in joining Dale Mayer's Reader Group, here is the Facebook sign up page.
http://geni.us/DaleMayerFBGroup

Cheers,
Dale Mayer

About the Author

Dale Mayer is a *USA Today* best-selling author, best known for her SEALs military romances, her Psychic Visions series, and her Lovely Lethal Garden cozy series. Her contemporary romances are raw and full of passion and emotion (Broken But … Mending, Hathaway House series). Her thrillers will keep you guessing (Kate Morgan, By Death series), and her romantic comedies will keep you giggling (*It's a Dog's Life*, a stand-alone novella; and the Broken Protocols series, starring Charming Marvin, the cat).

Dale honors the stories that come to her—and some of them are crazy, break all the rules and cross multiple genres!

To go with her fiction, she also writes nonfiction in many different fields, with books available on résumé writing, companion gardening, and the US mortgage system. All her books are available in print and ebook format.

Connect with Dale Mayer Online

Dale's Website – www.dalemayer.com
Twitter – @DaleMayer
Facebook Page – geni.us/DaleMayerFBFanPage
Facebook Group – geni.us/DaleMayerFBGroup
BookBub – geni.us/DaleMayerBookbub
Instagram – geni.us/DaleMayerInstagram
Goodreads – geni.us/DaleMayerGoodreads
Newsletter – geni.us/DaleNews

Also by Dale Mayer

Published Adult Books:

Shadow Recon
Magnus, Book 1
Rogan, Book 2
Egan, Book 3
Barret, Book 4
Whalen, Book 5
Nikolai, Book 6

Bullard's Battle
Ryland's Reach, Book 1
Cain's Cross, Book 2
Eton's Escape, Book 3
Garret's Gambit, Book 4
Kano's Keep, Book 5
Fallon's Flaw, Book 6
Quinn's Quest, Book 7
Bullard's Beauty, Book 8
Bullard's Best, Book 9
Bullard's Battle, Books 1–2
Bullard's Battle, Books 3–4
Bullard's Battle, Books 5–6
Bullard's Battle, Books 7–8

Terkel's Team

Damon's Deal, Book 1
Wade's War, Book 2
Gage's Goal, Book 3
Calum's Contact, Book 4
Rick's Road, Book 5
Scott's Summit, Book 6
Brody's Beast, Book 7
Terkel's Twist, Book 8
Terkel's Triumph, Book 9

Terk's Guardians

Radar, Book 1
Legend, Book 2
Bojan, Book 3

Kate Morgan

Simon Says... Hide, Book 1
Simon Says... Jump, Book 2
Simon Says... Ride, Book 3
Simon Says... Scream, Book 4
Simon Says... Run, Book 5
Simon Says... Walk, Book 6
Simon Says... Forgive, Book 7
Simon Says... Swim, Book 8

Hathaway House

Aaron, Book 1
Brock, Book 2
Cole, Book 3
Denton, Book 4
Elliot, Book 5

Finn, Book 6
Gregory, Book 7
Heath, Book 8
Iain, Book 9
Jaden, Book 10
Keith, Book 11
Lance, Book 12
Melissa, Book 13
Nash, Book 14
Owen, Book 15
Percy, Book 16
Quinton, Book 17
Ryatt, Book 18
Spencer, Book 19
Timothy, Book 20
Urban, Book 21
Hathaway House, Books 1–3
Hathaway House, Books 4–6
Hathaway House, Books 7–9

The K9 Files

Ethan, Book 1
Pierce, Book 2
Zane, Book 3
Blaze, Book 4
Lucas, Book 5
Parker, Book 6
Carter, Book 7
Weston, Book 8
Greyson, Book 9
Rowan, Book 10
Caleb, Book 11

Kurt, Book 12

Tucker, Book 13

Harley, Book 14

Kyron, Book 15

Jenner, Book 16

Rhys, Book 17

Landon, Book 18

Harper, Book 19

Kascius, Book 20

Declan, Book 21

Bauer, Book 22

The K9 Files, Books 1–2

The K9 Files, Books 3–4

The K9 Files, Books 5–6

The K9 Files, Books 7–8

The K9 Files, Books 9–10

The K9 Files, Books 11–12

Lovely Lethal Gardens

Arsenic in the Azaleas, Book 1

Bones in the Begonias, Book 2

Corpse in the Carnations, Book 3

Daggers in the Dahlias, Book 4

Evidence in the Echinacea, Book 5

Footprints in the Ferns, Book 6

Gun in the Gardenias, Book 7

Handcuffs in the Heather, Book 8

Ice Pick in the Ivy, Book 9

Jewels in the Juniper, Book 10

Killer in the Kiwis, Book 11

Lifeless in the Lilies, Book 12

Murder in the Marigolds, Book 13

Nabbed in the Nasturtiums, Book 14
Offed in the Orchids, Book 15
Poison in the Pansies, Book 16
Quarry in the Quince, Book 17
Revenge in the Roses, Book 18
Silenced in the Sunflowers, Book 19
Toes up in the Tulips, Book 20
Uzi in the Urn, Book 21
Victim in the Violets, Book 22
Whispers in the Wisteria, Book 23
Lovely Lethal Gardens, Books 1–2
Lovely Lethal Gardens, Books 3–4
Lovely Lethal Gardens, Books 5–6
Lovely Lethal Gardens, Books 7–8
Lovely Lethal Gardens, Books 9–10

Psychic Visions Series

Tuesday's Child
Hide 'n Go Seek
Maddy's Floor
Garden of Sorrow
Knock Knock…
Rare Find
Eyes to the Soul
Now You See Her
Shattered
Into the Abyss
Seeds of Malice
Eye of the Falcon
Itsy-Bitsy Spider
Unmasked
Deep Beneath

From the Ashes
Stroke of Death
Ice Maiden
Snap, Crackle…
What If…
Talking Bones
String of Tears
Inked Forever
Insanity
Psychic Visions Books 1–3
Psychic Visions Books 4–6
Psychic Visions Books 7–9

By Death Series
Touched by Death
Haunted by Death
Chilled by Death
By Death Books 1–3

Broken Protocols – Romantic Comedy Series
Cat's Meow
Cat's Pajamas
Cat's Cradle
Cat's Claus
Broken Protocols 1-4

Broken and… Mending
Skin
Scars
Scales (of Justice)
Broken but… Mending 1-3

Glory
Genesis
Tori
Celeste
Glory Trilogy

Biker Blues
Morgan: Biker Blues, Volume 1
Cash: Biker Blues, Volume 2

SEALs of Honor
Mason: SEALs of Honor, Book 1
Hawk: SEALs of Honor, Book 2
Dane: SEALs of Honor, Book 3
Swede: SEALs of Honor, Book 4
Shadow: SEALs of Honor, Book 5
Cooper: SEALs of Honor, Book 6
Markus: SEALs of Honor, Book 7
Evan: SEALs of Honor, Book 8
Mason's Wish: SEALs of Honor, Book 9
Chase: SEALs of Honor, Book 10
Brett: SEALs of Honor, Book 11
Devlin: SEALs of Honor, Book 12
Easton: SEALs of Honor, Book 13
Ryder: SEALs of Honor, Book 14
Macklin: SEALs of Honor, Book 15
Corey: SEALs of Honor, Book 16
Warrick: SEALs of Honor, Book 17
Tanner: SEALs of Honor, Book 18
Jackson: SEALs of Honor, Book 19
Kanen: SEALs of Honor, Book 20
Nelson: SEALs of Honor, Book 21

Taylor: SEALs of Honor, Book 22
Colton: SEALs of Honor, Book 23
Troy: SEALs of Honor, Book 24
Axel: SEALs of Honor, Book 25
Baylor: SEALs of Honor, Book 26
Hudson: SEALs of Honor, Book 27
Lachlan: SEALs of Honor, Book 28
Paxton: SEALs of Honor, Book 29
Bronson: SEALs of Honor, Book 30
Hale: SEALs of Honor, Book 31
SEALs of Honor, Books 1–3
SEALs of Honor, Books 4–6
SEALs of Honor, Books 7–10
SEALs of Honor, Books 11–13
SEALs of Honor, Books 14–16
SEALs of Honor, Books 17–19
SEALs of Honor, Books 20–22
SEALs of Honor, Books 23–25

Heroes for Hire

Levi's Legend: Heroes for Hire, Book 1
Stone's Surrender: Heroes for Hire, Book 2
Merk's Mistake: Heroes for Hire, Book 3
Rhodes's Reward: Heroes for Hire, Book 4
Flynn's Firecracker: Heroes for Hire, Book 5
Logan's Light: Heroes for Hire, Book 6
Harrison's Heart: Heroes for Hire, Book 7
Saul's Sweetheart: Heroes for Hire, Book 8
Dakota's Delight: Heroes for Hire, Book 9
Tyson's Treasure: Heroes for Hire, Book 10
Jace's Jewel: Heroes for Hire, Book 11
Rory's Rose: Heroes for Hire, Book 12

SEALs of Steel

Geir: SEALs of Steel, Book 6

Jager: SEALs of Steel, Book 7

The Final Reveal: SEALs of Steel, Book 8

SEALs of Steel, Books 1–4

SEALs of Steel, Books 5–8

SEALs of Steel, Books 1–8

The Mavericks

Kerrick, Book 1

Griffin, Book 2

Jax, Book 3

Beau, Book 4

Asher, Book 5

Ryker, Book 6

Miles, Book 7

Nico, Book 8

Keane, Book 9

Lennox, Book 10

Gavin, Book 11

Shane, Book 12

Diesel, Book 13

Jerricho, Book 14

Killian, Book 15

Hatch, Book 16

Corbin, Book 17

Aiden, Book 18

The Mavericks, Books 1–2

The Mavericks, Books 3–4

The Mavericks, Books 5–6

The Mavericks, Books 7–8

The Mavericks, Books 9–10

The Mavericks, Books 11–12

Standalone Novellas

It's a Dog's Life
Riana's Revenge
Second Chances

Published Young Adult Books:

Family Blood Ties Series

Vampire in Denial
Vampire in Distress
Vampire in Design
Vampire in Deceit
Vampire in Defiance
Vampire in Conflict
Vampire in Chaos
Vampire in Crisis
Vampire in Control
Vampire in Charge
Family Blood Ties Set 1–3
Family Blood Ties Set 1–5
Family Blood Ties Set 4–6
Family Blood Ties Set 7–9
Sian's Solution, A Family Blood Ties Series Prequel
    Novelette

Design series

Dangerous Designs
Deadly Designs
Darkest Designs
Design Series Trilogy

Standalone

In Cassie's Corner
Gem Stone (a Gemma Stone Mystery)
Time Thieves

Published Non-Fiction Books:

Career Essentials

Career Essentials: The Résumé
Career Essentials: The Cover Letter
Career Essentials: The Interview
Career Essentials: 3 in 1